LONELY EYES

ASPEN GOLD SERIES BOOK 12

BERNADETTE JONES

ISBN: 978-1-7357144-0-0

Cover photo licensed through: Depositphotos

Cover photo Artist: vishstudio (Andrei Vishnyakov)

Cover Design by: Banana Bread Designs

Interior design: by Cat & Doxie Author Services

Artist: Cassandra Hsieh

❀ Created with Vellum

To my children:
Your love and support mean the world to me.
All my love.

To all the chosen families:
Thank you for opening your arms and your hearts.
You show the world how it should be.

Authors Note

This novel is completely fictional. It contains adult themes, violence, sex, and language that may be offensive to some readers. This book is intended for a mature audience.

Lonely Eyes

There is an art to pursuit.

Keira is running out of time. The handsome stranger with a dragon tattoo says he can keep her safe, but he doesn't know the demons on her trail…

Will her mysterious past lead her to escape, or drag her back to living hell?

Owen Strong has suffered tragedy, but he's made a new family in Spencer, Colorado—one he will protect at all costs. When he finds determined Keira Hoa Thi, she rouses more than just trouble. Looking into her lonely eyes, he sees that everyone's in danger.

But she's come to the right place. He's the monster hunter.

CHAPTER 1

"What the hell?" Owen swore into the empty truck cab, struggling to see through the blinding downpour. Was that a kid hiking on the road? He leaned forward, squinting through the rain-dappled windshield, catching quick glimpses of the asphalt between the rapidly beating wipers. Luckily, he caught a second glimpse of the huddled form, slogging ahead on the empty traffic lane.

Easing completely off the gas, he fought the urge to slam on the brakes. He quickly shifted into the opposite lane and gradually guided the heavy tow truck around and past the hitchhiker walking along the highway. Why would someone be out in this mess?

Once past, he eased to a stop, steering as close to the edge of the mountain road as sensible.

He glanced at the clock on his dashboard, already knowing the time was well after midnight. Throwing the vehicle into park, he put on the emergency brake and switched on every flashing and blinking light the truck sported. Opening his door, he stepped onto the road. "What the hell are you doing walking in this storm? Don't you know how dangerous it is? I almost didn't see you. I could have hit you."

The kid took two steps backward and stopped, hiding in the shadows of the overhanging evergreens. Slightly-built, maybe five-five. From what he could see, Owen guessed him to be twelve or thirteen.

"Look, it's dangerous out here. Visibility is shit and there's all this lightning. How long have you been walking? Get in the truck and I'll give you a lift."

Still no response. Owen studied the teen's body language. He sensed that if he made a move the kid would bolt into the forest. With the cold rain and the lower night temperatures, he didn't want the kid freezing to death.

"You've got to be cold. It's another six miles to town. I don't think you're going to make it walking. You're already moving stiffly."

The kid tried to straighten, but under the bulging back-pack and rain soaking every inch of his body, he could barely stand.

"Let's make a deal. Use your phone to take a picture of my truck and send it to a friend. Then I'll give you a ride to town. No questions. No charge. Hell, I won't even talk."

Still no sound, but the boy at least shuffled his feet.

"I'm not one to let people die. What's it going to be?" Through the torrent of rain, Owen kept his gaze locked on the kid. Worst case, he could drive off and wait on the opposite side of the upcoming bend. He doubted the kid could walk much farther before he collapsed. Once he had fallen, Owen could pick him up and put him in the truck.

How had he gotten up here on the mountain in the first place? Owen hadn't passed any abandoned cars on his return from the accident. He thought of the collision site. Could the teen have been involved in the crash?

He studied him. No way he'd walked from the crash site. Who would dump a kid off in the middle of a storm?

The kid shifted again, this time awkwardly pulling a phone from his left pocket.

"Good choice. Take photos of the truck, license plate, and one of me." He pushed off the hood from his rain slicker. Tell your friend my name is Owen Strong and I'm from Spencer."

Motionless, the kid stared at his phone.

"Your battery dead? Look, you need to get into the truck. You need the heat."

The hiker took one step and collapsed.

"Damn." Owen sprinted to the fallen kid, instinctively weighing options and the best recourse. Most Spencer emergency response teams were still transporting accident victims from the crash. He could help quicker than calling. He had enough experience to deal with early stages of hypothermia.

Lifting him upright, he gently tossed the kid over his shoulder, scooped up the cell and headed to the truck. Pulling open the passenger door, he sat the kid on the seat edge and tugged the backpack from his shoulders, dropping the bag onto the ground by his feet.

Turning the kid to face the dash, he hooked him in place with the seatbelt. Confident the boy was secure; he slammed the door shut and grabbed the pack. Hell, the bag weighed more than the kid. Rounding the front of the truck, he tossed the backpack into the rear seat and stripped off his slicker, throwing it on the floor. He grabbed the blanket he kept in the truck, climbed behind the wheel, and cranked up the heat, making sure the vents pointed toward his passenger.

"Kid. Kid, can you hear me?" he asked as he wrapped the blanket over the teen's crumpled body. Gently, he tapped the boy's hooded cheek. No response. As the boy lay collapsed against the passenger door, Owen loosened the cinch on the hood, slid his hand under the fabric and checked for a pulse. The flesh was cold, but with slight pressure Owen found a steady beat. A good sign.

He needed to move off the shoulder of the road. It wasn't safe to have the tow truck parked on this stretch of the highway. Releasing the brake and shifting the vehicle into gear, he checked his mirrors and eased onto the highway.

Once he got them to town, if he couldn't wake the kid, he'd take him straight to the hospital. At least he was out of the rain. The trip to Spencer would take about fifteen minutes in this downpour.

He glanced to the side. The hood had fallen forward again. Now, in closer proximity, his passenger seemed even smaller than he'd initially thought. A knot fisted in his gut. If he hadn't driven by, would the kid have died? The weather wasn't frigid, but the temp had definitely dropped, and being soaked could chill a person quickly. The kid didn't have on a rain parka, or anything waterproof. Caught unprepared, even experienced hikers died in this weather. Owen didn't like the odds.

What the hell was this boy doing? The most probable explanation was that his passenger was a runaway.

Most kids took off for a reason. Taking the kid to the hospital would most likely send him right back to what he was running from. Owen tightened his hand on the wheel. One step at a time. Get the truck back to Rollie's and give the kid time to wake up.

KEIRA JERKED AWAKE. The car was moving. Had she fallen asleep at the wheel? With a gasp, she sat upright. Her eyes flew open and she reached for the steering wheel. Her hand landed on the dash. Lights from an oncoming car blinded her. She screamed.

"You're okay. I got you. You're safe."

A male voice seeped into her consciousness. "Who are you? Where am I?"

"You're in my tow truck. You were walking in the downpour, and I almost didn't see you. Then you passed out. I'm taking you to the hospital. You'll be okay. You're safe."

"No. No hospital. I'll be fine." She glanced around the cab. "Where's my bag? Where are we headed?"

"We're about five miles from a little town called Spencer. Do you remember walking on the mountain road?"

The rain had seemed to come from nowhere. She'd been walking for a while when the sky broke open. Within minutes she and her backpack had been drenched. She'd been so cold. The sound of a truck behind her had startled her. The big rig passed her and came to a stop. This huge man jumped out and offered her a ride. His voice and words sounded trustworthy.

People lied.

He'd told her to take a picture. That suggestion made her feel better, safer. "Yes. You stopped and offered me a ride."

"Good. We'll get you help."

"I don't need a hospital. I'm fine, really." She shot the stranger a glance. "Just drop me off in town."

"You a runaway?"

A gasp escaped her lips. She lifted her gaze to his, pushing her still-wet coat hood back, to see him more clearly. "Why do you ask that?"

He glanced at her and his eyes widened in the lights from the dash. "You're a girl."

She leaned against the door, slipping her fingers into the handle.

He held up his hand. "It's okay. You're fine. You're safe. I thought you were a guy. A kid. A boy." He shook his head and whispered. "Shut up, Owen."

She studied the man closer. He'd removed the billowy rain cape but he still seemed huge. His rain-slicked hair was pushed back from his face and plastered against his head. His jaw was shadowed. The rolled-up sleeves on his flannel shirt exposed muscular arms wrapped in a waffle-weave thermal shirt.

"Let me try this again. I'm taking this tow to the shop. Spencer is a small town, and at this time of night there won't be much open. My car is close, though, and I can give you a ride to wherever you need to go."

"Does this town have hotels?"

He glanced her way. "You didn't know where you were going? You weren't headed to Spencer?"

She swallowed. "I knew the next town was Spencer, but nothing else."

"How'd you get—"

"Does Spencer have hotels?" she asked, cutting him off.

"Yes, but the nice ones will be shut down for the night. It's tourist season and most will be booked anyway."

"Oh. It's a tourist town?" she asked.

"Yeah, but not crazy touristy. I mean, we double in size for a few months, but mostly it's a nice little artist mountain community. I'm not big on crowds, and this is my first summer here, but so far it's been okay."

He drove the truck around another bend, and the town unfolded before them. On the left, a large beautiful older home welcomed them with lights ablaze on the lower level.

Spencer. She'd arrived. Anticipation and trepidation vied for dominance in her chest. Tomorrow she would see the buildings and landscape in the daylight. She hadn't lied. Things had happened too fast for research.

"You didn't answer me. Are you in trouble? Are you a runaway?"

She gazed out the side window at the dark passing landscape. Runaway. Her whole life had been one desperate move after another. *Can you ever run away?*

Glancing back at the huge man beside her, she smiled. "You're a good guy. I appreciate your help. But I'm okay. Thank you for your kindness. Just get me to town."

"I have to drop off the truck. I'm willing to take you anywhere you need to go."

"What about the not-so-nice places to stay in this town? The other hotels?"

"How'd you get on that stretch of mountain? I didn't pass other cars. Did somebody dump you? Are you afraid? I'm friends with the local police chief. He can help."

Damn, he was persistent. "No. I don't need the police. I don't need anyone."

"Maybe we should take you to my friend, Gage. He's a doctor. He could check you out. How old are you?"

"When you offered me the ride, I remember you said you weren't going to talk. Did you forget?" she asked.

"No. But—"

"But what?"

"Is my ass going to end up in jail for transporting jail-bait?" He snapped out.

She couldn't stop the chuckle. "I'm over eighteen. You're safe. And, I'm fine. I can take care of myself. All I need is for you to drop me off in town."

With a sharp left, he took a side road and then another left, ending up back onto the main road they'd traveled on into town. A couple of minutes later, they approached the big old-fashioned stone mansion she remembered seeing as they'd driven into town, with welcoming lights in the lower level.

He glanced at her before grabbing his cell from the console and hit a button. "Hey Zoe, your lights are on. You up? Thought you might be. Hey, I've got a friend who needs a place for the night. Do you have any openings? Good. Thanks. We're pulling in now."

"This is Zoe's place," he explained. "She owns the Blue Spruce. You'll be safe and comfortable here. I wouldn't feel right dropping you off at any of the motels with open rooms. Do you need money? I can help you out."

"I have a little money. Is this place expensive?"

"No. Zoe is reasonably priced."

He guided the tow truck into the drive beside the Blue Spruce sign. The storm had ceased as quickly as it started, leaving the air fragrant with pine. Climbing from the cab, he grabbed her backpack from the back seat, and met her at the front of the truck. She walked beside him to the big porch where a woman waited to greet them.

"Hi, I'm Zoe Barlow. Welcome to the Blue Spruce."

Keira pushed the hood from her head and reached out a hand. "Hi. I'm Keira. I hope we didn't wake you."

Zoe smiled. "No worry. I was waiting for Chet to come home." She glanced at the crumpled vehicle. "Are there more wrecks to pick up?"

"No, that's the last one. Chet should be home soon," he offered. "Did you say you have coffee?"

"Yes, a fresh pot." Zoe looked at Keira. "Or tea and a snack. Complimentary with your stay, along with breakfast in the morning. Why don't we get you settled? You can take off those wet clothes and take a shower to warm up." Zoe sized up the dripping backpack. "I have something dry you can put on, and then you can join us for a bite to eat."

As they reached the second floor, Zoe advised Keira she'd be sharing the Jack-and-Jill bathroom. Handing her the key, she reminded her to come down for a snack.

The room was lovely. A colorful bouquet of fresh flowers graced a well-polished oak dressing table. An antique chest of drawers was pushed against the far wall. On either side of the queen bed, tables supported globe lamps in a soft green with delicate roses painted on the base. The intricately designed wrought iron headboard decorated the soft rose-colored wall between two windows.

Keira's artistic eye was drawn to the bed quilt. The traditional wedding pattern had been stitched on a soft grey background. The intertwining rings were teal, lavender, varying shades of pinks, soft blues and peach. The bed was stacked with matching pillows, comfortable and cozy with a fresh palette.

Nothing stark or sterile. No white walls. No clinically blunt furniture. The space was warm and welcoming. A gentle place to retreat and relax. If only she could.

Staying here and avoiding the larger chains would be beneficial—no national database. She had to keep under the radar; being caught was too dangerous for everyone. The only issue would be the price. She'd already been traveling four days, using more money than she'd hoped.

Tomorrow she'd check out the town and see if he still lived here.

Thirty minutes later, showered and wearing the sweatpants the kindly woman had insisted she take as a gift, Keira hesitated outside the doors of the dining room entrance. She nervously swiped her hands over the soft fabric. The matching baby-blue sweatshirt with the Blue Spruce logo was warm and comforting. She shouldn't be doing this, but she was hungry and alone. Zoe had kind eyes, as did the big man who'd found her. This one meal couldn't hurt.

She took a deep breath before entering the dining room. Owen sat at the table with her hostess and another older man. "Oh. I'm sorry. I'll come back."

Owen stood. "No. Join us. We were waiting for you."

Zoe glanced up and smiled. "You'd better hurry dear, or these two will have eaten everything. Tea or coffee?"

"Tea, please."

As she approached, the older man rose from his chair and held out his hand. "Hi, I'm Chet. I hear you'll be staying for a while."

"Um—uh, yes if I can afford the price, sir."

Zoe filled a cup, placing the saucer in front of the empty chair that Owen pulled out. "Sit. There's no charge for tonight since the night is almost over. We'll discuss the rest after we've eaten." Zoe glanced up, surprise lit her eyes. "Your hair! The braid goes well-below your waist. Have you ever cut it?"

"Yes, but it's been years. I've always found it easier to keep it braided or in a bun rather than messing with hairstyles."

"It must take forever to dry. Did you find the hair dryer? Do you need a second one? No wonder you were so cold. You must still be warming up."

"I will dry it when I go back up. I did see the dryer under the sink. Thank you." Keira took her place at the table, hoping no one had heard her stomach rumble. Other than coffee, she hadn't eaten anything for almost two days.

She surveyed the food laid out. Six large sandwiches were stacked on a plate, carrots, celery and pickles on another. Bowls of coleslaw, potato salad and mixed fruit filled the table center. There was another plate with cookies, brownies and cinnamon coffee cake.

"Oh, I should've asked, are you vegetarian?" Zoe asked.

Keira shook her head.

"Good. We have ham or chicken. I always hate choosing. Would you like to share half of each with me?"

"That's perfect." Keira agreed. Taking the coleslaw bowl that was handed to her, she added a scoop to her plate.

Passing the bowl to the right, she and Owen almost collided dishes as he passed left. He chuckled, switching hands, then making the transfer. The fresh crunchy salad was a treat to her vegetable-starved senses. The fresh fruit was ambrosia. They allowed her to eat in peace.

Keira was amazed at how quickly the food disappeared. The two men ate until the plates were empty. They discussed the big wreck on the highway and were thankful that the injuries incurred seemed to be treatable. When everyone was finished, the two men rose and started clearing the table. Keira joined them. The simple task grounded her, relieving her stress.

"Thank you for your help, Keira. Why don't you go get some rest? Breakfast is served between seven-thirty and nine-thirty."

"Please, Miss Zoe, how much is the room?"

Zoe smiled and glanced over Keira's shoulder. "If you'd like to stay, we could let you have the room for the next two nights. It's booked after that, but I can help you find another place. I have friends in hospitality, and we support each other all the time. The room was available, so you're helping us out. How does two hundred sound for the two nights? I'll need the room by noon on Friday."

Keira stifled a sigh of relief. She suspected they were giving her a break, but hoped the lack of customers was true. She wasn't in a position to turn down such a generous offer.

After excusing herself, she headed upstairs. Closing the door, she leaned against it and took a deep breath. The food helped. She no longer felt so anxious, and the trembly sensation had left her body.

She crawled into the soft luxurious bed, snuggling under the covers. The kindness, the food, the safety held fear at bay. Still wide awake, she stared at the ceiling. Maybe this would work. Maybe she could get free. If only she could find the man with the answers. Maybe then she could sleep.

Owen gave Zoe a hug, and led Chet outside.

"What the hell are you up to now?" Chet admonished.

Owen opened the driver's door, reaching inside to grab his wallet. Stepping back, he slipped five hundred-dollar bills from the sleeve and handed them to Chet. "Give that to Zoe. I told her I'd cover the difference on the room cost. Tell her I said thank you, and if there's a problem, have her call me."

"You didn't answer my question," Chet persisted.

Owen glanced up at the light in the upstairs corner bedroom. "Did you hear her stomach growl?"

Chet nodded.

"Her backpack weighs more than she does." Owen shrugged. "I think she's got trouble. I think she's running. She said she saw Spencer on a map. Maybe she can rest here, take a few days to think through what she's doing and where she's going. Nobody that young should be on their own."

"You can't fix the world, son."

Owen slapped his friend on the shoulder and climbed behind the wheel. After starting the engine, he rolled down the window. "If you think she's trouble, have Zoe let me know."

Chet patted the hood and headed back inside.

Owen sat for a moment, studying the light in the upstairs corner room. A slight shadow drifted across the window frame. He'd been shocked that the kid turned out to be a woman. A beautiful woman. She'd been ravenous. He didn't think she'd noticed Zoe slipping extra food on her plate. She'd been pacing herself, consciously trying not to show her hunger.

Zoe had noticed as well. A genuinely good person, she'd assessed the situation and known exactly how to handle Keira. Serving everyone until the food was gone, making sure that Keira kept getting refills. She'd even caught on when the cost came up and he'd brushed his nose with a finger.

Yes, the room had been empty due to a last-minute cancellation. Still, the Blue Spruce was a landmark and coveted destination for its location and reputation. There would've been a customer waiting in the morning. He realized that the two hundred Zoe had whispered in his ear was below what she could normally make renting the room. He'd tried to give her enough to cover the cost.

He watched as the woman walked past the windows again and the light went out. His chest tightened, a disturbingly familiar intuition when trouble was near.

Voices in the hall woke Keira with a start. Jumping from the bed, she glanced around in a panic. The Blue Spruce. She looked down at the sweatsuit she still wore. She glanced at the clock on the table, surprised it was already eight-thirty. How had she slept this late? She was wasting time.

Washing up and refashioning a quick braid in her hair, she checked the clothes she'd hung to dry. They were still wet. Damn.

Leaving the suite, she made her way to the breakfast room. An older twosome sat at the table in front of a window, and a young couple with a baby and toddler occupied the table nearest the entrance. Her hostess filled a coffee urn at the breakfast bar and checked the assorted trays.

Zoe glanced up and smiled as Keira approached. "Good morning. Did you sleep well?"

Keira smiled back. "Very well. Thank you."

Zoe handed her a plate. "I just put out fresh coffee and tea. These are the pastries and fruits. We make eggs, waffles and pancakes to order. On every table you'll find a menu for the day's selection. I'll give you time to decide and be right back to take your order."

Keira made tea and chose a cinnamon cake and a bowl of cantaloupe before sitting at a secluded two-person table by the window. Warm in her hands, the green tea was a perfect temperature and soothed her.

She'd managed to reach her destination. Now what? How would she go about finding him without calling attention to herself? She needed to be discreet. She couldn't leave a trail to be followed.

A lovely younger woman with curly black hair took her order and headed back toward the rear of the house. The woman paused in the doorway and glanced back at Keira. A flutter of unease crossed over her as she watched the woman retreat into the kitchen.

While she waited for her breakfast, the other diners left. A few minutes later, Zoe came out with her eggs and bacon.

"Are you here visiting friends or family?" she asked.

Keira smiled and repeated her refrain. "No, I'm slowly making my way across the country. Taking a break between semesters while I decide on a new major."

"You're backpacking?" Zoe asked in disbelief.

Keira blushed and looked away. She'd never been a good liar. "My car died and I've been walking, hitchhiking, and taking buses when I could afford them." She met Zoe's gaze. "I was hoping with the tourist traffic, I could find a job in Spencer to build-up my cash reserves. Waitress, bar work, cleaning. Can you tell me a little more about the town? Where I might get work?"

Zoe studied her intently, then seeming to make a decision, she nodded. "Eat your breakfast, then we can talk."

The food filled the large plate, but Keira devoured every bite. Being full was a luxury. Between fear, anxiety, and being broke, she'd been cautious on her food purchases. Peanut butter and crackers had gotten her through the first two days. The two after that, she could barely remember.

Zoe returned to gather her empty plates. "If you're planning on staying in town for a while, we need to find you a place. Before I forget, I'm sure all your clothes got soaked. Gather your laundry and meet me in the hall at the back. We'll start your wash, then we can sit in the parlor while I arrange flowers. I'll tell you about the town, where you might find a job, and maybe we can find you a room."

They started laundry, and Keira followed Zoe back to the parlor. The black-haired waitress who'd taken her order was in the room arranging fresh flowers in a vase. Nine additional vases sat on the sidebar waiting to be filled, and a second table overflowed with fresh flowers. The woman glanced up and paused, brown eyes searching. Keira swore she could *feel* the woman's scrutiny.

"Vianna, this is Keira. She got caught in that awful storm last night. Thank heavens Owen found her, and we had that last-minute cancellation." Zoe crossed to the table and selected a vase.

"Hi." Keira forced a smile. The other woman met her gaze and her eyes warmed as did her smile.

"Want to help us arrange the flowers?" she asked.

Keira considered the table filled with beautiful blossoms, colorful dahlia, lilies, roses, delphinium, hydrangea, carnations, and gardenias. "What a variety. They're all lovely."

"Mom grows most of them in her backyard and only has to order a few. She has quite the garden. I can show you later."

Keira took in the two women; they didn't resemble each other in the slightest.

Zoe smiled. "This is my daughter-in-law. She's married to my son, Ryder. I'm blessed that she calls me mom." Zoe winked. "She's going to be a mom herself. And I'm almost as excited as Ryder."

Vianna chuckled. "Thank god you aren't as overprotective as he is."

Keira relaxed. Her fretfulness and trepidation had her seeing suspicion where there was none. These people had no reason to believe anything other than what she told them.

"I'd love to help. Do you have a set design?"

"Oh no. Have fun. We have them all over, in every guest room, on dining tables, and in the entryway…. which reminds me that one needs to be redone today. I'll go grab the container." Zoe took off.

Keira selected a vase and several flowers, then joined Vianna at the table. Zoe returned with a large mason jug that she placed to the side and selected a smaller jar. Zoe and Vianna giggled and joked as they filled their vases, stealing what they called 'select blooms' from each other. For a few moments Keira immersed herself in the colors, fragrance and composition.

She finished her arrangement and studied the design. How long had it been since she'd been able to create for the simple joy of creating? No expectation, no deadline, no guilt —the simple combination of white flowers with complementary scents and the leafy greenery.

"That's stunning," Zoe exclaimed.

Keira drew herself back from her contemplation. The two women stared at her with shining eyes.

Vianna nodded. "Lovely." She tugged her cell from her pocket. "I'm taking a photo so we can remember what you did."

Zoe chuckled. "I love flowers and all the different colors. My tendency is to keep adding to a vase because I want the whole garden in one place. But this is exquisite. Simple and elegant. Soothing."

"The whole design is relaxing," Vianna added.

Humility flooded Keira. "No, yours are lovely and vibrant. Mine is plain."

"Eye of the beholder," Zoe said with a smile. She retrieved the large vessel used for the entryway. "Please, will you do this one to welcome our guests?"

Surprisingly moved Keira nodded, letting their praise for the beauty of her design wash over her. Only the beauty, no other demands.

They worked in companionable silence for a few minutes before Zoe spoke. "You mentioned you need work. How long do you think you'll be staying?"

"Not long. A few weeks." Keira kept her gaze lowered.

Zoe cleared her throat. "You need something off the books."

Keira met her eyes and nodded.

"That's going to make it a little harder," Zoe admitted. "Most businesses in town do a full background check. We may not be the lodge, but we want the business they bring us."

"The lodge?"

Zoe hesitated, then glanced at Vianna. "You haven't heard of Aspen Gold Lodge?"

"No."

"Aspen Gold Lodge is an exclusive resort for people with lots of money and prominence who don't want to be bothered by paparazzi, autograph seekers, or political opponents. The lodge is self-contained, but their business does bring attention to the area. Everyone in Spencer is security conscious."

Oh, shit. An abundance of security was the last thing she needed.

"How'd you get here dear?" Zoe asked.

"A trucker gave me a lift when my car died at a truck stop. He's the one who said I might be able to get work here."

"Why—"

Keira needed to stop the questions she sensed coming. "Please, tell me someone will give me something for a week or so."

"Obviously, you could work at the floral shop, but she can't afford help this summer. You mentioned you could waitress. The places that pay well and where you could make the best tips would be Spampinato's Fine Italian or The Golden Grill. They both require a full background check. The hotels I'd send you to also have a set staff for tourist season. The Back Porch Bar would be okay. Although, if you want bar work, I'd go to the Wild Card first. Ace runs a tight ship, and he watches out for his staff," Zoe explained.

"He'll sometimes give a traveler a temp job," Vianna offered.

"True, but with Ruby pregnant, I hear he's been a little pickier."

"Ace?" Keira asked.

"Ace Joseph. He owns the Wild Card Saloon. He inherited the property and business from his father and his father's father. Spencer is an old town and many families who live here are multi-generational." Zoe paused, "We also have to find a place for you to sleep. I'm booked solid starting Friday, the seventeenth." Zoe stood. "Can you girls finish the flowers? I'm going to make a couple calls to see if anyone has an opening."

When the bouquets were finished and the parlor cleaned and put back in order, Keira turned to Vianna. "My laundry should be done. I'm going to get dressed and walk into town."

"There are bikes out front if you'd like to borrow one. Zoe won't mind."

"Thank you."

Vianna walked with her to the hall and paused. "You stopped in the right town. There are a lot of good, caring people here. I'm sure you'll find help."

Keira smiled, nodded, and turned toward the laundry room.

"Keira," Vianna called.

She turned back to the open parlor entryway. The probing expression on the other woman's face sent a chill up her spine.

As though changing her mind, she smiled. "I'm glad you came here."

CHAPTER 2

*a*t six the next night, Owen rode his custom motorcycle along the highway. He traveled the same route he'd taken the night before when he'd picked up Keira. He didn't like unanswered questions. The fact that she'd been walking after midnight on an isolated stretch of highway nagged at him. He'd been on that same road and hadn't encountered another vehicle for over ten miles. How had she gotten to where he'd found her?

After having followed the road up the mountain to the accident site, he traced the return trip back down, hunting for what he might have missed. Taking a leisurely pace, he waved to other vehicles to pass him. A few miles from where he'd found the girl walking, he noticed a pull off.

Angling off the main road, onto the slightly wider gravel, he studied the muddy soil. A set of tire tracks marred the ground before disappearing over the edge. Shutting off his bike and making sure the kickstand held in the still-damp ground, he dismounted and followed the trail.

At the ledge, he stopped and looked down. Several hundred feet below a robin-egg blue little car rested awkwardly. He glanced down the highway toward Spencer. Five miles walking in the rain would soak a body to the skin and start a chill. Especially if you weren't dressed for the weather.

He lifted the cell from his pocket and hit the speed dial number. "Hey Hunter, I think we've got a problem."

He dropped a pin for his friend, the chief of police, and headed back to Spencer to get Rollie's tow truck. By the time he returned, Hunter had the area cordoned off. They had about an hour of daylight left.

Hunter greeted him. "Officer CloudWalker hiked down. The car was empty. Keys were still in the ignition. He said there were no suitcases, bags, or trash. Nothing. The vehicle was completely clean. He feels it's a little too clean. No license plate, in-transit sign in the window. He did find a Louisiana College parking sticker on the rear passenger window. He was able to read all but one number. "Let's get it towed and we'll talk more at Rollie's."

Driving into the auto repair yard, Owen glanced in his rearview mirror. Hunter was right behind him. He motioned for him to join him in the patrol car.

"I know that look on your face, Owen. How'd you find this vehicle? And what's really going on?"

"Last night, I'd picked up a car at that accident site on the highway."

"Joe Cavanaugh's boys had that one, right?"

"Yes."

"Nasty, but no one died," Hunter commented.

"I was driving back when that second downpour hit. Heavy and hard. I was crawling. Which turned out to be good. Literally, in a flash of lightning, I see a kid walking on the side of the road. I offered him a ride. The kid dropped like a rock before he could get to the truck. I picked him up, put him in the seat and headed to town and the hospital.

The kid came to as we got to Spencer. He, it turns out, was a she."

He watched the muscle in Hunter's jaw twitch, knowing his friend was struggling to contain his anger and fear. In the spring, two members of their chosen family had been threatened and almost killed. Knowing there could be more trouble coming, everyone in their group was on high alert. With all the disturbing incidents Spencer had seen this year, Hunter didn't like surprises.

Quickly, Owen continued. "I asked if she was a runaway and how she got where she was. She evaded almost every question I asked. She did tell me she was over eighteen and that she'd seen Spencer on a map. She was cold, shivering, soaked, and her stomach rumbled like a freight train. I think she was afraid of me. She wanted me to drop her off in town."

He met his friend's gaze. "I-ah couldn't do that. Zoe was up. I called her. She'd had a last-minute cancellation. I took the girl there."

"You took her to my aunt? What the hell were you thinking?" Hunter shouted.

"I'd seen Chet at the wreck and figured he'd be going back to Zoe. I expected she was waiting-up for him. I went in with the girl. Zoe got her dry clothes and told her to settle in, then come join us for a bite to eat. Chet showed up while we waited and the three of us had a few minutes to talk. Keira came back—that's her name—and we ate together. She seemed scared, on edge. She's tiny, delicate. She ate like she hadn't eaten in days."

"My aunt, Owen? What were you thinking? Why didn't you call me?"

"I mentioned the hospital and she freaked out. I mentioned I knew the chief of police and she seemed even more upset. I think she might be a runaway.

"I called Zoe first thing this morning and again at lunch to make sure nothing was wrong. She said everything was fine. Keira seemed like a sweet girl. Polite, respectful and quiet. I guess she helped them with flowers today. She told Zoe she wanted a quick part-time job where she could make a little money to move on. A job where they won't want references. Both Zoe and Vianna think she's running from someone." Owen ran a hand through his hair. "Aw, hell. I thought it was smart at the time."

"What made you reevaluate?"

"I lay in bed last night questioning how she got where she was on the highway. Nothing made sense. And honestly, because of the nightmare with Ivy and Gage, I'm just kinda suspicious of everything, so I took a ride after work and found the tracks. They were about five miles from where I picked her up. She could've dumped that car."

"Call Ivy and Gage. Find out where they are and tell them we need to meet. Someone could be coming after them again." Hunter grabbed his own phone and hit dial. "Zoe, where's the girl?"

KEIRA SAT cross-legged on the bed in her room at the B&B. Zoe had given her a tourist map for the town, showing the attractions and shops. All afternoon and evening she'd wandered the streets, studying the map carefully. Her grandmother's instructions played over and over in her head.

Once you get there, spend a day investigating your environment. Find how to get out of town quickly—buses, cabs, bike rentals, whatever is convenient and fast.

Find the best places to hide: abandoned buildings, barns, campgrounds, libraries.

Whenever you go to the restroom, change something about your appearance. Your hair, your glasses, your shirt, a hat. Trade out your shoes. Rings or no rings. Add or take away a decoration on your backpack. Never do the same look more than once in a day. If you make subtle changes, people will describe you differently, and you make it harder to be found. But always have one small memorable item to catch attention. People rarely look past the novelty. If asked, they would say the girl with the beaded feather, or the red scarf on her head.

Once settled, keep your day appearance the same and save your traveling disguises. Find him. Then you know what you need to do.

Keira emptied her purchases from the bag. Knowing she could count on two more days of breakfast, she'd bought the largest sandwich available at the Cold Slice. She could eat half tonight and put the other half in the ice bucket for tomorrow. Stopping in the dining room before going upstairs, she grabbed a juice and water bottle. Securing them in her backpack, she poured a cup of tea and wrapped two cookies in a napkin to take to her room.

Pulling the hidden pouch from the backpack base, she counted through her stash. Seven hundred sixty-five dollars was all the money she had left. Setting aside the two hundred she needed for the room, she put the rest back in hiding. She wouldn't have to pay for gas, but she needed to save enough cash to get out of town.

She thumbed through the four fake IDs she carried. Zoe said the Wild Card might hire her. The California ID she chose listed her age at twenty-three, her correct age. She had a supporting university ID.

Laying out the seven burner phones on the bed, she placed the one marked number four in an easy-access pocket of her bag and secured the rest in the hidden pouch. Monday she would receive the call. Hopefully, she would have something to report.

"DESCRIBE HER," Officer Ivy Vaughn said.

Owen glanced across the table in his loft apartment at the woman who'd become a sister to him. She and her man, Gage Ewing, had already suffered enough this year. Ivy's government position had left her with a bullseye on her back. Gage had been an informant for the DEA on a drug cartel. They were both lucky to be alive.

They were family. He needed to protect them. "She's Asian, I believe. Around twenty to twenty-five, she looks younger at first. About five-foot-four. Maybe one hundred and five pounds. Her black hair was in a thick braid that hung at least six inches past her waist. Dark brown eyes, almost black, warm skin. Delicate features. A little-bit of a woman. Almost b—"

Ivy cocked her head. "Almost what, Owen?"

He met her gaze. "Breakable. Like those delicate glass animals at the art gallery."

"I'll reach out to my old contact, Donavan, at the government agency I worked for," Ivy said.

Hunter nodded. "It's probably nothing, but we aren't taking chances. Owen is going to transport the car to the forensic team tonight. We'll reach out to the college tomorrow and see what information they can give us on the vehicle or owner."

Hunter glanced at Owen. "Chet agrees with your assessment. The girl is skittish. Most likely afraid and on the run. I think we need to get a photo to search through the runaway database."

"Let me. I'm off tomorrow." Owen offered. "I can go unnoticed, and if she does see me, I think she'll be okay. She might trust me a little."

Rising from his chair, Hunter glanced from Gage to Ivy.

"Just in case, be on guard, and keep in touch. If she dumped that car, she could be your kind of trouble. Any idea when your ex-boss is going to get his mess cleaned up so you're out of danger?"

Ivy shrugged. "He's working on it."

Hunter hmphed and headed out the door.

It was after midnight before Owen got back to Spencer from the forensic lab. He took the long way home, driving past the Blue Spruce. The corner room where Keira stayed was dark. What was she running from?

He dropped the tow truck off at Rollie's and walked the short distance to his barn. As he approached the barn door, the motion light didn't come on. The moon was bright enough to see a good-sized tree branch on the ground. Glancing up, he noticed the motion light dangled awkwardly.

His night vision was good, and if Gage or Ivy came to workout they'd drive. He'd get the light fixed in the next few days. His inside security was tied to his phone and computer. He rarely even locked the barn. He was a light sleeper; life had trained him to be easily woken.

That same instinct was what made him wonder about the girl, Keira. Something was wrong. He could sense trouble; he wouldn't rest easy until he knew if it was *her* or if danger followed her.

KEIRA WALKED into Willa's Studio and was instantly capti-vated by the art. She'd strolled past the shop yesterday and resisted the urge to go inside. Today she gave in.

Conscious of her bulky backpack, she carefully drifted from one painting to the next, taking in the colors, the grandeur of the nature scenes, the touching portraits of children at play, lovers in love and the humanity of the aging. The artist was speaking to her, giving hope to the paintings she knew she still had inside her.

Tears filled Keira's eyes, and she swallowed hard. She had to leave, to get away before she broke down. She'd almost reached the door when a voice from behind the counter halted her.

"Paintings have always had that effect on me. The first time I was taken to a museum, I spent the afternoon in tears. Thank you for honoring me. Have a lovely day."

Keira looked up into the knowing violet eyes of a striking woman with short silver hair. Emotionally undone, she nodded and scurried out.

She walked through the park to the opposite side and sat on the bench that faced across the road to the Wild Card Saloon. Her breathing was still uneven. She knew the woman. Willa Samuels. Would Willa remember her and who she really was? She was so close. She couldn't be found. Not yet.

Leaning against a brick wall between two buildings, Owen snapped another picture of the woman he'd been following. He skimmed through the last few shots, confident he'd gotten good facial angles for recognition.

In one photo, she'd stopped to pick up an empty pizza box someone left on a park bench. She glanced straight in his direction as she tossed the garbage into the trash. When she'd stopped a ball from going into the street and threw it back to the kids playing, he'd gotten a perfect profile. In another, she'd smiled kindly as she conversed with an old woman walking her dog. God, she was enchantingly beautiful.

Two hours ago, Keira had rushed out of Willa's studio, almost in tears. Since then, she'd sat cross-legged on the park bench across from the Wild Card, eating a bag of chips, then an apple, drinking water, and pretending to read a book or her phone. She scrutinized each person who came and went from the saloon.

His chest tightened. He didn't want her to be dangerous. He didn't want this to be about Ivy and Gage. He couldn't let anyone hurt his family. Never again.

She stood, brushed off her jeans, and crossed the street to the sports bar entrance of the Wild Card. He waited fifteen minutes before he sauntered down the street, stopping to read the menu taped to the window near the door. At first, he couldn't find her, and then he noticed her approach from the hall that led to the back. Apparently picking up an order, she took a seat on one of the take-out benches.

Something was different. He studied her closely. The jean jacket was gone, replaced by an oversized blue shirt. Multiple bracelets sparkled from the wrist of the hand holding her cell. The red tennis shoes were now strappy white sandals, and her braid was twisted into a knot on top of her head.

He instinctively began unpacking what he'd witnessed: The changes were enough to confuse identification attempts, while not drastic enough to call attention, in the moment. She was smart to make the change at a place where the order taker and the person delivering the food were two different people. If someone asked for a description of the young woman, they'd get conflicting information.

She lifted her gaze from her phone and nervously scanned the room, then shifted her attention higher, glancing through the window.

Owen stayed in place, unmoving, still reading the menu. She wouldn't notice the guy in the Broncos ball cap and blue-grey plaid shirt. He knew how to blend in. But in spite of her attempts, to him, she was not so inconspicuous. What was she up to? Who was she looking for?

When she rose to pick up her order, he walked down the street and secured a new position to observe her.

She exited the restaurant and crossed into the park, taking a seat on a different bench to eat her lunch. She was still in position to see who came and left the Wild Card.

Owen followed her the rest of the afternoon and evening until she returned to the Blue Spruce. He watched from the street until the light came on in the corner room. Distant shadows played across the curtains as she undressed. He stayed until the light went out.

Walking down the street, he slipped his phone from his pocket and texted.

I've got the pictures.
I'll meet you at Gage and Ivy's.

CHAPTER 3

$\mathcal{F}$riday night, Ace walked out of the storeroom, down the hall, and crossed to the bar. He carried three bottles of top-shelf whiskey. The weather was warm and the community needed a distraction. The Wild Card was hopping tonight.

He glanced over to the table where Ruby was taking an order. The three yahoo tourists at the table were flirting big-time. Granted, the flowy dress she wore disguised her baby bump, and she used her order tray as a cover up. She carried her pregnancy with style and grace. But, how clueless could they be? He made a mental note to tell the staff "no more rounds" for that table.

Ace shot a glance to where Hunter drank his iced tea at the end of the bar. Damn, he could see the smoke pouring out of the man's ears. Ruby loved her fella, but she didn't take it kindly when he interfered. The girl could handle herself. He chuckled. The night could get interesting.

Placing the bottles on the shelf behind the bar, Ace turned back to the room just as one of the men placed a hand on

Ruby's arm. A chair scraped on the old wood floor. He turned to Hunter. "Sit. She's got this."

Ruby patted the man's hand and leaned forward whispering something near his ear. The tourist pulled back instantly. She smiled at his companions, finished taking their orders and crossed to the end of the bar.

Hunter cuddled her to his side as soon as she was within reach.

"Three kamikaze, and three drafts," Ruby ordered.

Ace nodded. "Problem?"

"All's good," Ruby replied.

"He touched you," Hunter snapped.

"I handled it."

Hunter scowled. "What'd you say to him?"

Ruby glanced at Ace, then met Hunter's glare. "I declined his offer and told him I don't do peashooters, not since I married the badass police chief who carries a really big gun."

Ace chuckled and glanced at his friend. Hunter wore a smile, his manhood obviously soothed.

The next hour flew by. Owen and Gage popped in and Hunter joined them at the table always kept in reserve. At Ruby's insistence, Ace took a break and took a seat with them.

Ace glanced around the table at the men with whom he'd become so close. For years, he'd been on his own. He had acquaintances, employees, but no friends. Now with Ruby insisting that he come to Sunday dinners, Gage checking his health, and Owen stopping by to do minor repairs at his house, he felt almost content. Almost fulfilled. Almost like he had a family: sons, daughters, and as Ruby proclaimed, a soon-to-be grandchild.

Almost.

Ace studied his unfinished draft. He didn't like the month of August, and it was fast approaching. Years past, he'd always taken the first half of the month off and gone into the mountains, escaping to mother nature.

To remember.

To forget.

Ruby walked up to their table. "Any refills?"

Ace cleared his throat. "I'm thinking of taking a vacation. I usually have extra bar help, but Jimmy isn't available for additional shifts this year, and the kid who's covered for the last four years isn't coming back this summer. Do any of you know someone who could fill in for a couple weeks at the beginning of August?"

He avoided Ruby's too-knowing gaze.

"I can bartend, a little," Owen offered. "I may not be the best at the newer drinks, but I can fake most stuff. I could get here by six-thirty most nights, if that would help."

"I'm here waiting for Ruby," Hunter added. "As long as there are no major police calls, I can help cover."

"I can work the bar," Ruby offered. "I'll talk to the waitresses from the other side and see if they can pull extra shifts to work the tables. I'll work on a schedule." She paused. "Is everything okay, Ace?"

"Thanks. I appreciate the help." Pushing to his feet, Ace patted her shoulder and walked to the supply room. Closing the door behind him, he shut his eyes and leaned back. How many more years would he have to endure this? He dropped onto his desk chair and reached for his private bottle.

OWEN GLANCED at the others as Ace walked away. "Something's wrong. Gage, does he seem sick to you?"

Gage frowned. "No, but he has seemed distracted for a while. I'll bring my bag tomorrow and tell him it's time for his check-up." He lifted a brow at Ruby. "Unless you could get him to come to my office."

She shook her head.

"Did you forget how hard we fought to get him to you the last time?" Hunter snorted, then glanced across the room. "Something has been off for a couple weeks. I thought it was me. But you've noticed, too?"

They nodded. "He said 'the last four years', which makes me think that he takes this time off each year. Gage you've been here, do you remember him taking vacations?" Owen asked.

"I've only been a regular at the Wild Card for about a year-and-a-half. I do vaguely remember coming in about this time last year and thinking that Ace didn't seem healthy. But after a few weeks, he gradually began looking better."

"Ruby, can you pull Jimmy aside and see if he can tell us more?" Hunter asked.

Ruby rose from her chair. "I'll talk to him now. If Ace comes back out, keep him away from us."

Much later, Ace returned from the backroom, a slight stagger to his walk. Seeing Deke at the reserved table, he pulled up a chair and joined him.

Sitting at the end of the bar, Owen pushed his empty bottle aside. He glanced to where Ace and Deke sat. He hadn't noticed either man talking. They simply sat at the same table, lost in their own thoughts—dark thoughts, by the tension on their faces.

As she crossed to the reserved table with two coffees and a couple sandwiches, a concerned Ruby met Owen's gaze.

The crowd had started thinning out. He'd nursed his last beer for an hour, his mind too unsettled to allow sleep. He'd seen Keira come in, but had hesitated to approach her. Instead he'd waited and watched.

Keira sat alone in the corner, a half-finished draw in front of her. He followed her gaze as she watched Rollie and his wife wrapped in each other's arms on the dance floor, then as she studied where her fingers wrapped around her mug. Her shoulders drooped with an exhaled sigh, and she glanced at the couple again. Her gaze appeared desolate. The loneliness in her eyes twisted his heart.

"Last call," Jimmy called out over the din.

Several guys had gathered around the large table by the door. Two of them stood and made their way to the bar, two others sat, opening up a sightline to the corner booth.

Zoe had informed him that Keira had checked out right on time, paying the money that had been agreed upon. She told Zoe that she'd found a place to stay on her own and thanked her for her kindness. Hunter and Ivy had been keeping an eye on her today, but lost her when they'd been called to a domestic disturbance.

Ruby walked past.

"Hey, Ruby, splash a little draw in a mug for me."

She frowned. "You don't drink draw?"

"Ruby, help a guy out here." He nodded toward a group of women chatting on the dance floor.

She widened her eyes and mouthed an 'Oh'. Smiling, she handed him a mug. "Good luck."

Taking the frosted mug, he slowly made his way to where Keira sat. Casually, he glanced at her and raised his eyebrow when she looked up. "Hey, I know you. You finally dry out?"

She frowned for a second before recognition set in. "Hi. Yes, I'm dried out. Your friend was very kind. Thank you for your help."

"Can I buy you a last call?"

She glanced at her drink. "No, I'm fine. Thank you."

"Waiting for someone? Or can I join you till closing?"

She glanced quickly toward the next table. "Sure."

One of the guys from the big table snorted. "Good luck with that one. She's an iceberg."

Owen maneuvered his bulk into the booth and smirked at the guy, obviously a tourist looking to score. "Maybe she's just got class."

The guy awkwardly pushed to his feet, using the table to stabilize himself. Within seconds, Deke came up behind and placed a hand on the troublemaker's shoulder, in a grip firmer than it appeared. Ace approached from the side and slipped the bottle from the man's hand. He then turned his steely eyes on the others at the table. "It's closing time, fellas. Take your friend home to sober up, and you might be welcome in town the rest of your stay."

Two of the guys at the table chugged their newly purchased beers, got up and filed out, supporting their loud-mouth friend.

Ace turned to Keira. His gaze narrowed slightly. "Sorry for the inconvenience, ma'am. Owen here will see you safely home."

Owen glanced at Keira. She stared wide-eyed at Ace, then at Deke. Her hands trembled on the table. A muscle throbbed at her temple, and her breathing escalated. She swallowed, then nodded.

Ace studied her a moment longer, then walked away.

Deke leaned against the wall and gazed out the window, making sure the rowdy men didn't hang around outside the Wild Card.

Owen waited. Keira glanced at him, her eyes filled with emotions he didn't understand. Relief? Panic? Recognition? Doubt?

"Restroom." She slid from the bench, slipping her backpack on as she headed quickly down the hall.

Owen watched her walk away, trying to reconcile her

reaction to the men threatening her. Or had her reaction been to Deke? Ace?

Shit. She's cutting out the back. He rushed out the front door and ran to the side street. He caught sight of her as she raced onto Willow Road, heading west. Careful to keep his cover, he followed her.

She kept to the shadows, but moved too quickly to go unnoticed. His first assessment was reinforced. The girl knew enough to fool the untrained observer, not enough to be stealthy. Was she an anxious runaway, or someone on the hunt?

Owen's concern grew as she passed every hotel and continued toward the lumberyard, located at the edge of town. Where was she going? Did she plan on sleeping in the open?

When she headed up the unmarked drive to his barn, he almost laughed. He watched from the trees as she crossed to the unlocked barn door, glanced behind her, then slipped inside.

The barn appeared rustic and a little unkept from the outside, but after seeing his equipment on the inside, there was no way she could think it was abandoned. Could she?

Definitely a novice. Now what was he going to do?

Soundlessly, Owen entered the barn. He watched from the shadows as she made her way around the equipment with the help of a pen light and headed down the hall to the restroom. She'd been here before. She must have found the place empty over the last couple days and decided the building was safe enough. He supposed the unlocked door might have added to her assumption.

A few minutes later, she returned carrying her backpack and crossed to the crash mats. From her bag she pulled a water bottle and a jacket that she rolled up like a pillow.

Owen flipped the light switch.

She spun, stifling a scream with her hand.

"Breaking and entering is a crime. I could call the cops." He spoke from the doorway. "Or you can talk to me. Explain what your problem is, and maybe we can come up with a plan that keeps you safe."

She shook her head, took a step back and reached for her backpack. "I only wanted to sleep for a while."

"You thought this place was abandoned?"

"I found this barn a few nights ago. Every time I came by, it was empty. The door was unlocked. I—I thought maybe I could sleep here tonight."

"Okay, lesson one. Did you see a lot of dirt or debris on the floor? Is the electricity working? Did you watch the place for twenty-four hours on multiple days? Never assume a place is unused until you've looked for signs of neglect or monitored the activity over several days. But before lesson two, why don't you tell me what's really going on?"

Shoulders slumped, she shook her head. "You can't help."

He shrugged. "You might be surprised. I've helped other people. Why don't you talk to me?"

She studied her hands for a moment, then straightened. "What are you doing here? Did you follow me?"

He couldn't help but smile. "You might say that. Ace did tell you I'd make sure you got home safe. This is my home."

She glanced around. "Home? This is a gym no one uses."

"Look up." He waited for her to lift her gaze. "I live in the loft. This is where I workout with my friends. We have jobs with changing shifts, so the door is open. If someone gets a couple hours in the middle of the night, they can walk in." He glanced at his watch. "In about four hours we'll have company. This week, Saturday is our day to get in a solid workout, plus we have kids coming for practice."

He continued to study her, then decided to take a chance. "I'm going to assume you're running from something or someone. Truthfully, you suck at hiding. You've got the right ideas, but your execution is bad. You can stay here and I'll teach you, or you can take off again. My guess, you won't last two days before 'whoever is after you' finds you. From what I can tell, you're scared, broke, and alone."

She plucked at the wristband on her cotton shirt, refusing to meet his gaze.

"Come clean with me. I can help. If they're out to harm you, I know how to protect you. I can teach you to survive."

Raising her gaze to his, she asked. "What do you get? What will it cost me for your noble gesture? Free labor? Free sex?"

Owen was surprised by the fire and anger in her response. On the plus side, it was a good sign that she could learn and survive. Downside, someone had hurt her, and she'd lost all trust. "All I expect in return is that you respect my home and my friends, that you pick up after yourself, and you do me the courtesy of not stealing anything. You do anything illegal on my property and I'll personally turn you in. You're welcome to any food you find in the refrigerator. You can sleep down here or follow me upstairs and sleep on the couch. Upstairs is air-conditioned. My friends will be here at seven in the morning."

He headed for the stairs at the far side of the barn.

"I can't pay you."

Owen turned to face her. "I'm not asking for money. Or free labor. Or sex. I don't know what scum you're running from, but I'm not like them. If you want my help, ask."

This time he continued up the stairs, leaving the door to the loft open. She lacks some judgement; she's untrained, but possesses an unexpected layer of fire, he thought. Not a boy or a girl, definitely a woman.

Fifteen minutes later, he sensed her presence in the

doorway as he finished cooking scrambled eggs. "You hungry?"

She nodded.

"The toaster is on the counter. Butter the bread that popped up and throw on a couple more. I'll dish up. You want milk or water to drink?"

"Water."

She put her bag by the door and crossed to the sink to wash her hands before going to the toaster.

"Plates are in the cupboard above your head."

After dishing up and pouring drinks, he took his place at the counter, indicating she should sit across from him.

She ate almost the whole meal before seeking his attention. "Can you teach me to hide better?"

"Yes."

She ate a little more. "I need money, a job. They told me that sometimes the Wild Card will hire people for a short time."

"You ever bartend?"

"No, but I can waitress. How hard could a drink order be?"

She was lying—not about waitressing. She was too eager. She wanted a job at the Wild Card for another reason.

"The owner gets there at around ten-thirty in the morning. Your fake ID good quality?"

She paled.

"For a couple weeks, they'd probably pay you under the table. But they'll want to see an ID." He shrugged.

"How can you tell if an ID is phony or not?" she asked.

"Usually by how much they cost. If you've seen enough, it's easy to spot a fake from experience. Bar owners see a lot."

"It was expensive."

"Then try it. But when you do, act confident. Hand it to them like it's the real thing. Speak your experience with conviction and meet their gaze. Don't look down or away. You have to believe the lie you're telling."

Standing, he cleared the empty plates and loaded them into the dishwasher. She brought over the remaining dishes and then wiped down the counter.

"I'm going to take a shower, then hit the rack. There's extra bedding inside the bench by the couch. Want to use the bathroom first?"

She nodded and he pointed her in the right direction. She'd taken five steps when he stopped her. "Lesson two. Always keep your bag with you when you're on the run. If it's not on you or within reach, it can disappear. Bus depots, shopping malls and gyms usually have lockers where you can rent a key. Whenever you get to a new town, you need to check that out first. I know that the Wild Card will provide you with a locker. I hope you have a good place for your money. Are you wearing a money belt?"

"Money belt?"

"Never mind. We'll find one tomorrow."

She crossed the room and grabbed her backpack.

Owen watched the slip of a woman disappear into the washroom. He could teach her how to run, how to hide. He'd rather help her so she didn't have to.

Thirty minutes later the hot water from the overhead rainfall faucet beat down on Owen's head. Voices rattled around inside his mind. *What are you doing now? You can't fix everyone. You can't save yourself. How can you save anyone else?*

Shaking his head like a dog, dispersing the voices, he squeezed soap into the palm of his hand and lathered his body. She was so damn tiny compared to his bulk.

She wasn't some street hustler after her next mark. She'd worried about paying for a room, and then paid Zoe the agreed upon price without skipping out. Nothing was stolen from the B&B. Hell, Zoe said she even helped out with the flowers and folded sheets. After she'd left, they'd even found a thank you note and tip for the maid. The players he knew wouldn't have gone that far to make a good impression. Those actions were ingrained manners.

He squeezed shampoo onto his hair and scrubbed his scalp. He wondered if Keira always wore her hair in a braid. His attention fixated on the silken rope, imagined letting the shiny thick tresses slide through his fingers, burying his face in the scent and softness. When loose it would hang well below her waist. He closed his eyes and envisioned a midnight waterfall pouring over his body. Her body. Desire billowed—a storm cloud threatening to erupt.

Whoa. Stop. Don't go there. He reached out and twisted the temperature to cold. Fuck. What was wrong with him? She was a scared young woman who needed help, not some guy hitting on her while she was vulnerable. He stood under the water till his body and blood cooled.

Stepping out, he dried off and crossed into the connected walk-in closet. He grabbed a pair of boxing shorts from the drawer and tugged them on, then studied the stack of T-shirts. Damn, he hated sleeping in anything. Snagging the top shirt, he dragged the well-worn fabric over his head.

Walking out into the bedroom-living room, he noticed Keira lay fully dressed on the couch with a lightweight blanket from the bench bunched at her knees and a pillow under her cheek. "You can get a little more comfortable than that. Maybe take off your shoes and socks. I swear, I'm not going to jump you."

"I don't know you. How can I be sure I can trust you?"

He ran a hand over his damp hair. "You don't. So, let me give you lesson three. Unless you're prepared to really stab someone, ditch the knife you have in your backpack sleeve. If you're prepared to kill someone, keep it on your person. Where you have it now makes it a better weapon for an attacker than a defense for you. You can give it to me, or if you're going to toss it, at least wipe it clean when you dump it."

He shut off the lights and crawled into bed. She was right —how could she know he was trustworthy? "Do you know anyone who served in the military?"

"Not really."

He spoke from the darkness inside his heart. "I was in the Army. I saw combat. When you experience the danger, you realize your promise to have your brother's back is more than talk. Those people become family. Battle is life or death. My word, my promises, mean everything to me. But you don't know that. Yet. But I'm telling you so you can understand."

He cleared the lump in his throat. "While I was at war, my sister was abducted and murdered. I would never hurt an innocent person."

"What about a person who wasn't innocent?" she whispered.

CHAPTER 4

"*H*elp me! Help me!" a young voice screamed. Keira sprang up from the couch, instantly awake. Was she dreaming?

"Help me! Help me!"

A shrill whistle split the air, again and again.

The sounds came from the lower level. Grabbing her bag, she crossed to the window overlooking the room below. Three adults and four children of varying ages occupied the space. Her eyes were drawn to Owen.

He stood beside a teenage girl dressed in baggy sweatpants and a T-shirt. Raising his hand, he gave the beaming girl a high-five before reaching down to assist a slightly younger boy wearing a padded vest from the mat.

In the ring, another man in shorts, T-shirt, and headgear boxed with an older boy dressed just the same.

A woman in a sports bra and shorts, with a long blond braid, worked with a younger dark-haired girl teaching her strategic steps. Keira recognized the movements as Tai Chi. Sadness hiccupped in her chest. Her grandmother practiced similar moves.

Tears filled her vision. Grandma had to be okay. In two days, Grandma had her doctor's appointment. Keira had to wait until then to call and check on her.

Owen lifted his gaze to where she watched from the window. The man's sixth sense was uncanny. He seemed to be everywhere and nowhere at the same time. How had he known the flat ripple in her bag was a knife? How could he know she was running?

No one could ever know the truth. She must stay cold. An iceberg, exactly like the drunk had said. Years ago, she'd become an expert at hiding her emotions. Or so she'd thought.

He tilted his head, silently inviting her to join them.

Glancing at her watch, she frowned in surprise. Could the time really be nine-thirty in the morning? How had she slept at all with a strange man less than ten feet away? She hadn't even heard him leave the room.

He was right. She had no survival skills. Walking to the kitchen, she removed the knife her grandmother had given her and placed it on the counter for him to find.

Turning, she headed to the back to change. There was a job she needed to land.

HUNTER USHERED RUBY through the back door of the Wild Card. "Babe, I really don't think you should be here."

Ruby turned and cradled his cheek. "I *know*, you shouldn't be here. You, Owen, Ivy, Gage, are all overreacting. First let me remind you that Ace and Deke are more than capable of taking care of themselves. You have nothing but a gut feeling that she is after someone in the family. First it was Ivy and Gage, now it's Ace or Deke. All this concern simply because of how she *looked* at them. That reminds me,

I need to talk to Owen about his conspiracy theories. He started this.

"I'm sure you're jumping to conclusions about this woman because of what happened this spring. I talked to Zoe, and she feels the girl is scared, probably running from something, but harmless." She stroked her husband's cheek. "You, my fierce protector, know more than most about what nightmares women suffer. Let's give her a chance. Maybe she needs our help."

"Owen was right about the car."

"Really? You've traced it back to her already?"

"Well no, but there was a car there."

Ruby shook her head and pressed her lips to his. He wrapped his arms around her and deepened the kiss.

"Get out of my way and get a room," Ace's gravelly voice broke in. "What're you two doing here anyway?"

Ruby broke the kiss and whispered, "Raincheck."

She turned to Ace. "Well, if you're going to take off, I think we should go over the inventory. I also wanted to catch the other waitresses and start working on a schedule. Hunter's off duty today. He offered to help stock, freeing me and you up to do the mundane paperwork."

Hunter took his cue. "I'll put on the coffee. Want me to start with the beer or the liquor?"

Ace nodded. "Beer. Go ahead and unlock the door while you're there."

Ruby suggested they work at the bar so they could go through the current inventory and compare what was left with the recent increase in summer sales.

Thirty minutes later, the door opened and a young woman walked in. Ruby recognized the woman from the pictures Hunter had shown her. She glanced at him across the bar and he winked.

Ace glanced at the new arrival and cleared his throat.

45

"Can't serve for another five minutes, but you can take a seat and we'll be right with you."

Tentatively the girl stepped forward, then seemed to bolster her courage and crossed the distance with her shoulders back. She put out her hand. "Hi, my name is Keira, and I'm hoping to find a temporary job. Zoe Barlow at the Blue Spruce said that maybe you could use some help."

Ace studied the girl so long that Ruby slid off her stool and took the girl's hand. She smiled. "Hi. I'm Ruby and this is Ace. Hunter is behind the bar. How do you know Zoe?"

The girl glanced at Ace, then turned her attention to Ruby. "I stayed there a couple nights and she recommended I come here."

Ruby shot a quick glance to where Hunter was washing glasses, then to Ace who seemed transfixed by the girl.

"Why don't you, Ace and I go over to the table, and you can tell us a little about yourself. Would you like coffee?"

"Could I have water, please?"

Ruby glanced to where Ace still sat motionless. "Hunter, would you get water for me and Keira, please? Ace, bring your coffee and join us."

Keira took a drink as soon as Hunter brought the water, and Ruby followed suit. She waited until Ace joined them before starting the conversation again. "What brings you to Spencer?"

"I'm on my way to California. My car died, and I hitched a ride with a trucker. He said that Spencer was a tourist town and I might be able to get work here. I need to make enough money to buy a bus ticket."

Ruby nodded and glanced at Ace. He seemed content to let her continue. That, in itself, was disconcerting. When it came to the saloon, Ace was always outspoken. "Do you have a resumé?"

The girl glanced at the water glass she gripped. "No. I didn't think I'd need work before I got back to college."

"Oh, you're a student. Where do you go?"

"Southern Cal."

"What's your major?"

"Bachelor of Arts in Art History."

"How exciting. Do you want to paint, sculpt, curate a museum, or what?"

"I like to create. I'm not interested in management." The girl glanced from Ruby to Ace. "But I can do other things, other jobs. I've been a waitress at several places." She studied Ruby. "Are you the owner?"

Ruby smiled. "No, Ace is the owner. But as you can tell, he has me do the talking during interviews." Ruby nudged her boss. "The strong silent type."

Ruby took a sip of water. "How old are you, Keira?"

"Twenty-three."

"May I see your ID, please?"

The girl retrieved a driver's license and university ID from her pocket. She took a drink while Ruby reviewed the information.

"Keira Long. Twenty-three," Ruby read out loud.

"You can start today." Ace pushed back his chair and stood. "Ruby will get you settled." He glanced at Ruby. "I got something to do. Can you take care of things till Jimmy gets here?"

Without waiting for an answer, Ace walked down the hall and out the back door.

Ruby glanced toward Hunter. She didn't like the grim expression on his face. She also didn't like the way Keira's gaze followed Ace all the way out the door.

When Keira glanced back at her, Ruby smiled. "Let's go to the back room and get the paperwork filled out. I'll make copies of your ID, and we'll get you set up with a locker. Are you okay to start today?"

"Yes, starting today would be perfect."

They both rose, and Keira studied the room. "Where should I put my glass?"

Ruby chuckled. "Leave it, you'll get enough cleaning duties once you start. Hunter will pick up this time. Follow me to the back."

Hunter watched the two women go down the hallway. Sliding his phone from his pocket he dialed as he crossed to the table. "Ivy, I need you to come pick-up a glass for prints and DNA. I'll have it on the floor in Ruby's car. The girl's starting a job at the Wild Card today. And Ivy, check with the office to see if we've heard anything on the Louisiana parking tag. Tell them it's a priority."

He slipped on a rubber glove and placed the girl's glass in an evidence bag. Going behind the bar, he concealed the evidence bag in a paper bag and headed to Ruby's car.

ACE WALKED out the back door and down the street, placing one foot in front of the other until he arrived at the Gold River and was forced to stop. His chest hurt, his head throbbed, and his eyes felt swollen. He sank onto a boulder at the river's edge.

It must be the dreams. The dreams hadn't let him sleep well in several nights. The dreams and the memories. After seeing the girl yesterday, last night had been particularly tough. The loss. How could he forgive? How could he forget? He hated this time of year.

He closed his eyes and concentrated on breathing in and out. Soon the prayers of his forefathers filled his heart and mind. He began to chant softly, praying for peace and focus.

KEIRA WIPED off the table and glanced at the clock over the bar. Five p.m. All afternoon she'd trained with Ruby, going over the menu for the sports bar, pizza garden and the saloon. She'd explained how Ace had expanded the original saloon as the other properties had become available. Because she was new, Keira would start in the pizza garden and sports bar. Ruby had worked side by side with her until an hour ago when she'd explained she needed to finish the schedule and order liquor.

Another bartender, Jimmy, came in and finished restocking with Hunter. He'd told her Hunter wasn't an employee, but he helped out when he was here, because Ruby was his wife.

Ace hadn't returned.

At five-thirty, Owen came in, dressed in jeans and a white dress shirt, cuffs rolled up displaying his tattooed forearms. The crisp shirt hugged his muscular chest and biceps. His stubble beard had been neatly trimmed. He seemed more imposing now than he had this morning when he'd been on the workout mats.

When he passed her and rounded the end of the bar, he nodded at Keira, and then shifted a smiling Ruby in for a hug and a kiss to the top of her head.

"Leave my woman alone, asshole," Hunter chided in mock displeasure before clasping Owen's hand and giving him a shoulder bump.

Ruby waved her over.

"Keira, Owen is going to help tonight until Ace returns. He and Jimmy will be behind the bar, and he'll help you clear tables as he can. Lacey will work the saloon. You and Dawn will be in the pizza garden. I put you on the clock starting at eleven. You'll need to clock out at eight. Are you up for a full eight hours today?"

She nodded. "I can work longer if you need me."

"Not on your first day. Hunter and I are going to grab dinner. Will you join us? We'll talk about a start time for tomorrow while we eat, and I can answer questions you may have. I'm going to leave for a little while because I close tonight."

Ruby idly rubbed her baby bump.

A shuffle behind the other woman drew her attention over her shoulder. Ace walked up behind Ruby.

"No. You'll eat, then go home for the night. I talked to Owen. He'll cover your hours. You're off tomorrow. Don't come in." He turned her to face him. "I'm sorry I left you to handle everything. Thank you."

Love was evident in Ruby's eyes as she stared at the older man.

"Are you okay? I was worried," she admitted.

"I know. It won't happen again." He regarded both women. "Go sit, rest your feet. Both of you." He glanced at Hunter. "Take care of Ruby and Keira. I'll get behind the bar."

They did as instructed until customers arrived.

At eight, Owen approached Keira in the pizza garden. "Ace said to tell you your shift is over, and you can leave. Go clock out. I wanted to tell you the barn and loft doors are unlocked."

"Owen, I—"

He shook his head. "Just go. You're going to hurt more than you think. In fact, you should use the soaker tub. I won't be back until about three. When you go in the barn door, the motion light will come on."

"There was no light before," she said.

"The light was broken. I made the repairs today. The outside light will come on when you approach, as well. Once inside the barn door, the security keypad is on the left. Hit the red button to arm the system. If you don't set it, I'll know and come to check on you."

She nodded her understanding, and he walked away.

Twenty minutes later, Keira arrived at the barn, entered, and set the alarm as instructed. Walking up the stairs to the loft, she marveled at how heavy her backpack seemed. Ruby and Owen had been right. She started to drop the pack on the floor near the door, then remembered Owen's second lesson, and laid it at the end of the couch. He'd left a note on the counter, telling her to take whatever she needed from the refrigerator. She got a juice and headed to the bathroom, grabbing her pack as she passed.

The more she thought about it, the more appealing a long soak sounded. Pulling her shampoo from the backpack, she turned on the faucet and tested the temperature. Disrobing, she wrinkled her nose at the beer and food smells attached to her clothes. The scent thrust her back to when her mother would force her to work tables at her gentleman's club. Cigarette and cigar smoke from the private rooms, booze, sweat and sex—the sensory memories turned her stomach.

To pull herself back to the present, she grabbed body wash from the shelf and squeezed the gel into the water stream. A puff of suds erupted releasing another scent, a woodsy, clean, manly scent. She stepped into the tub and lowered herself into the warm water. Breathing deeply, she relaxed, surrounded by the heat and oddly comforting reminder of Owen.

OWEN LET himself into the loft from the upstairs deck. Silently, he crossed the kitchen into the living area. The air conditioner hummed in the background. Keira was deeply asleep on the couch.

He studied her from eight feet away. She lay on her side facing the room, legs tucked up in a pseudo-fetal position, one hand folded under her cheek. A towel wrapped her head resting on the pillow. She must have washed her hair. The corner of her shoulder was exposed by the lightweight blanket. She wore the Blue Spruce sweatshirt Zoe had given her. Her backpack, jacket and shoes were neatly arranged at the end of the couch where she could grab them quickly. Good girl. She'd listened. How much time did he have to teach her more?

While searching for his sister's killer, he'd worked for the most successful skip tracer in Chicago. When the old guy had been young, he had also been a bail bondsman doing bounty hunter work. As he'd gotten older, and after being shot twice, he'd cut that side of the business. When Owen hooked up with him, the man was getting ready to retire permanently. Since Owen willingly offered to learn both sides of the business, the skip tracer gladly passed on the tricks of the trade, not all of which were above board—some of his clients operated in the underworld. The job paid well. At the time, Owen needed the money and experience to fund his search for Oona's killer.

Owen never shared his unique talents or contacts with anyone, but sometimes he wondered if Hunter suspected. Admittedly, he still kept his fingers in the water. An occasional influx of cash was good financially, and the practice kept his mind and skills sharp. A man never knew when he'd need to revisit the past. When reviewing the copies of Keira's IDs, he'd instantly known they were fake.

He let his gaze travel her form one more time. Beautiful, delicate and fragile. Easily trampled and destroyed by careless people. His gut told him she was just what she seemed.

But something ugly was going on around her. Damn, he hoped there were logical explanations for the doubts in his mind. He wanted to believe she was innocent.

Turning, he headed for the shower. He needed to wash off the bar smells and attempt to rinse away the distrust. The sweet scent of her flowery shampoo surrounded him and mixed with his own woodsy soap. He inhaled deeply, feeding the growing need. The two fragrances entwined like lovers. But then the cold rush of reality hit him.

If she was the innocent she appeared to be, then she was too good for him, for what he'd become. If she had brought trouble, family came first.

He returned to the living room. Placing the money belt he'd purchased and one of his survival knife's on top her backpack, he crawled into bed. He'd saved the knife she'd left him in a bag in case Hunter needed evidence. Tomorrow, he'd learn what self-defense moves she knew. Then while she worked at the Wild Card, he'd search for her on the internet.

THE SMELL of bacon gradually pulled Keira from sleep. Grandma always made bacon with eggs benedict for her on the rare Sundays they were allowed to be together. She snuggled into the pillow and shifted her hips. Her body ached, and her eyes felt glued shut. Five more minutes. Keira bolted upright and glanced toward the kitchen.

Owen stood at the stove, turning bacon. Reaching for a coffee mug, he glanced toward her and leaned a hip against the counter. "Good morning." He studied her as he took a swallow of his coffee. "What time is your shift today?"

Again, she hadn't heard him come in. How had she missed him moving around in the kitchen? The man was a ghost.

"I start at five and work until close. Ruby wants me to get used to the evening shifts, because I'm going to help cover while someone else is gone."

Owen nodded. "I'm helping out later today. Breakfast is almost done. We can talk while we eat."

She headed toward the kitchen, stopping when she noticed the items on top of her backpack. "What are these?"

He nodded to where she waited. "Bring them over here and we'll talk. I'm a big eater, especially in the morning." Owen spoke as he placed several plates on the counter. He pulled out a stool and sat. She took the seat across from him, again. Bacon, eggs, toast, pancakes and fruit filled the plates. He topped off his coffee mug. "I started the hot pot if you want tea."

Loading his plate, he'd passed the selection to her. She hid a grin. He *was* a big eater. After eating in silence for several moments, he pointed toward the flat canvas belt.

"Lesson four. The money belt has six compartments. Separate your IDs and memorize which set is in which compartment. You don't want to fumble getting out the wrong ID. Handle your money in the same way, never keeping it all together. One ID should be hidden in your shoe in case you ever get separated from your money belt. It's double protection if you lose your bag."

Grabbing a small cardboard box from beside the door, he sat. Lifting the oblong case from the counter, he palmed the small tool. "This is a soldier's field knife, more practical for someone surviving on the streets. Not as lethal as a self-defense knife, which is what you had, but safer for someone who hasn't had training. This unit was engineered for survival, not specifically as a weapon. You could gut a fish or small animal for food. Its size makes it easy to conceal. It will fit into a compartment on your money belt. We're going to go through each component and practice. It doesn't do any good to have one of these and not know how to use it properly."

Owen showed her how to open each section and went through the obvious and not-so-obvious uses. For the bottle opener, he made sure she could open a beer bottle and a jelly jar. For the can opener, he'd given her a can of tomato soup, which took her forever to open. Then he went over the screwdrivers, scraper and reamer.

Last, he placed an apple, orange and grapefruit in front of her. He showed her the quick release for the knife and how to properly put the blade back in place. "You can cut meat, bread, even twigs with the blade."

He studied her intently. "However, this particular blade has been sharpened." He flicked his thumb lightly over the knife tip and a thin streak of blood appeared on his flesh. "The point is highly sharpened. A person could kill someone if they knew what they were doing. Someone takes it away from you, they could kill you as easily."

Keira watched the blood roll down his finger and drip onto the counter. She glanced up. "I couldn't kill anyone. I'd die before I could take someone else's life."

"Why is your life worth less than someone else's who is attacking you?"

She shifted her attention to the table. "I just don't think I could."

"Defending yourself doesn't always mean killing the other person. Sometimes self-defense means hurting them enough to get loose and run away. Running away is always where you start." He handed her the apple. "Stab the blade into this, cut it in half, and then peel off the skin."

When she finished, she glanced up. He handed her the orange. "The skin is tougher, more resistant. Stab it, then remove the blade. Do it three times."

The grapefruit was last. He stood in front of her, the fruit held between his palms. "This time I want you to grip the knife in your fist like you were stabbing down or out from your chest. Aim for the center."

"Not while you're holding it! I could hurt you."

He smiled. "At this range, you aren't going to miss. Trust me, I won't let you get to me."

On the first attempt, she didn't breach the rind.

"Harder. Like you mean it."

The peel resisted, but with a little more force the blade slid in. A warm sluice of juice washed over her hand.

"Again quickly. Don't lose your grip."

Responding to the command in his voice, she pulled out and plunged the blade again. The sticky fluid sprayed her hand and forearm. Releasing the knife, she stepped back in horror. "No. No more. I can never do this."

"Look at me," he demanded. "You're alone. Asleep in a doorway. You hear someone approach. Are you going to lay there and let them kill you? Or are you going to defend yourself long enough to get away? Extreme situations call for extreme actions. Every strike isn't a kill. But one hit can equal escape."

"I could never…."

"The will to live is strong. None of us know what we'll do until confronted."

Removing the knife, he washed it under the faucet and directed her to always make sure to dry it properly. Closing the blade, he placed the knife on top of the money belt and slid them toward her.

She glanced up. "How much do I owe you for these?"

"Nothing. They're spares I had lying around."

"No. I have to pay my own way or I can't take them." She put her hands over the items to slide them back.

He laid his much larger palm over hers. "Keira?"

She enjoyed the warm flesh covering hers. In spite of his

size, she didn't feel threatened. His low-pitched voice calmed her. The relaxed, unhurried way he moved never seemed threatening. Inhaling once and releasing the breath, she met his gaze.

His lips tilted in a gentle grin. "A long time ago someone helped me, gave me mental and physical tools to survive. Now, I do the same. Allow me. Let me help. Let me be a friend."

She studied his unwavering, deep blue eyes. The past six years, she'd lived in a gilded cage, a torturous existence, unable to trust anyone, not even the ones she should have been able to depend upon. Now a complete stranger had taken her into his home, fed her and given her—trust. She didn't deserve his support, but for now she couldn't resist. Nodding, she slid her hands from beneath his comforting hold.

"Do you have self-defense training?"

She shook her head.

"I'd like to give you a few basic lessons. But if you'd rather have a woman show you, my friend from yesterday, with the long blond hair, would come today and work with you. Your choice."

"You. I know you."

"Good. I'll clean up while you pack your money belt. I want you to keep it on you from now on." Pleased, he gave her a hundred-watt smile that threatened to take her breath away. The genuine pleasure transformed his normally expressionless features; he was strikingly handsome. She wondered if he even realized his appeal. She wished she could draw him to save the memory for after she was gone.

CHAPTER 5

The evening shift at the Wild Card started out slow and gradually got hectic. Keira worked nonstop in the pizza garden and sports bar, but whenever possible made her way into the saloon to clean tables. Ace and Owen worked behind the bar in an easy choreography, each shifting and turning to complete the work, effortlessly avoiding each other.

Straightening from the table, she studied them, realizing they both bore the same expression. Neutral. No emotion. Nothing gave away their thoughts, while Jimmy, the part-time bartender, talked the whole time. Owen and Ace rarely engaged in conversation except to take an order or greet those she realized were good friends, like the long-haired blonde and the man with her. Both Ace and Owen simply completed their tasks quickly and efficiently and moved on to the next. They never fidgeted.

Their eyes, however, never stopped. Both watched, searched, observed what others didn't notice. What did they see in her?

Ace glanced up and met the dark, soulful eyes of the girl he'd avoided all day. She'd been watching him and Owen covertly throughout the evening. More than once, he'd sensed her study. Embarrassed she'd been caught staring, she dropped her attention and fumbled with the dirty dish tray, crossing into the pizza garden and out of sight. The kid was more skittish than a homeless mutt. She was making his life hell.

He glanced at the clock. Midnight.

Owen crossed behind him. "Something wrong?"

"Nah. Going to the office. I'll be back. You good?"

Owen nodded.

Ace leaned over the back of his office chair, placed his palms on the desktop and hung his head, his long braids brushing the old oak. He swallowed hard. Two more weeks and he could leave. Two more weeks watching the beautiful dark-eyed child, the midnight hair, the girl who personified the remembrances of all he'd lost—two more weeks of heartbreaking memories.

Last week he'd made a decision and gone to his lawyer. His affairs were in order. In two weeks, he'd go into the mountains, as had his father's people before him. He was proud of his Cheyanne and Arapaho ancestry. Proud of his service to his country and to his fellow soldiers in the Navy. Proud of his accomplishments and the success of the Wild Card.

Pride couldn't bring back the dead.

A knock on the door jerked him from his dark reverie. He straightened. "It's open."

Gage walked in, Ruby right behind him.

"What're you doing here?" Ace groused at Ruby. "I thought I told you not to come in today. It's your day off."

"I'm not working. I came to see my favorite fella."

Ace glanced from Gage to Ruby. "Well, I'd say we got a

problem. Your old man hears you talk about the doc that way and we'll have blood on the floor."

Ruby laughed. "I'm talking about you. Hunter knows where I am, and he's keeping Ivy company."

Suspicion working its way into his mind, he studied the two. "What are you up to?"

Gage placed a black bag on the desk. "It's past time for your six-month check-up. We figured if we trapped you in this dinky little office, we could get the exam over with and have you back behind the bar in record time."

"Don't need no check-up."

Ruby reached out and took his hand in both of hers. "Ace, I asked Gage to come. I've been worried about you. I don't think you're sleeping right, and I know you aren't eating enough." She paused and the concern in her eyes was evident. "I need to ensure nothing is wrong. I can't help but worry about you. With the baby coming soon, I need to know you'll be with Hunter and I."

She slipped forward and wrapped her arms around him, leaning her head against his chest. Ace closed his eyes. He didn't want to be needed. He didn't want her to care. He didn't want to fail. Still, he couldn't stop from worrying about her.

"Fine, take my temperature."

Gage smiled. "We're going to do a little more than that, but I'll be quick. I need you to take off your string tie and shirt. I'm going to listen to your heart and draw blood."

Ace nodded at Ruby. "Go back to your man. I won't run Gage off."

ONCE THE PIZZA GARDEN CLOSED, Keira spent her time in the sports bar. Occasionally, she'd venture into the saloon to check for dirty plates. She noticed Ruby and Hunter now sat with a man and the blonde who'd been at Owen's. She wondered if he'd been the man boxing with the boy. Ruby met her gaze as she stood in the opening between the saloon and pizza garden. She waved her over. Hunter nodded at her approach.

"How was today? Any problems?" Ruby asked.

"It was fine. Lacey and Dawn helped a lot. I was busy, which I like."

"Good. Let me introduce you to our friends. If you ever have questions or concerns about the Wild Card or town, feel free to reach out to them. We're family. This is Doc Gage Ewing. If you have any medical issues, his office is on Brook Park Road and Third. He also works in the ER. And this is Ivy. She works with Hunter."

Keira shook hands with them, marveling at the easy acceptance they seemed to have. It was as if working here made her one of them. She'd been isolated for so long, she'd forgotten how good it felt to have friends.

"Would you like another round since I'm here?"

Before they could answer, the main door opened and a police officer walked briskly to the table. "Hey Chief, we've got a domestic disturbance you need to know about."

Hunter pushed back his chair. Planting a kiss on the top of Ruby's head, he pulled car keys from his pocket and put them on the table. "Gage, will you get Ruby home?"

The man nodded. Ivy leaned forward and gave the doctor a quick kiss and followed her boss.

Clutching her service tray to her chest, Keira stepped out of the way and followed them as far as the exit to the sports bar. Cutting through the closed pizza garden, she headed straight to the ladies' restroom. They were cops. Now what was she going to do?

OWEN WATCHED Keira disappear into the other side of the business. Realizing Hunter and Ivy were police, her eyes had widened to the size of saucers. Her reaction was a clear indicator that she had a fear of—or issues with—law enforcement. Too expressive. No survivor skills.

He glanced at the clock. One more hour until closing time. Leaving Ace behind the bar, he grabbed a tray and made a sweep of the tables and booths in the saloon. Stopping at the table held in reserve, he asked, "How'd the check-up on Ace go?"

Gage shrugged. "Nothing I can say. Ace is Ace. He did promise to stop by the office next week. I gave him HIPAA papers to complete. As he told us, he's looking forward to taking a couple weeks off."

Owen raised an eyebrow. "You don't think he is?"

"He gave the right answers. But his word choices lead me to think it's more. I'm going to talk with Deke tomorrow and see what he knows."

"Maybe we shouldn't let him go alone," Ruby responded.

"Let's see what Deke says. We've got a few days." Gage replied.

Owen collected the empty bottles from the table and carried them back to the bar.

Around three, the last of the closing staff from the sports bar and pizza garden came through the connecting door. Owen had seen Keira walk past the outside window around two-thirty. He wondered if she'd gone back to the barn. Her obvious distress at Hunter and Ivy being cops worried him.

Owen walked Ace to his truck a few minutes later. "I'll come work the bar again after my shift at Rollie's tomorrow. I want to get familiar with as many drinks as possible before you go on vacation. Going someplace special?"

Ace looked off into the distance and shook his head. "Just a hike up the mountains."

"I've been looking at the local trail maps. Like to hike myself. You have a particular trail you like to follow?"

"I stay away from the trails," he grumbled as he climbed into the truck. "Need a ride?"

Owen shook his head. "I like the walk. Tomorrow."

What he didn't like was the older man's evasiveness, or the distant look in his eyes.

Letting himself into the loft, Owen noticed Keira's huddled form on the couch and released a silent breath of relief. As he walked past her, he knew she only pretended to be asleep. He kept going, letting her charade play out.

After cleaning up, he crawled into bed. She'd curled against the back cushion and now slept. Perhaps she found it easier to fall asleep knowing she wasn't alone. He could've been a gentleman and given her the bed. As big as he was, he'd have ended up on the floor so he could lay flat.

An image of her in his bed flashed in his mind—her body spooned against his, her hair across his chest. He swallowed a groan and rolled onto his side. Do not go there, he reminded himself. If her driver's license held any truth, she was ten years his junior. Regardless of her bravado, or whatever mess she was in, she was an innocent. Too good for the likes of him.

AT TWELVE-THIRTY MONDAY AFTERNOON, a police car pulled into the parking lot at Rollie's Auto Body Shop. Standing under a vehicle on the hydraulic jack in the auto bay, Owen glanced toward the sound. Smiling, he grabbed a rag from his back pocket and wiped his hands as he walked out to greet his friend. The expression on Hunter's face didn't bode well.

"As we suspected, the parking sticker on the car led us to a college student in Louisiana. The kid said he sold the car three weeks ago to an older Asian woman who paid cash. He signed over the title and explained to her that she needed to register the vehicle and get plates. He doesn't remember if she ever gave him a name."

"An older woman can't be Keira." Owen shoved the rag in the back pocket of his coveralls and placed his hands on his hips. "I have a hard time thinking she could've stolen the car. She's not a professional. I'd know if she was acting. Maybe someone gave it to her."

"I believe you. I think we were off base when we thought she might be here hunting for Ivy or Gage. I got a great big, I-told-you-so from Ruby on that one. But something is going on. Did you see the look on her face when she realized Ivy and I were cops?" Hunter asked.

Owen grimaced. "You saw that, too."

"You make headway on the fake ID?" Hunter asked.

"I have a few guys working on it, and I contacted a tracer I know. DogWidABone is his name. He's good. He works out of Texas, where I think this may have come from, actually, even though the address is California."

Hunter raised an eyebrow. "DogWidABone."

"It's his alias. Might sound silly, but he has a reputation for never letting go until he gets what he wants. No clue about his real name," Owen offered.

"Do I want to know your alias?"

"Nope. Any hits on the finger prints?"

Hunter shook his head. "Too soon. She still at your place?"

"Yeah."

"Watch your six, buddy. Innocence can be deceiving. Listen to your gut, but stay alert."

Owen stood in the drive as Hunter drove away. His instincts shouted something was wrong, and could be serious. Shame they weren't telling him what.

Keira glanced at the clock over the bar. Five-forty in the afternoon. Grandma would be calling. They had limited minutes for which to talk. She glanced around the bar. According to the other waitress, Monday nights, during baseball season, meant a crowd. Business would pick up in another hour. Placing her dish bin on the rack, she wiped her hands and headed down the hall to the back door. If anyone asked where she'd gone, she'd tell them she'd been in the restroom.

Pulling her burner from her pocket, she paced back and forth behind the building. *Call Grandma, call.* Five minutes passed. Panic gripped her. She checked the phone making sure she'd turned on the button. Was something wrong with Grandma? She waited five more minutes. Still no call.

Her hand trembled as she stared at the screen, begging the phone to ring. She desperately needed to hear Grandma's voice. She had to know she was okay. If she didn't call in one more minute, she'd break the rule and dial her.

She rubbed her forehead and wiped the tear from her cheek. 'You must never call me. I call you. Promise me.'

The ring broke the silence. Keira spoke in Vietnamese. "Grandma, are you okay?"

"Hush, dear. I'm fine. We cannot talk. My appointment got changed to tomorrow. I will call then at this time." She paused. "Are you okay? Are you there?"

"Yes."

"Did you find him?"

"Yes," Keira responded again.

"Good. Watch him. We talk tomorrow. I love you."

Keira stared at the silent phone; tears continued to fall. It was too brief. Grandma was gone again.

Wiping her face once more, she ran to the dumpster. She struggled to open the phone, dropping it in the process. Scooping up the device, she pulled apart the case like she'd practiced. Removing the battery, she stomped on the metal square then threw it into the trash. Racing in the opposite direction, she deposited another section into a different receptacle. She placed the third part in her pocket to be disposed of in the bar trash, then slipped back inside.

Owen waited at the corner of the building and watched Keira enter the back door to the Wild Card. This delicate marionette was involved in a dangerous game. He wondered who was pulling her strings.

That evening Owen worked behind the bar, occasionally glimpsing Keira as she crossed between rooms.

She came into the saloon and cleared tables around midnight, and once more around one. After last call, she came in with her backpack and sat at the bar. She smiled at Ace. "Dawn told me I should go ahead and clock out. The sports bar cleared out early, and the cleanup is already done. I thought I should check with you."

"You're good to go. Thanks for asking." He nodded and crossed to the opposite end of the bar.

Owen smiled at her. "If you want to wait, I'll walk to the barn with you. Jimmy is staying for cleanup. I was leaving early as well."

She held his gaze for a moment, then shook her head. "I'm okay. I'll grab the shower first. I was wondering if I could use your washer and dryer."

"Sure, go ahead. I won't be far behind you."

He watched her walk out the front door, finished the glasses he'd been washing and said his goodbyes to Ace and Jimmy. Making his way out the back, he headed toward home at a leisurely pace, giving her a few minutes of privacy before he got there, but then they would talk.

A vision of her under the rainfall faucet with her long black hair loose against her bare back flashed through his mind. He imagined it would hang just past her perfectly rounded butt.

He gave his head a shake. Clearly, his libido and brain weren't communicating. Maybe he'd do a little bag work before going up to the loft.

Voices drifted on the breeze, and pulled him from his thoughts. He couldn't make out the words, but the tone was quarrelsome. One man tried to calm another. The sound came from about a street over and a little ahead of him. He moved out of the light and followed the sound.

"Come on, Princess. I know you're interested. No need to pretend. If you want to keep it on the lowdown, we're good."

"Leave me alone. Please." Keira's voice reached Owen.

Owen picked up his pace. Rounding the corner, he took in the situation. The three drunk tourists who'd been in the Wild Card the other night had Keira blocked against a brick wall. He slid his phone from his pocket. Knowing Ivy was on duty, he ran his thumbs over the keypad, texting a message.

Problem over by St. Mark's Church on fourth.
Get here.

Stepping forward, he secured the cell in his pocket before he spoke. "Why don't you guys step away from the young lady and move on?"

The loudmouth turned and gave him the once over. He hesitated for a second, then gave his buddies a grin. "Why don't you mind your own business?"

"Not my style." Owen shrugged and glanced at Keira. "You okay?"

She nodded.

"Keep your back against the wall. Everything will be fine. This won't take long." He turned his full attention to the three guys. He'd sensed their movement and knew each man's new position. Shifting his own stance, he moved away from Keira. Loudmouth angled to the left, and the other two flanked him. "She asked you politely to leave her alone. Go back to your hotel, sober up, sleep it off. Maybe tomorrow you can get lucky with someone who's interested."

"Why don't you fuck off and mind your own business?"

"I can't. She's a friend."

Loudmouth laughed. "So, the Ice Princess played you the other night, too. Cock tease." He stumbled. "She's been eyeing me all night."

"Was this douchebag at the sports bar tonight?" Owen asked without shifting his attention to her.

"Yes," she responded.

"You should've told me or Ace. We would have handled it."

"I didn't realize. I'm sorry."

"It's not your fault. Ivy's on the way."

Loudmouth made a drunken grimace. "Ah, the big guy mustn't be that tough. He had to call his girlfriend for support."

"You guys don't want to do this." In the alley nearby a vehicle rolled to a stop and a door opened. He glanced at the three bullies in front of him. They were too caught up in their own bravado to hear anything. A movement in the shadows let him know Ivy had arrived.

"What do you guys want?" Owen asked.

"She's coming with us. She's been promising all night, pouting those lips, giving us the eye. She knows what she wants."

"Well, there's the problem. I heard her say no as I walked up. To be sure, I'll ask again. Keira, do you want to go with these guys?"

"No!" Her shocked reply came out loud and clear.

"Did you promise to have sex with them?"

"No. I was their waitress. I didn't even speak to them except to get their order."

"What the fuck are you doing, man?" Loudmouth slurred. "You think you can step in and take over once we got her primed? Go fuck yourself. She's ours."

Loudmouth lunged at Owen, with his two friends close behind. The first man was down before the others got close.

"Police! Everyone stand down," Ivy shouted.

Momentum and bluster propelled the other two men forward. Owen took one solid punch to the side and a grazing clip to the chin before he had them flat on the ground. He stood over Loudmouth and glanced at Ivy.

Ivy tossed him a pair of handcuffs and went to where the other men landed. "You have the right to remain silent...." Securing them with zip ties, she finished reciting the Miranda Warning.

"You motherfucker. You set us up. We didn't do anything," Loudmouth shouted as Owen tugged him to his feet.

Another patrol car arrived and Officer Levi Ephraim stepped out. "Where do you want me?"

"I parked around the corner. Let's put two in your car, then I'll get mine. Mr. Strong, please wait by Officer

Ephraim's patrol car." Ivy glanced toward Keira. "Ma'am, please stay where you are. This'll only take us a minute."

Ivy approached Keira. "So that you know, what occurred after I arrived is recorded on my bodycam."

"I don't want to file a complaint. I just want to go. They didn't touch me. They just talked trash and stuff."

"Were you threatened?" Ivy questioned.

Keira met the woman's eyes, slightly taken aback by the understanding she saw. She nodded.

"I get it. They didn't touch you. Nothing happened, except they scared you. You don't want to create a fuss. You want the whole incident to go away. No one needs to know. Owen got here in time."

"Yes."

Ivy lowered her notepad and met Keira's gaze. She softened her voice. "See, the issue I have is that these assholes are predators. They did it together to justify their actions, bolster their courage, and to overpower their victim. I'll wager this isn't their first time. I guarantee it won't be their last. Not everyone has an Owen in the background. If someone doesn't speak up, they'll keep assaulting women. Success will be their rationale for continued behavior. After all, you didn't complain."

"I didn't encourage that guy. I was doing my job, paying attention to when they needed refills. That's all." She met Ivy's gaze.

Ivy relaxed her posture, glanced away, then returned her focus. "I'm working with a little girl. She's learning how to protect herself. She's twelve. A couple bullies tried to coerce her into a car. They had plans for her. Like these guys had for you. She got lucky. Someone helped. I know another little girl who didn't have anyone to help."

Keira remembered the girl she'd watched from Owen's loft window, practicing Tai Chi with Ivy. She thought of the intense concentration on the child's face. Now she understood. "I'm only here for a short time. I may not be able to come back to testify."

"File a report. Get this event on record. With video conferencing, if the courts need more information, we can swear you in through live video. Make sure this assault shows on their records."

All Keira could envision was the little girl working out at the gym. "Okay."

Hours later, Owen slid the barn door open and ushered Keira inside. "You're exhausted. Go on upstairs. I'm going to do a quick workout, then shower down here."

"This is your home. I can use the facilities down here."

He smiled and shook his head. "I need to release some steam. This is SOP for me."

At her quizzical glance, he explained. "Standard Operating Procedure. Now get going before you fall flat on your face."

Keira glanced up at him, concern evident in her eyes. "But you have to work at the garage soon. You should sleep. It's my fault you even got involved. They could have hurt you. You were out-numbered."

He reached to brush a loose tendril of hair off her face. "No. You have no fault in any of this. We were both lucky I was nearby. It would have been a lot worse if they'd touched you."

"What do you mean?"

"It would've gotten ugly." Owen shook his head. "Go to bed now, Keira. I'll watch over you."

CHAPTER 6

"What did you mean, 'it would have gotten ugly'?" she pressed.

Owen gritted his teeth and stepped back. He'd listened to the bullshit for the last two hours as the would-be rapist tried to pin the evening's events on Keira. The old rage roiled in his chest.

With verbatim testimony from each one, it was easy to tell these douchebags had done this before, likely been caught and probably gotten off.

""I'm trained. I can take care of myself. Now let it be, Keira." Darkness lurked at the edges of his mind, threatening his control.

"No. No, you meant something else. Tell me."

He took two more steps back and let it out. "Had they touched you, there would've been a beatdown. Definitely, some broken bones and a whole lot of payback. No one hurts the people in my family."

She retreated a step, in turn. "I'm not related to you."

"Family are the people we choose to let into our inner circle. In my book, blood is no assurance you're called family.

Now go and get some sleep. You're safe." He paused. "Unless you're afraid of me now?"

She met his gaze, then turned and headed up the stairs to the loft.

He watched her go. No lies. She needed to understand there was a violence within him. A violence he would call on to protect her, but never use to hurt her. If she couldn't accept that, then he'd find another place for her to stay.

After preparing for bed, Keira crossed to the window overlooking the barn floor below. Owen had turned the lights low and stripped down to loose-fitting shorts. His feet were wrapped, and he wore thick fingerless gloves.

He punched the hanging bag in a series of strikes, then spun and kicked the same bag. Repeating the process over and over, only alternating which hand or foot he led with, his broad shoulders glistened with sweat as did his hair, but he didn't stop. She felt his ferocity. Was he imagining the three men as he pummeled the bag?

She watched from above. The ripples on his abdomen and perfectly formed pecs affirmed the intensity and dedication of his workouts. His taut thighs bulged and smoothed with every step. She'd seen the tattoos on his forearms but only now did she realize there was ink covering his right chest and shoulder. His body was beautiful. Worthy of a sculpture. One she wished she could do.

When he'd worked out with the young girls he'd wore longer shorts and a T-shirt. He seemed painfully aware of his size and how he could be intimidating. If he saw her as a woman, he hid his awareness well. He'd called her a friend. What would he think if he knew how much she was savoring this moment? How would he feel knowing she saw him as desirable?

As Keira studied the imposing man, she realized he'd never frightened her. Ironically, she knew of smaller men that had petrified her. The fluid way he moved, his aware-ness of where his body was relative to others, his calmness generated confidence in his thoughtfulness. His gentleness with the children and Ruby gave credence to his devotion to those he cared about. No, he didn't frighten her.

She envied the family he had created. What if her coming to Spencer put one of them in danger? She wished she'd never come to the Wild Card. But what choice did she have?

The description of what he'd have done had the bullies touched her, hadn't terrified her. But the resolve in his eyes—that he might do something terrible to defend *her*—that was terrifying. She didn't need more guilt on her conscience. There were already too many mistakes for which she had to pay.

THE FOLLOWING DAY, when a car pulled in front of the open bay door, Owen glanced up from the engine he was inspect-ing. Hunter sat in his patrol car and rolled down the window closest to where Owen worked. "You eaten lunch yet? I've got Cold Slice sandwiches."

"Give me five and meet me in the back at the picnic table." At his friend's nod, Owen washed up and grabbed a couple drinks from the vending machine. He exited through the back door to the outdoor employee break area.

After dividing the sandwiches and chips, they'd both made headway into their meal before Hunter spoke. "Ace cancelled poker tonight. Said there was too much to do before he took off."

Owen met the other man's gaze. "Odd. Ace loves poker night."

"Yeah. Gage talked to Deke. He confirmed Ace takes off in

early August every year. He tried to talk to him once but got shut down, hard."

"And Deke let it go?"

Hunter snorted. "When he couldn't get answers, he did what Deke always does. He started digging. He admitted he didn't find much. Ace served in the Navy during the Vietnam war, honorable discharge and medal. Everyone in town knew when he got discharged because his dad was excited that he was coming home. But he didn't show up for several months. When he got home, he never talked about it to anyone. People in town speculate he lost a friend."

Owen stopped eating and stared at Hunter in surprise.

"Shit that's harsh."

They finished the rest of their lunch in silence, each lost in their own thoughts of love and loss. Sometimes Owen wondered if the heartbreak of losing his sister Oona would ever heal. Did Ace suffer the same guilt for his friend?

The repair shop was slow, and Owen left early to get to the Wild Card. Keira worked eleven to seven today, and afterward he planned to work with her on her self-defense skills. He thought of the phone battery he'd retrieved from the dumpster. He needed to find out what she was hiding.

KEIRA STRUGGLED TO BREATHE. Ace was the one going away. She'd heard him talking to the man with the silver beard. Oh God, nothing was going right. Now what were she and Grandma going to do?

Glancing at the clock, five-thirty-five, she made her way down the hall to the back door. Grandma would be calling and they would discuss the new development. When the phone rang, she answered in Vietnamese.

"Grandma?"

"Yes, dear. We don't have much time. Are you well?" Quang asked.

"Yes, Grandma. And you?"

"I'm fine. He is very angry about your disappearance. But I don't think he suspects our calls. What have you found?"

"We haven't talked yet. I was hoping tonight. But we have a problem…. Grandma, what's that noise? Grandma, Grandma, what's happening… Quang Hoa. Grandma…" Her phone went silent.

A door slammed behind her. Keira spun around.

Ace stood behind her, his face drained of color. "What are you saying? Why are you saying that name?" Ace staggered back clutching his chest, the trash bin landed at his feet. His eyes seemed to lose focus. "Who are you? Am I dreaming?"

"No. No." Keira yelled, dropping the phone. She raced forward to catch him as he slid down the wall.

"Ace!" Owen raced across the back alley, stopping abruptly behind her. "What's going on?"

She looked up at him. "I don't know. He just… I'm sorry. I'm sorry."

"Is Gage here?" Owen asked, kneeling beside Ace.

"No."

"Ruby? Hunter? Deke?"

"Deke. Deke is here."

"Get him now." Owen took Ace's wrist and checked for his pulse. "Have him call 911."

Ace grimaced, struggling to catch his breath. "It's okay. Tell Ruby I love her. Daughter. Time. Ready."

"Like hell you are," Owen snapped. "You've got a grand-baby on the way. Can you tell me what you're feeling?"

"Chest tight. Hard to breathe. Dizzy."

Deke came up behind him. "Spencer Fire Department is on the way. Gage was at his office. He's running over and should be here any second. What happened?"

Owen glanced around. "Where's Keira?"

Deke turned. "I don't know? I thought she was behind me? I'll find her."

Mere seconds later, Gage slammed through the back door, black bag in hand. He motioned Owen to the side, and knelt beside Ace. Slipping his stethoscope in his ears. "Sitrep."

"I was across the alley," Owen stated. "He walked out the back door with the garbage bin. Keira was out here on the phone. I couldn't hear her but something she said seemed to upset him because he dropped the garbage and I heard him ask her who she was. He clutched his chest and staggered back. Said something about dreaming. He told me his chest hurt, and he couldn't breathe."

Gage nodded and continued to check vitals.

The SFD Advanced Life Support Vehicle sped through the back lot entrance. Stepping out of the way, Owen spied the burner phone lying on the drive. He scooped the device up, dropping it into his pocket. "I'll get Ruby and we'll follow you to the hospital."

He walked in the back door, meeting Deke's concerned stare. "I've already contacted Hunter. He's picking up Ruby, and they'll meet us at the hospital." He paused. "The girl is gone."

FROM HIS POSITION against the ER waiting room wall, Owen watched Hunter talk on his cell, with Ruby huddled against his side on the plastic double seat. Owen crossed the space when the other man hung up.

Hunter looked up as he spoke. "Ivy says no luck. Keira's bag is gone from the Wild Card. Ivy swung by your place and she's not there. She said to tell you the blanket and pillow were folded on the couch. There was a note and money on the kitchen counter. Ivy left them for you."

Hunter grimaced in disgust. "I've got everyone looking, and I contacted Joe Cavanaugh. He said he'd have his people keep an eye out as well. Technically speaking, Keira hasn't done anything wrong. Until we can talk to Ace, we can only ask her to speak with us and explain."

Owen nodded. Once they had word on Ace, he'd search for Keira himself.

It was another hour before Gage came through the double doors. He waved for Ruby to stay seated and pulled over a chair. "First, why are you still here? I told you I'd call." He shook off her silent scowl. "We've run the tests. Ace didn't have a heart attack. Since I had him here, I ordered a full battery of tests. I won't have the results for a couple of days."

Gage met Hunter's steely gaze. "He won't talk other than to tell me his symptoms. Since he hasn't filled out the HIPAA papers, I can't say more."

Ruby lifted tear-filled eyes. "But he'll be okay?"

Gage gave her folded hands a squeeze. "Yes. I'll watch over him."

Ruby released her pent-up breath. "Okay, we can work with this." She glanced at her husband. "He comes home with us for a while."

"For as long as he needs, babe," Hunter agreed.

"Deke and I will handle keeping the Wild Card running," Owen added. "So Ruby, you be with Ace as long as he needs you."

"Have you found the girl?" Gage asked.

"No," Hunter replied.

Gage shrugged. "It'd help if we could talk to her. I've informed him we need to monitor him for twenty-four hours. I'm not releasing him tonight. I've given him a mild sedative, and a meal is on the way. Once he's eaten, I will give him another sedative. I want him to rest. I'll be here to guarantee he does what I ordered. Food and sleep are my two biggest concerns right now. Ruby, I know you're dying to see him, and I do want you to work your magic. He's being transferred to a room now. I'll have someone get you as soon as he's settled."

"Will the sedative knock him completely out?" Ruby asked. "Because if not, he'll be sneaking out in the middle of the night."

"I'll confirm he's monitored closely all night." Gage stood and glanced at his beeper. "He's settled. Ruby and Hunter follow me."

Owen stopped at the saloon on his way home. Deke had taken charge with the help of Jimmy and the other regular staff. He'd also called in extra help from the lodge.

"How's he doing?" Deke asked as he wiped down the bar.

"Doc says he should be okay. It wasn't a heart attack." Leaning against the end of the bar, Owen surveyed the room. "She hasn't come back?"

Deke shook his head.

"This is my fault. I sensed something was up. I haven't been able to nail it down yet, and Ace paid because I missed it."

"If not for you, she wouldn't be on our radar at all."

"A lot of good that did."

"We still don't know what's going on. She didn't do anything. In fact, you said she rushed over to help when he went down. I've still got my people checking on her." Deke studied him for a moment. "You're attracted to her and want to protect her because you sense another wounded dove. But you don't trust why she's here. Your head and instincts are at odds. That's my take."

Owen evaluated Deke's words. He was right. He'd tried to deny his attraction. He'd told himself he was doing a good deed, but that wasn't the whole truth. He wanted to help Keira so she'd see him and want him, the same way he wanted her. He wanted her even though he knew she had secrets, maybe even demons.

"Trust yourself." Deke said.

Owen straightened. "I'm going to find her. I—we need answers."

He followed the back streets to his barn. After checking the potential hiding places on one route, he backtracked the path she'd taken the night the drunks followed her, and then every other path he'd watched her walk. Hours later, he'd come up empty and headed home.

Even though Ivy had checked the barn, he went through each nook and cranny himself before heading upstairs to the loft. He studied the money and folded paper on the kitchen counter. He'd never wanted money from her.

Forcing himself to open the note, he read her words. *I'm sorry. I didn't want anyone to get hurt. I hope Ace is okay.*

He glanced blindly out the kitchen window. There was a reason she'd come to Spencer and dumped her car. He'd felt certain she was searching for something. The something, was Ace. What could the old man possibly possess to bring her here?

Owen dropped the note. At first light, he'd try to track her again.

Crossing the loft, he inhaled her lingering sweet flowery scent as he walked past the couch. Entering the bathroom, the lotus fragrance of her shampoo seemed stronger. He glanced around the room. She'd left nothing behind. He studied the closed entrance to the interconnecting walk-in closet. Silently, he opened the door. Keira lay huddled in the far corner, curled around her backpack, fast asleep.

Keira shifted, the dream slowly dissipating. She'd been running, again. Regardless of which version of the terror she tried to escape—an open road, a crowded city, the dense forest—she could always feel the hot breath and billowing fire of evil on her heels.

She squeezed her eyelids tightly shut and hugged her pack to her chest. She wanted out of the nightmare, but that would never happen. Not until the monster won. Pushing to a sitting position, she took a deep breath. The cedar scent from Owen's clothing met her consciousness, beating back the lingering terror of her dream. *He protected what was his.* A long-abandoned yearning filled her—if only she was his.

Opening her eyes, she started when she realized the object of her wandering mind sat silently in front of her. "How long have you been there?"

He glanced at his watch. "Three hours. After I left the hospital, I looked for you. I found you here around four this morning."

"Is Ace okay?"

He nodded.

Thank god, she silently prayed. "I was only going to rest for a minute."

He rose in one fluid movement and held out his hand. "I think you had quite the scare. You probably needed the sleep. We'll talk in the kitchen. Hand me your pack, and I'll put on coffee and tea."

He asked for compliance with steely expectation. All the mistakes she'd already made bombarded her. In over her head, and clueless as what to do, he might be her only chance. Others were depending on her, and his advice and expertise were her best shot. Putting her hand in his, she rose to her feet.

After splashing water on her face, she joined him in the kitchen. He'd poured her tea and his coffee into mugs and plated sandwiches. She couldn't suppress her smile. In deference to his size, there was one for her, three for him. He'd already started to eat.

"I know it's not breakfast, but quick and easy were on the menu." He shrugged. "I didn't eat last night and I bet you didn't either."

In silent agreement, they both ate, then cleaned up the kitchen and carried their mugs into the living room. He gestured for her to take a seat on one end of the couch and sat opposite her. Taking a drink of his coffee, he simply waited.

She shifted her position, folding her legs to her side. Glancing to where he sat, she marveled once again at his ability to be so still and silent. Plucking the hem of her shirt, she cleared her throat and dared to meet his gaze. "I thought Ace was having a heart attack."

"We all did. What happened?"

"I'm really not sure. I was on the phone." She bolted upright. "Oh no, the phone. I have to find it."

"Don't worry. I found it."

"The battery."

"I shut it off."

"Thank you." Another mistake. She sighed in relief and lifted her tea with trembling hands and took a swallow. Lowering the mug, she met Owen's gaze. "I need to talk to Ace. I have a message for him. It's private."

"What did he hear that upset him?" Owen asked.

"I didn't know he was there. I don't know what he overheard. What did he say?"

"He hasn't said much. What's this about?" Owen asked.

"I told you. It's a private message I need to give him."

"No."

"What do you mean? It's his decision, not yours."

"No."

"You can't stop me."

"He's still in the hospital."

"You said he was okay," Keira exclaimed.

"They're monitoring him."

"I need to see him." She jumped to her feet. "I have to talk to him."

"Sit down, Keira. You aren't going anywhere. And you won't be seeing him until Doc releases him. What do you need to tell him?"

"I told you. It's private."

"I'm telling you, you won't get within ten feet of him now without someone by his side."

She paced back and forth in front of the couch. Now what? She paused and turned on him. "What do you mean, now?"

"He's in the hospital. Ruby's scared and watching him like a hawk."

Keira hesitated. Oh no, she and Grandma never discussed what to do if he had another family. "She's his daughter?"

Owen held her gaze, but didn't answer her question. "We found the car you ditched. Hunter traced hairs found in the vehicle to you. He also located the original owner who sold the vehicle. At this point, he has reason to believe it's stolen property. Why don't you tell me what's going on?"

Keira's stomach lurched. "I'm going to be sick."

Two days later, Ace sank into the leather chair in Ruby and Hunter's living room, leaned his head back and closed his eyes. Doc had refused to release him unless he'd promised to stay with Ruby for at least two nights and not to work at the saloon for the same duration.

Ruby switched shifts, and they'd just finished dinner for

the second night. Damn, she could cook. He smiled to himself. Being here felt like he had a real family. Since the two of them had moved into this house, she'd been insisting he come for Sunday dinners. She kept talking about how he'd have to take time off to be with the baby. She claimed she needed him. His chest tightened in a good way. When he thought of Ruby and the baby, his heart swelled. The last two days had been nice.

The couch rustled. Opening his eyes, he sat up. Ruby perched on the end nearest him. Hunter stood stiffly by the window. He glanced from one to the other. "Spit it out girl."

Hunter was the one to turn around and speak. "Ace, I need to know what Keira said that upset you. Did she threaten you in some way?"

Taken aback by the question, Ace could only stare. Hunter was dead serious. *Well, hell.*

"No, she didn't threaten me. She wasn't talking to me. She was on the phone. She took me by surprise, that's all."

"What do you mean?"

"She was speaking another language, and I recognized it."

Knowing his heritage, Ruby asked, "Cheyenne? Arapaho?"

"Vietnamese."

"Hmm." Hunter waited.

Ace met their gazes. "I was stationed in Vietnam during the war. I learned a little of the language."

"Was it the fact she spoke Vietnamese or something she said?" Hunter pressed.

Damn stubborn boy, Ace thought. He wouldn't let up till he got what he wanted. "I thought I heard her say a name I knew. She said, Quang Hoa."

Hunter ran a hand over his mouth then sighed. "The girl wants to talk to you. Do you feel up to it?"

"Now? I'll be back to work tomorrow."

"No. I have reason to believe she stole a car. I don't want

her alone with you until I know more. Owen will be here too."

"Ace. You don't have to do this unless you want to," Ruby cut in.

Ace stood and began pacing the room. A thousand questions bombarded his mind. He'd heard the girl say "Grandma", then "Quang Hoa". Could the name be a coincidence? In two weeks, he planned to be gone. He was tired. He needed peace. Now was the time to rip off the band-aids and be done. "I'm fine. Let's get on with it."

Ruby got up and took his hand. "Ace, we love you. We'll be with you."

He smiled and hugged her, kissing the top of her head.

Hunter typed a text, and a few moments later Owen ushered Keira into Ruby's home.

"Let's meet at the table. I've made coffee and tea, or I have juice," Ruby offered.

Ace noticed Keira seemed as nervous as he felt. Well, at least he wasn't the only one. Band-aids. "You need to talk to me. Talk."

She looked at Owen, then back at him. Locking her fingers, she placed her clasped hands on the tabletop then met his gaze. "I came here to find out if you are the Ace Joseph who was in Vietnam in 1973."

"Yes."

"Were you in the Navy?"

"Yes. I was assigned to a Navy vessel in Saigon at the time."

"Did you know a street vender named Quang Hoa Thi?"

His heart thundered in his chest, and he gripped the coffee mug in front of him with two hands. "Yes."

"Are you still married to Quang Hoa Thi or did you divorce her?"

CHAPTER 7

*a*ce's pulse pounded in his head and tears filled his throat. The dreams and now this. Over and over he relived losing her. How much more could his heart take? He swallowed twice, then whispered. "She died in a reconstruction camp after I left."

Shock blanched Keira's face. "Who told you that?"

He closed his eyes and inhaled deeply, then released the breath. Ruby took his hand. A calmness came over him, telling him to release the pain.

"My assignment on the ship meant I was able to go into town on a regular basis. I bought my meals from her. She sold food on the street corner, and I fell for her the first time I laid eyes on her. She practiced her English with me and I worked on my Vietnamese.

"Every time, someone went to her cart, she would greet them and make conversation. She remembered everyone and asked about their families. I could tell how kind and thoughtful she was. She had the most beautiful smile.

"I started walking her home when she was done for the day. When she wasn't working, she would take me to temples and gardens and tell me stories. I told her about Colorado. I tried to teach her to play poker. I would make her laugh and smile and she would take my breath away.

"One day, we were together holding hands, walking through the market and someone started yelling at her, condemning her. I realized then she was in danger. It wasn't safe for her to be seen with me.

"I didn't want to leave her, but she'd been promised to someone else. He'd been gone for almost three years. In all that time, she only received two letters from him. Still, her family's pressure was strong.

"I tried to be patient, content with loving her. That day she admitted she hated the thought of being forced to marry her promised suitor. I asked if she could love me. She said she already did, regardless of how her family felt. The end of the war was near, and the situation deteriorated fast. We applied to be married via the military channels, but the paperwork was slow coming through. The officials weren't working with us. We got married in town. Two weeks later I was shipped out."

Ace clenched his fist at the remembered frustration and anger. Damn bureaucrats. The officials in charge only cared about having the paperwork filled out and the number of immigrants coming into the country. They never considered the lives that were affected, the pain of separation and loss.

"I wrote every day while I was on the ship. Quang had a friend who could translate. We made an arrangement where I sent my letters to the friend, and she would forward Quang's letters to me through the military base. Our plan was that I'd send for her as soon as I got the approval. Saigon fell while my ship was in route.

"When I got back to the states, I immediately applied to have her brought here. I even paid the extra money to expedite the process. I continued to write to her, but communication wasn't like today. Letters took weeks to arrive."

He paused, lost in the past. His eyes clouded over.

"Ace," Ruby whispered.

Blinking twice, he took a deep breath. "My time was up. I was discharged. I stayed near the base and waited for three months while they processed my request for Quang to join me. The first month there was no news. A fellow soldier who was still in the Navy agreed to check for me.

"I heard about the horrors of the reconstruction camps. I also heard a few people were able to escape them by hiding. Scuttlebutt is hard to confirm. No real information was coming to those of us waiting. Then my letters started coming back. All but three were returned. I never received any letters from her. Still I waited.

"After three more months, my friend contacted me. He'd learned she'd died. There were lists of the dead from the internment camps, and her name was recorded. I came back to Colorado. I tried to make a life, but it wasn't the life I wanted or had dreamed of with her." He scoffed, "A year later I got permission from the government for her to join me."

He studied his clasped hands on the table. "If only they'd let her come with me. If they'd have helped us, she wouldn't have been left behind. She wouldn't have died."

Speaking of his loss, saying the words out loud, expressing the long-buried feelings for the first time, drained him. Insurmountable grief swelled in his chest and clouded his mind.

He glanced at the girl. "Why are you here now, after all these years, asking these questions? Do you know where she's buried? Can I bring her remains here for burial? I want her here with my family, to rest with me."

Keira swallowed back guilt. She'd done nothing right. This wasn't the miraculous rescue they'd planned. This man was no longer a name on a piece of paper. This was a living, breathing, feeling man who obviously loved and grieved her grandmother deeply. She was ripping his heart apart. They should have thought this through.

"Quang didn't die in the camps," she managed through her constricted throat. "She escaped into the country and hid for a couple of years. Eventually, she made her way to the United States. She was one of the boat people. The relocation group sent her to Houston, Texas."

She watched helplessly as his face drained of color, his jaw dropped as he struggled to speak. "You're telling me, my Quang is here? In the United States? When did she come here?"

"Sometime around 1978."

"What? Why didn't she come to me? Why now? Who are you? How do you have this information?" Ace asked, doubt filling his voice.

"I know, because she sent me to find you. Quang Hoa is in trouble. She needs your help."

Ace started to rise. "Where is she? What kind of trouble?"

"Wait a second, Ace," Hunter interrupted, calmly placing a palm on the man's shoulder. "Let's think this through."

He glanced at Keira. "We need the truth about you. The only hard evidence I have is your false identification, and that you were in possession of a car we believe may have been stolen. Let's start with who you really are. I want proof. And believe me, I will verify."

Keira reached under her shirt.

"Stop."

Keira froze, meeting Hunter's gaze, his hand intentionally resting on his weapon. "My ID is in a money belt around my waist." She nodded toward Owen. "Ask him. He gave it to me."

"Don't move your hands. Owen, help her."

Owen placed a hand on her shoulder. "Stand up, Keira. Pull your shirt up enough so I can grab the ties." He glanced at Hunter. "I also gave her a soldier's knife that she carries in the belt."

He unfastened the belt, laid it flat on the table and pushed it toward Hunter. He urged Keira to sit back down.

Hunter removed the four IDs and knife from the belt.

"My real name is Keira Hoa Thi. Quang is my grandmother."

"She remarried?" Ace's eyes revealed fresh anguish.

Tears stung Keira's eyes. Would the truth bring this man any peace or only more pain? Too late to go back, she answered. "No Ace. She never remarried. My mother was your daughter. I'm your granddaughter."

Ace stared at her. Unblinking. Unmoving. As though in a trance or lost in his mind.

Hunter walked to the side door. "Gage, we need you."

Keira glanced around as Gage and Ivy filed in. Family, Owen called them. She longed for people she could depend on.

Owen took her hand and led her away from the table, allowing Gage access to Ace.

Gage spoke softly to Ivy. She went to the kitchen, returning with a glass of orange juice and placed it in front of Ace.

"Drink," Gage instructed. He glanced at Hunter. "Another shock, I take it."

"Yeah. A lot of those going around, I'm afraid," Hunter responded. He glanced at Ivy. "Would you mind going out to my patrol car and grabbing my DNA kit? I need a couple saliva swabs and evidence bags."

Keira volunteered saliva and a hair sample, as did Ace. She also wanted to be sure. She glanced up at Hunter. "In my money belt, the last compartment isn't empty. There's a baggie with Grandma's hair and another with some of my mother's hair. Part was from her hairbrush, the rest was from her body.

"Body?" Ace asked, with a catch in his voice.

How could she and Grandma have been so selfish, and insensitive? Shame filled her, and she struggled to contain the tears. "I'm sorry, Ace. I'm sorry. I didn't mean to tell you that way. She died two weeks ago."

Ace pushed shakily to his feet and walked to the window. In his reflection, Keira could see tears streaming down his cheeks. Ruby rose and went to him, wrapping her arms around him from behind.

What had she done? Remorse and self-disgust filled Keira's chest. She buried her face in her hands. Her mother was gone. Grandma was in danger. And now, she'd brutally wounded an innocent man.

Strong hands urged her from her chair, and she was engulfed in warm woodsy heat, comfort she didn't deserve. Why hadn't they all run away? Sobs broke from her chest in wave after wave, sobs she'd been forced to keep inside. Her mother hadn't been a kind or loving mother, but she had been her mother. Damaged by her own failures, she'd tried in her own dysfunctional way to make Keira successful. At least Keira wanted to believe she'd made decisions for her benefit.

She realized new hands stroked her cheek and back. Ace stood at her side and opened his arms. Owen released her into his embrace. She didn't understand the words he whispered into her ear, but she felt the consolation of the message. She and Ace grieved their loss together.

Ace led her to a chair and sat beside her. Ruby was there with a cool washcloth and a supportive hug.

"I'll have all your samples tested for DNA matches. I'll also be running checks on your real ID," Hunter explained.

"No, don't! If you do, he'll know." Keira exclaimed, the present dangers coming back into focus.

"Who'll know?" Ace asked.

"The man who is holding my grandmother hostage." Keira turned a tear-filled gaze on the older man. "Please, I need your help."

Hunter glanced at Owen. "I think we need more chairs."

When everyone was seated, Hunter nodded to her. "From the beginning."

Keira glanced at Ace. "A few years ago, my mother married her business partner, Dracon Escott."

"Where is your father?" Ace interrupted.

"Dead, we think he was killed in Afghanistan. But I didn't know him. Mom had a one-night stand with a military pilot from the base, close to where we lived in Texas. She never saw him again. Another pilot she knew from the base told her he died."

"Mom was an entrepreneur. She dabbled in a lot of—opportunities. Dracon was a client at my Mom's club. Shortly after they met, I started college and moved out. After they married, Mom and Grandma moved in with him. He's a bad Man. Recently, Grandma and I learned that Mom was planning to leave him. She was going to file for divorce. But she died."

Keira paused and took a drink of water. "Grandma and I were supposed to inherit Mom's half of her business, her house and investments. But the day after Mom died, Dracon produced papers stating that in the event of her death, he'd have medical and financial power of attorney over Grandma. He then had reports from a doctor that my grandmother had never seen, stating she suffered from dementia and was under his care and had been for months. Now Dracon is forcing her to go to that doctor's office once a week, where he writes more false reports. She does not have dementia."

She met Ace's gaze. "Grandma is quiet, but always watching and listening. By far the smartest of us all."

Ace nodded in silent agreement.

"About a month ago, when Mom started talking about leaving Dracon, Grandma got nervous. She sensed something was very wrong. She started making copies of legal documents and stashing money aside. She was going to get a place of her own, but she didn't get that far. When my mother died, she became a prisoner. Dracon has someone with her at all times, or she's locked in her room with a guard outside the door."

"How do you know this if you didn't live in the same house?" Hunter asked.

"Grandma learned from my mom how to use burner phones. Mom always had them stashed around the house, and Grandma has found little moments to call me.

"But I didn't see her until my mom's funeral. We were never allowed to speak Vietnamese in front of Dracon, but he couldn't make a scene in a public place like the funeral. We met in the restroom, where she gave me money, the IDs, the hair, and keys to her car. I was to come here and find you."

Ace studied her carefully. "How can I help?"

"Please understand, I never knew about you until the day Mom died. And I've told you what little Grandma confided in me. She said when you were shipped out, you took the marriage certificate with you. You needed the papers to send for her. If you're still married to her, you'd be her legal guardian, and the documentation would get her out from under Dracon's control. You were our last hope." Keira paused and glanced at Ruby. "But if you're still married to Ruby's mom…"

Ruby placed a hand over Keira's. "Ace took me in when I

was in trouble. He's been like a father ever since. We chose each other."

Ace glanced at the concerned faces around the table. His head pounded; his heart tightened. He didn't know what to believe. Quang was alive. All these years, she was alive. But she hadn't come for him. Had she not loved him, like he loved her? Why hadn't she found him? He pushed from his chair. "I'm going home."

Ruby stood. "Ace, please stay. One more night. You agreed."

"I have to go. I need to think."

"Ace, you're scaring me," Ruby whispered.

Keira watched as Ace embraced the other woman. They latched onto each other as though gripping a life line, unable and unwilling to let go. Weathering the storm together.

Aware of the skeptical eyes on her, more alone than ever, Keira longed for the comfort of her grandmother. Of warm arms to hold her and keep her safe. Someone to care. She envied these people's obvious love and concern for each other. A strong arm draped over her shoulders, and a large warm hand stroked her arm. She glanced up into Owen's compassionate blue eyes.

Hunter straightened. "Ivy, can you take Ace home and stay with him until he's settled?"

The woman gave Keira a contemplative glance, then nodded to Hunter. Gage eased her into a hug and whispered in her ear before giving her a quick kiss.

Gage left right after Ace and Ivy.

Hunter gently stroked Ruby's check. "Babe, I'd feel better if you went up to bed. I know you're going to have a hard time sleeping, but for the baby, will you go rest, please?"

"Hunter, I'm afraid. I don't think he should be alone."

"Don't worry. Ivy will be staying. She'll give him space,

but watch over him. Now give me some love and go rest. I'll be up as soon as we're done talking."

She gave him a kiss, then shot Keira a glance. Leaning her forehead against Hunter's chest, she said, "Be gentle, my love."

Hunter went to a drawer and pulled out a legal pad and pen. He slapped them on the table in front of her. "I want to know why you have all the fake IDs. And don't fucking lie to me."

Keira held his gaze for a moment, realizing this man wouldn't make a good enemy. "My mother and grandmother didn't have an easy life. They learned to hide and change IDs to stay alive after Saigon fell. They had to move often when there was a risk of being found. Once they made it to America, there were language barriers and, although Grandma spoke a little English, Mom spoke none when she first got here. Like I said, it was hard.

"When I was growing up, my mom didn't always run strictly legal businesses, or what some would call reputable businesses. We moved a lot. Then Mom and Dracon owned a lucrative gentleman's club with plenty of energy and banking guys coming through. They also dealt in stolen merchandise. Mom had this frantic need to be prepared in case we needed to take off. She'd have new IDs made fairly often. These were pretty recent. Grandma found them in with some legal documents.

"She always kept important papers and several burner phones on hand in a go bag. She taught us that if we were ever on the run, to use burners only once and then destroy them. She'd planned to run from her husband. Whenever I witnessed them together toward the end, their interaction was strained and often verbally ugly."

Hunter studied her. "I want names and numbers. Your mother, grandmother, step dad. You have three fake IDs. I assume there are more. I want every name for every fake ID they've ever used. Every business your mom owned or partnered with, every address where you lived together and on your own. I want the date your mother died, where the funeral was and where she was buried. I want—hell I want everything."

"Mom never got IDs for Dracon, so I don't know for sure if he has fakes, but I would bet money he does," Keira explained, then started writing. Almost thirty minutes later, she lay the pen down and slid the pad across the table to Hunter. He flipped through the pages and made a few notes on a separate page.

"May I use the restroom, please?"

"It's in the hall."

Once she left the room, he glanced at Owen. "Keep a close eye on her. I'll expedite the DNA. I wrote down the basics for you, so you can do your own search, and I'll get the rest to Deke. I'll also talk to Jakob and see if we can use his lawyer. Her real license, if we can believe it's real, was issued in Texas. Anything your friend can do for us?"

Owen nodded. "I'll contact him."

"I've got a bad feeling about all of this. You realize Ace is going to want to rescue this woman."

"Yeah," Owen agreed.

"Watch your back, brother."

"You DIDN'T NEED to walk me in, but thanks, Ivy. See yourself out." Ace hurried across the entrance and headed upstairs to his bedroom.

He sank onto the edge of the bed. Lifting his hesitant hand from the mattress, he opened the drawer of the small bedside table. He removed the framed black and white photo. Quang. His Quang was alive. All the years he'd grieved her loss, she'd been in America. All these years. All these lonely years.

He'd had a daughter. A daughter he'd never meet. He wondered if she had been as beautiful as her mother.

He also had a granddaughter. A lovely young woman. Her lips and smile had been the key. With a shaky finger, he traced the lush lips of the only woman he'd ever loved. From the first moment he'd seen Keira, something about her had troubled him. When she talked, he couldn't take his eyes off of her. He'd blamed his disquiet on the time of year. He'd married and lost Quang in August, and every year the memories flooded back.

Keira's smile was like her grandmother's. Her stature and the graceful, almost dancing way she moved, was also like Quang. But her cheekbones and eyes were reminiscent of his family. He could see that now.

What had her mother looked like?

Laying the framed photo on his pillow, he got down on his knees and pulled a plastic tub from under his mattress. Opening the tightly closed case, he removed the aged bamboo box holding his prized possessions. Kneeling at the bed's edge, he carefully laid out his mementos. Twenty fading photos of his love, a dried lotus flower and the government papers allowing him to bring his wife to America. Their marriage certificate lay at the bottom. In the corner was the jade pendant she'd given him on their wedding day. The chain was fragile now, and he only wore it when he went into the mountains in August. Carefully, he slipped it over his head.

Gently replacing the items, he put the box back in its protective case and slid it under the bed. Crawling onto the mattress, he laid his head on the pillow. Holding the photo to his chest with one hand and clutching the jade stone in the other, he closed his eyes to dream.

Ivy stayed in the shadows by the door and watched the old man drift off. She wondered if he'd realized he'd been speaking the whole time. She didn't know the words, but she understood the meaning. Tears streaming down her cheeks, she tugged her phone from her pocket.

Gage, I don't tell you enough. I love you with all my heart.

OWEN FOLLOWED Keira up the stairs to the loft. She stopped in front of the couch and glanced over her shoulder. "What do I do now?"

He met her wary gaze and released a sigh. "Same as you've been doing. But you'll be with someone at all times until we know what's going on."

Her eyes widened.

He lowered himself onto the side chair and motioned for her to sit. "Ruby was the catalyst. Her family had died, and she was on her own. Ace gave her a job when she needed one, and watched out for her. She saw he was alone and lonely. She adopted him. The rest of us—myself, Hunter, Gage, Ivy, Deke— were all brought into her family by choice.

"We were all alone, each of us with a past and none of us innocent. With the exception of Ruby, we're a misfit bunch of your-worst-nightmares. But we are family now. Threaten one, and you threaten us all." He warned.

"For now, I'm willing to believe what you said tonight, but I also know you're keeping more secrets, secrets that could prove dangerous to my family. I'd like to think I've proven I can be trusted. But I understand trust is hard. When you're ready, I'll be here. But don't wait too long. For now, you should get some rest."

He waited until she was asleep on the couch before he rose and fired up his laptop at the kitchen counter. He reached out to his friend, DogWidABone, first, then started his own search. At three, he shifted back to the living room chair, taking the laptop with him.

Not much luck on traditional search sites, he did find that Keira had been a promising art student, she'd won several scholarships, and was a finalist for something called the "Future Generation Art Prize", but then she'd dropped out midterm her sophomore year of college. She had no presence on social media, no phone number listed in her name, and her last residence had been on what appeared to be a private compound. The listing trail for the location was one shell company after another.

There'd been even less info on the grandmother. Her mother's obituary was short and sweet, stating little more than she'd died and been cremated.

He needed a power nap. Leaning his head against the back cushion of the chair, he closed his eyes. The one obvious fact he'd discovered was that someone was urgently searching for Keira.

The message from Dog pinged his cell at four a.m.

*MAN, **what the fuck are you into? Back away. Get a burner and call this number.***

I'm shutting down the connection you used.

CHAPTER 8

*K*eira woke to find Ivy in the chair across from her.

"Owen said you need training. I usually do a power drink, workout, then eat. Can you be ready in five?"

"Umm, yes."

"Do you have anything besides those tennis shoes?"

"Sandals."

"Stick with the tennis shoes and dress as if you were going to work at the Wild Card. This is real-life training."

When they got downstairs, Gage was running on the treadmill in the workout area.

"We're going to work on escape moves. I'll teach you the move, then show you the execution on Gage. Then you'll practice. The goal today is to break loose and get away. Always pay attention to where you are, where others might be hanging out. Head for the highest concentration of people. There's a lot to cover. Let's get started."

OWEN WASHED up and met Deke and Hunter behind the garage. They were already at the picnic table. "Rollie said to tell you he's going to start charging for using his office."

Hunter slid a small paper bag across the table. "Tell him it's payment."

"What is it?" Owen asked.

"A cupcake from Cookie's."

"He'll like that." Owen pushed the bag and the sandwich to the side and popped the top on his pop.

Hunter eyed the discarded food before asking, "What'd your contact say?"

"Dog would only talk to me on a prepaid cell. He says Escott has some of the best tech guys he's ever seen working for him, both traditional and dark net. They can back-trace anything. He warned they've probably already got us in their sights.

"Keira's stepdad is squeaky clean in the public eye. Big benefactor to the humanities and tight with local government officials in Houston. He has half the lawyers in the state on his payroll and uses the law for manipulation and fake papers to get what he wants.

"In reality, Dracon Escott is about as dark as they come. No surprise, the gentlemen's club is a front for his illegal businesses. He runs drugs, weapons, people, stolen goods— you name it, he has his hand in the pie. No way Keira's mom didn't know what he was into.

"He remembers a few years ago, Escott paraded his wife and daughter around at charitable functions pretending to be a family man.

"About four years ago, the daughter, who must have been in college, vanished. Supposedly, she went to Europe to study. There was speculation her disappearance was something else."

Hunter raised an eyebrow. "What something else?"

"The mom was smart and almost as devious as Escott. She started a little political blackmail ring through the club, hidden video of sex workers with VIPs, that kind of thing. She had another side game Escott was cashing in on, but he couldn't get any details on that one. There was talk that he took the girl to keep the mom in line."

Owen studied his drink, twisting the can around.

"What else did he say?" Hunter pressed, pushing his own food aside.

"He has three recommendations. His first piece of advice was to back away and pretend we never heard of Dracon Escott. Quit searching, because if he hasn't already, he'll find Keira and then he'll find us. His second suggestion was to buy the girl a one-way ticket to as-far-away-as-possible and drop her off at the airport."

"And his third recommendation?"

Owen looked up from his drink. "Get my affairs in order."

Hunter pushed off the bench and tossed his garbage in the wastebasket. "Guess life was getting boring. We'll get everyone together at the Wild Card after closing."

Thinking of Dog's final suggestion, Owen watched his friends, Deke and Hunter, walk away. *Chances are good it's already too late. He's probably locked onto you searching for him. The girl is the key. He's after her. Bring the heavy guns and burn the motherfucker down. Because now the only way to save yourself and the girl is by cutting off the dragon's head.*

Owen grabbed his untouched lunch. He needed to talk to Rollie. Today would be his last day at work. After the meeting tonight, he and Keira were taking off.

He hoped their disappearance would be enough to protect Ace and the rest of the family. Would he be able to protect Keira on the run?

After work, Owen headed to the barn. When Ivy had to report for her shift, Deke had come and stayed with Keira.

The plan was for him to go with her to the Wild Card where they'd work until closing.

Entering the loft with steak and potato takeout from Pearls Café, he learned Keira was in the back preparing for her shift. Deke rose from the chair at the kitchen counter and nodded for Owen to join him on the upper deck. They stood where they would have a clear view when Keira came out of the bathroom.

"Willa called me," Deke said. "Jakob mentioned Dracon Escott and she recognized the name. The last few years he's become a mover-and-shaker in the art world. Willa also remembered Keira. She said Keira was quite the prodigy, but once Dracon became her step-father, her work changed dramatically. Her paintings became sloppy and boring. Escott is an egocentric asshole—Willa's words—who sees himself as a real art connoisseur. Over the last few years, he's been building a name for himself as an art collector and dealer, brokering deals for the hard-to-find market. Recently there's been a hint he's brokered forgeries, but buyers who were duped won't admit their losses as it would taint their whole collection."

Deke paused and glanced inside. "When I hung up, I tried to talk to Keira about her art and Escott. She became very quiet, guarded. I could feel the anxiety practically pulsing through her. Then clearly and carefully, she explained she has 'a little talent, but nothing like the masters. She also said that Dracon Escott was an exceptional judge of new and rare art."

Keira entered the kitchen, and Owen turned to Deke. "Can you stay while I take a fast shower?"

Deke nodded, speaking softly. "Owen, make sure you're thinking with the right head. There's a good chance she's not the innocent you think. She could be involved with some shady art dealings."

Later, Owen carried their dirty dinner plates to the sink and scraped the scraps into the disposal. "You start at seven. We have a little time before we need to head out, if you want to take a short nap. It'll be a late night."

When she didn't comment, he covertly lifted his gaze and studied her. Her attention was locked on her thumb, flicking over and over the edge of the steak knife. Unease settled in his chest. What was she thinking?

Keira studied the knife in her hand. Earlier, Deke was talking to someone on his cell. He told the other person that if Dracon had killed the wife to get the grandmother's inheritance, he'd have no problem killing Ace. Only she knew the inheritance wasn't what he wanted. Dracon wanted the golden goose. He wanted her.

A drop of blood bubbled on the tip of her thumb.

Grandma was a hostage. Ace would die or become another tool against her. If Keira was gone, would he release Grandma and let Ace go? The sound of the garbage disposal shocked her from her rumination.

"Keira, go rest. It's going to be a long night."

"No, no, you rest. I know you were up after me. Let me finish cleaning up the kitchen. And then I'll lay down for a few minutes. Why don't you do that power thing you do."

He chuckled. "Power nap. No. But I'll work on my laptop."

As she scraped the rest of the food into the garbage disposal, she glanced at the knife again. Could she do it? Could she slice her wrist and be done with all of this? If she died, Dracon would have no reason to keep Grandma locked up. She flipped the switch on the garbage disposal and cringed at the powerful grinding sound. She shut it off and watched the water swirl down the drain.

Did she need to die? Maybe she only had to be damaged. What if she no longer had value? Like the quiz—if you had to lose one of your senses, which would you forfeit? Not the colors of the world. Not the scent of the flowers. Not the sound of laughter.

What about touch? What about a finger or two? She flipped the switch back on. Would he let them both go?

Letting the water flow over her left hand she slid her fingers along the lip then dipped the tips over the rim. She wouldn't have to see anything. She'd read that people have lost entire limbs and never felt it until later when the phantom pain comes. The damage would be done before she knew it. She slid her fingers a little farther into the hole. *You can do this. Don't be afraid. Don't be a coward. Do it for someone else. Just do it.*

A firm grip clamped her wrist before she could make the final plunge. The grinding stopped with the flip of a switch.

"I don't think this would end with you losing a hand."

Her chest was weighted down with despair. "It's my fault.

"Ah, Little-bit. You're breaking my heart." Owen turned her around and put one broad palm under her butt and lifted her. "Wrap your arms and legs around me. I got you."

He held her. She was safe for the moment. She wrapped her legs around his waist and her arms around his shoulders, and buried her face in his neck. He barely knew her, yet he cared enough to hold her, protect her. Her tears erupted like a water show, and she couldn't stop them.

She cried until there were no more tears. Her head pounded and her body was drained. Still, she clutched him as tightly as possible, absorbing his heat and the comfort he offered. For the first time in forever, she felt supported and protected. He stroked her back, his hand warm and gentle.

She kept her eyes closed, while he rocked her back and forth for a while then set her on the counter. Holding her securely against his body, he bathed her face with a warm cloth.

Something shifted inside her, awakening a desire she'd never exactly experienced—a need for someone of her own —someone to share her sorrows, someone to touch and to touch her. A long time ago, she'd accepted she was the Ice Princess. Her ability to shut down and shut out had kept her from insanity. At this moment she didn't want to be sane. She wanted to feel and experience life, the days and nights. And love. She wanted something for herself. Something to cherish for a lifetime.

Lifting her head, she speared her fingers through his hair. "Kiss me. Please kiss me like a woman. Like you want me. Like I've dreamed of being kissed by you."

He groaned and cupped her face.

The feather-soft brush of his mustache and shadow-beard teased. His lips were warm and gentle on hers. He used the tip of his tongue to paint the soft flesh of her lips. She returned the action, then waited for his next move. Gently, he sucked her lower lip. She reciprocated. He nibbled her upper lip. She responded in kind. He growled and thrust his tongue past her lips to battle with hers.

Her limited experience hadn't prepared her for the scalding heat of his kisses. He wanted her. She could feel his desire in the strength of his palms as he brushed them up and down her sides, in the rough, needy sounds emanating from his throat. The arch of his hip against her throbbing core signaled his escalating hunger.

She wanted him, wanted his strength to lean on. She needed his courage to learn from. His honor to guide her on the right path. Most of all, she craved his touch, to live beyond regret.

She gripped him more tightly, holding him against her until she couldn't breathe, couldn't think. Releasing him, she leaned back and gasped for air. "So good. Again."

Owen was crazy for her, and wondered if he would ever get enough of her. "My pleasure."

Clutching her head with a palm, Owen devoured her lips and mouth. Sucking, sipping, thrusting, savoring her sweet responses and gentle gasps. He ran a hand over the gentle curve of her hip where she sat on the counter. Sliding a thumb under her shirt, he mindlessly sought the silken warmth of her back. The span of his hand nearly covered the breadth of her waist. With a groan, he buried both hands under her top, memorizing the sweep of her form, from hip to shoulder and back down.

Owen pulled back. The second foray had been even more exhilarating than the first. His body was on fire, but he knew she wasn't ready for all he wanted to give.

This woman. This little-bit of a thing had him so wound up he could barely think. When he'd realized she planned to hurt herself, he'd nearly come undone. Still, he struggled with his own realization. Innocent or not, he'd protect her.

He leaned his forehead against hers and simply held her until their breathing returned to normal. Lifting her feather-like weight, he walked to the living room and sat on the couch with her on his lap.

"Look at me, Keira."

He waited for her to lift her dark gaze. "I want to help you. But we're running out of time. I feel it. Come clean with me, now. One-hundred percent. Trust me."

Doubt flitted across her features. He realized the fear had a stranglehold on her. Her silence had become a defense so ingrained she didn't appear capable of breaking out. If he was going to be able to help her, he had to force her to open up.

"Dracon Escott is a dangerous man. You already know that. Your grandmother is in danger, as are you, and now you've put Ace's life on the line. How many more people are you going to endanger by withholding the truth?"

"I'm scared. I don't know what to do. I keep trusting the wrong people."

Owen met her fear-filled gaze. "I'm not the wrong person. Talk to me. Start at the beginning. Talk, Keira."

She fingered the pearl snap on his white dress shirt. "I loved art, and I always took classes at school. When I was very young, teachers told Mom I was talented. She started me in private classes. As I got older, she enrolled me in class after class and hired all kinds of private teachers. The more awards I won, the more classes she signed me up for. But it never felt like work. It was just my life.

"When I was in high school, she worked at the gentlemen's club as a host, securing big clients to come in. The owner wanted to retire, and he sold the business to her. She had big plans to elevate the clientele. In two of the private rooms she asked me to replicate famous paintings as murals.

"I was excited for the challenge, excited to see if I could do it. I really took my time. She encouraged me, saying I should make them perfect. She loved my work, and she used those rooms for the most sophisticated clients and big spenders. Dracon became a client, and he always asked for those rooms.

"I was starting college. I lived at home and still worked for Mom, but I was allowed a little more freedom to come and go as I pleased."

"Wait," he interrupted. "Your mother had you working at the club?"

She kept her attention transfixed on the flap of his shirt. With a hand under her chin, he insisted she look up. "Have you ever told anyone about this?"

She shook her head.

He chose his words carefully. "I was a soldier, saw battle,

came home and saw more bad shit. I've done things I'm not proud of. I hit a wall a while back and needed help. I learned that we sometimes need to talk it out. This is a no judgment zone. I am a safe place. You need to get it out at some point. You don't have to tell me, but did she force you to service clients?"

"I didn't dance. I dressed the part and waited tables, mostly."

"Mostly," he asked, then answered his own question. "Dracon."

She nodded. "Twice he asked for a lap dance. Mom was working the partnership deal at the time." She glanced up. "It was only a lap dance. But I didn't like it."

Sliding from his arms, she stood and walked to the window overlooking the gym below. He gave her a moment, but then followed, standing behind her.

"I started dating a boy at college, another art student. He was nice and we did things together, like museums. We could talk about art, and he listened. I liked him. I moved in with him." She turned, shoulders back, and met his gaze. "I didn't want my first time to be with one of my mom's clients."

He nodded his understanding.

"I also told my mom I couldn't work for her anymore, because school was too hard. She didn't need me anymore. Their partnership was solid, and she'd married Dracon as an added bonus. A couple months later, Mom asked me to paint a birthday gift for Grandma. She asked for a reproduction of one of her favorite paintings, a small Rothko. I said no, but my boyfriend talked me into it, saying it was good practice and there was no harm in hanging it in an old lady's bedroom."

"Did you do the painting?"

"Yes." Anger laced her voice as she continued. "And then Mom gave it to Dracon. Later, he sold it as an original." She slapped her palm against the window. "My own mother. She essentially gave me to him."

Owen cupped her shoulders, massaging the tension with his thumbs and waited for her to begin again.

"A few months later, Grandma's house caught fire. She didn't get hurt, but was obviously shattered. That night, Mom insisted Grandma and I come to dinner at Dracon's house, at his gated residence. While we dined on an awkwardly elaborate meal, my stuff was moved to a building on his property—they just broke in and moved my stuff. At the same time my grandma was moved into the main house where mom and Dracon lived.

"After dinner, he and my mother invited me to join them in the library. He informed me of my 'relocation'. They explained it was for my own good. The painting had sold as an original, and he had a bill of sale with my name on it. He warned if I ever told anyone, I'd go to jail for life for art fraud and Grandma would be humiliated from the shame and embarrassment of my deception. He claimed he was worried that she would do something to harm herself."

She spun around to meet Owen's gaze. "I didn't sell the painting or even want to do the forgery. But how could I fight his fake document? And I never believed the fire at Grandma's was an accident. The whole thing about my grandmother's embarrassment was nothing more than a death threat."

Keira fisted her hands at her side. "And my mother's response to the threats was to remind me how talented I was to be able to copy the masters so perfectly, as if being a forger was something to be proud of. She didn't even consider that I might want to express my own talent and visions."

Betrayal and pain filled her eyes. Owen felt a strong

impulse to hold her and comfort her, but he sensed there was more.

"After that night, Grandma and I were prisoners. They brought in private art teachers, and I painted what Dracon told me to paint. Once a week, I was allowed to visit with my grandma in the garden with my assistant present, who was nothing but a glorified guard. When a project ended, I was given a weekend with Grandma as a reward, but we remained in the compound under watch. For over three years.

"The night my mother died, Dracon came to my quarters and informed me he possessed bullshit medical proof I was emotionally unstable and that my mother's dying wish was for him to care for me. After the funeral, I'd be moving to the big house with him.

"That same type of phony papers as the fabricated medical proof claiming Grandma had dementia. Reports his family physician prepared without ever seeing her. The same fake doctor claimed he'd been treating my mother for an on-going health issue. She'd supposedly been in a lot of pain. That bastard said it was his 'documented opinion', that her death was an accidental overdose of her pain meds.

"My mother hadn't been sick. She wasn't in pain. But Dracon has doctors, lawyers and the police on his payroll, he can do anything, say anything he likes.

"Grandma and I were frantic to escape. But we weren't able to talk until the funeral, where she told me her plan. I tried to tell Grandma it wouldn't work, but she was convinced it would because we wouldn't be dealing with people in our home state." She looked up at him. "I never knew about Ace. Not a thing. Mom wouldn't allow Grandma to talk about the past. Now I understand. Grandma wants to see Ace one more time. She deserves that."

She flattened her hands on his chest. "I swear, I'll gladly

go to prison. I'll testify, I'll do anything, but I somehow have to get Grandma and Ace to safety first. I'd even go with Dracon if I could make this right for the people I've put in danger. I swear, Owen, I've told you everything. I've told you the truth. If we go to Hunter now, can we stop this?"

Owen believed her. She'd confirmed Dog's assessment of Dracon Escott's reach. He had his own experience with the control of evil men with money—his sister's killer flashed through his mind. This was another chance. He made himself a promise to fight Keira's demons with her, to set her free.

He eased her into his embrace. "I've got you. I'll protect you. You aren't alone anymore. You have a family who cares now. Working together, we'll think of something."

CHAPTER 9

$\mathcal{F}$riday night and the Wild Card was packed. Arriving at the bar, Owen asked Ace to assign Keira on the saloon side and switch Lacey to the sports bar and pizza garden.

Now that he'd touched her, tasted her, knew the pleasure of holding her in his arms, Owen struggled to keep his hands off Keira as the night wore on. He wanted her in his arms so he could keep her safe. Throughout the evening, he'd kept her in his sight while checking every customer who walked into the bar, an almost impossible task, since it was full-blown tourist season.

The last employee to leave for the night, Jimmy, paused at the door. "Anything else you need me to do, Ace?"

Ace shook his head and the young man left. Owen locked the door behind him.

Hunter argued with Ruby in the corner while the rest of them took a seat at the biggest round table in the bar. He'd obviously lost because they both joined the circle, taking the seats to the right of Ace. Owen sat next to Keira and directly across from Ace. Ivy and Deke sat on Ace's other side. Gage had an ER shift at the hospital and was going to catch up later.

Ace cleared his throat. "I have the marriage document from our wedding and my government-issued documents stating she can come live with me. I'll do whatever I can to help Quang. She can come and live here. I'll take care of her. I won't fail her this time."

"Ace, please give her a chance to explain when you meet her," Keira spoke. "You didn't fail her. I don't think it was her choice to not find you. Since I learned of you, I've tried to remember conversations. I think she and my mother fought about you. My mother was difficult. I do remember Grandma once saying her love was lost to her. But I was little, and I didn't understand. Another time she told me to make memories to savor in the hard times. Maybe, she was remembering you. I hope she gets the chance to speak."

He nodded. "I'll listen. Now what do I need to do? Can I go get her or do I send her a ticket to come here?"

"It's not quite that easy, Ace," Owen replied, then reported his findings through his friend DogWidABone. At Keira's request, he gave an outline of her life under Dracon's control, and the situation with her grandma. Keira spoke about the forgeries and assured Hunter she was prepared for the consequences if only they could help her grandmother.

"Can you call her?" Owen asked.

"No. I have to wait for her to call me. If I try to reach her, he may figure out we are contacting each other. The only time she's not being watched and is able to talk is when she's at the doctor. I'm nervous. The last time we talked, something happened. I think she dumped the burner in the toilet."

"Explain how you use the phones."

"We each had ten. She labeled each one, from one to ten. Each phone has a match. When the call is over, we destroy them by breaking them apart and smashing the battery. Most burners can't be traced if they're only used once. My mother learned that trick from Dracon.

"Grandma has the master list of phone numbers written in Vietnamese in her diary. We didn't have a lot of time to plan and only the twenty phones she'd stockpiled to share."

"Okay, when will she call again?"

"Monday around five-forty."

"Okay," Hunter spoke up. "I've got a lawyer working on the power of attorney issue. At first glance, she believes Ace would have primary rights. If we can get Quang here and get another doctor's evaluation, preferably two doctors to prove her competency, she should be able to debunk medical concerns, and the guardianship rights would become a non-issue. Ultimately, she wouldn't require a guardian. She'd be free to do and go wherever she wants." He glanced at Ace. "We assure her safety first. Then the two of you can decide how you want to proceed."

Ace nodded.

Hunter continued. "I want you both to know that I still want proof of paternity. We should have the results Monday afternoon."

"I want proof, too," Keira added. "What about my mother's murder?"

"You said she was cremated. The doctor would need to turn state's evidence for us to prove anything." Hunter glanced at Ivy. "If this prick has been pulling this shit for years, I can't believe he isn't on someone's radar. Hell, Willa's heard rumors. We're crossing a lot of state and federal boundaries here. We need someone who could give us a hand with federal law enforcement. Someone who maybe owes us a favor."

Ivy stood and headed down the hall toward Ace's office. "On it."

Owen spoke up. "I have a new backdoor to Dog. He

doesn't like Dracon much. Thinks he may have been the one to make a couple of his friends disappear. I'll see if he'd be willing to do recon around the compound. Getting Grandma out of there could be a problem. Doing it at the doctor's office might be our best shot.

"If Dracon's team is as good as Dog says, I'm worried he may have traced our searches back to me or Deke," Owen continued.

"My searches weren't on lodge equipment," Deke interrupted. "If he followed it back, it's going to dead end at a company located in Australia. I've given them the heads up to be watchful and let me know if they see any back traces."

Owen turned to Keira. "Is there any way Dracon could have known about Ace?"

Keira shot a worried glance at the older man. "I don't think so. Mom usually told people he was dead, and Grandma was forbidden to talk about him."

"That could work to our advantage," Owen said thoughtfully. "Your grandmother was very smart to pull hair from your mother's body and her hairbrush. We can crossmatch the DNA from grandmother, grandfather, mother and daughter. If everything matches, we have a lock on our case."

"If I'm the only one he can back trace and he sends someone here to get Keira, they'd look at my place," Owen confirmed. "I'll talk to Ivy and Gage. Keira can start staying with them. As a precaution, we should relocate Ace."

"No." Keira and Ace said simultaneously.

"I can damn well take care of myself," Ace proclaimed.

Keira glared at Owen. "You promised to take care of me. I don't want anyone else. I feel safe with you."

"Okay. We stay together at least until the call on Monday." Owen glanced at Hunter and Ace. "Since my name and property may already be on Escott's radar, let's take the call at my loft, just in case. We let him think she only has me."

He paused for a moment. "Deke, you have the fake backstory stuff you'd collected on me back when we were after DeMitri. Right?"

"Yep. Why?"

"I scrubbed all internet history. Put it back out there with a couple tweaks. Make sure his people have to work for it, but let him find my background. Clean it up a bit, so he thinks I'm just an Army grunt who's only trained as a mechanic. Let him see the bouncer history and who I worked for in Chicago. Let's give him a reason to think I'm an opportunist. We may need that persona."

Hunter frowned. "Owen what're you up to?"

"I don't know. I've got a feeling."

Ivy walked back into the room as they all got up from the table. "My ex-boss, Donavan, at the government agency will check into this guy and get back to us. He has both our numbers, Hunter."

OWEN PULLED the truck onto his gravel drive. He checked the security system on his phone, making sure all systems were live with no breaches, and then he risked a glance at Keira. She sat huddled against the door, staring blindly out the side window. He doubted she even realized he'd stopped the vehicle.

"It's going to be okay. We'll safeguard you."

She turned concerned eyes to him. "And how many of you will be hurt in the process? I should go back. I've put all of you in danger. Now that Hunter and your other friend know the truth, maybe they'll be able to find the proof and stop him. I can bargain with. I could go back in exchange for him letting Grandma go. Then she could be with Ace, and he'd take care of her."

"That's not how evil works, Little-bit." He got out of the truck and pushed the button for his barn security before rounding the vehicle to open her door. Hands on her waist, he lifted her down. "Come inside. It's been a long day. After we clean up, we'll both feel better."

Finishing before her, he put on hot water, plated the butter cookies and made the tea Ruby sent with him. She'd said it was soothing and might help Keira sleep. Meanwhile, his mind spun.

If he and the family were going to succeed, they needed a solid plan and more information. One thing was for certain. He'd do whatever it took to end this. He'd worry about the future once he knew Keira, Quang and Ace were safe.

He glanced up from behind the island when Keira walked out of the bathroom wearing one of his T-shirts.

"I forgot my clothes. This was on the shelf. Is it okay?" she stammered, smoothing the fabric over her midriff.

Okay? He'd never wash that shirt again. He'd forever picture the neckline hanging off her delicate shoulder, the rest draping her tiny form like a dress.

"It's fine. I imagine it'll be more comfortable to sleep in than the jeans you've been wearing." Damn, he could imagine the hem of his T-shirt sliding up her thighs as she shifted in sleep. "Do you want a pair of my boxers?"

She chuckled. "They wouldn't stay up. The shirt already comes to my knees."

Did she wear a tiny little thong? Or boy briefs? Was she wearing panties at all? He swallowed, the want filling his chest and pulsing below his waist.

"I made tea. Ruby said it'd be good to settle your nerves. Want some?"

She smiled and nodded, crossing to the opposite side of the breakfast bar. Quickly, he filled a cup and slid it across the granite, hoping she'd miss the bulge filling the front of his sweatpants. "You hanging in there?"

She took a sip of the tea and gave a little shrug. "I'm really scared for Grandma. She's strong, but—"

"Don't worry yet. She's still a bargaining chip for Escott. I doubt he'll do anything drastic before he knows where you are. I pulled up an aerial view of your last address. There were several buildings and one pretty big house. It's a fenced compound. Is that where he kept you?"

"Yes. He calls it Dragon Crest Estates." She screwed up her face. "Mother said he believes naming his compound adds to his importance."

"Let me guess, he named his dick, too?"

She rolled her eyes. "Mother said he called it king dragon."

"What is he, a ten-year-old?"

She laughed. Exactly what he'd hoped for.

"When Dracon and my mother first married, we kept our house, and he'd come and stay. He said he loved the modest household.

"Grandma lived in her own quarters behind our house, in a converted garage. When he came over, I'd go stay with her. When I moved out and started college, there were weeks when I didn't see them. I visited Grandma, but stayed away from them. The fire at Grandma's and moving us to the compound gave him the ultimate control.

Dracon made sure that I discovered at that time that my boyfriend had been getting money from him and had been keeping tabs on me for Dracon the whole time we were together. He made sure I realized his reach was wider than I expected.

Owen opened his laptop and pulled up the aerial view of the compound. He pointed to a rectangular structure resembling a monolith with large windows on the top floor. "Is this the one?"

"Yes. My sterile, suffocating, white cement prison." She shuddered. "The building is perfectly climate controlled for painting and the storage of paintings. Every product I could possibly want to work with was provided. As you can see, there's natural light from all directions, automatic shades and rolling walls to create shadows. My food was prepared and brought to me. I had a TV, but he controlled the times I could watch. I was there to work, to paint. To produce."

"Were there locks? Could you get out?"

"There was a stairway to the roof. I could go up there to get sunshine and fresh air. A little patio setup had a lounge chair and table. An emergency release button unlocked a door that led directly to the guard who watched over me. If I was on the roof, so was he. There was no actual way for me to leave on my own. The guards had keys and key codes."

"You were a true prisoner."

She nodded. "A year later, I found out he owned the original of the first Rothko painting I'd done. He actually owned several masterpieces. Eventually, I'd painted a copy of each for him. After I'd done a couple of the paintings, I overheard a conversation between him and my mother. I believe what he did was show the original to a buyer, but deliver my forgery, keeping the original for himself. Later, the paintings I copied were from pictures, videos, books, documentaries and the occasional visit to a museum. I think as I completed those replicas, he paid someone to break into museums or private homes and replace the originals with my forgeries."

"Why do you think that?"

"I lived and painted on the upper level of the building. He has his own private show room on the first level. That's where he invited people to come see what he had for sale. One day my mother took me to his private studio to show me how good I was. She was ecstatic that I could paint like the masters. She showed me several of the paintings I'd duplicated, but when I studied them, I was certain I was looking at the originals not my copies. I hated what I was doing. I threatened to stop painting, assuming there was nothing they could do to force me. He was furious that she'd shown me his collection."

"Keira, can you remember all the pictures he made you paint and write me a list?" She nodded and he got her a notepad and she started writing.

"Did he ever ask you to paint anything of your own?"

"A portrait of him. I think he hung that over the fireplace in the main house. He sat in a chair in the studio and watched me the whole time. He made me start over three times until he was satisfied with how he'd been presented."

"How long did it take?"

"Weeks. He was difficult and sometimes insisted on just sitting there without letting me paint. He was different after I finished the portrait." Finishing the list, she placed the pen on top. She studied her fingers then plucked on her shirt sleeve.

A dark suspicion slithered across Owen's mind. "Different how?"

"He was around more. Checked on my work more, that's all."

"Does he have a particular artist he favors for his personal collection?"

"No, not a specific artist."

"A style?"

"He likes nudes." She collected their dirty dishes and crossed to the sink, then turned back to him. "The human body is beautiful in all its varying sizes, shapes and colors. I would love to have done *Chloe*, by Jules-Joseph Lefebvre, or paint like Goya or sculpt like Rodin. But I never wanted to pretend to be those artists. I wanted to do my own work. I dreamed of making my own art."

"Did he ask you to do something else after the portrait?"

"Weeks later." Rubbing her forehead, she continued. "Two or three weeks before my mother died, he brought me a photograph. He wanted me to paint it. I said no. It was a photo of me."

"You were naked," he guessed.

Folding her arms across her waist, she bent her head.

"You can tell me."

"It was a photo of me getting out of the shower. But I never took that photo. I don't know how he got it. After that, I was uncomfortable all the time. I felt like I was being watched. I was afraid to sleep. When he showed me the photo, I told my mother. She told me to forget it, that it was only a picture. But I could tell she was furious."

"He probably had hidden cameras installed."

"On Wednesdays I got to spend time walking the gardens with Grandma. That same week she told me something bad was going on at the house. Mother and Dracon were fighting continuously. Mom had even thrown a vase at him.

"Grandma told me she was making plans to get the two of us away. I needed to be prepared to do exactly as she said. She sent a basket of flowers with me when I left. In the bottom were five phones and a backpack."

Owen grinned. "I think I'm going to like your grandma. She's one clever lady."

Keira turned and smiled back. "She'd like you. Honor and integrity are important to her. Though she'd worry about you crushing me in bed."

Owen's head jerked up, his eyes went wide. "I-uh. Don't —why?"

You can do this, she told herself. Even if their coming together wouldn't mean anything to him, it would mean the world to her. Never had she met a man with such a good heart.

Grandma always said, '*when you lose all, you can cherish the memories*'. If she ended up back in hell, she wanted these memories.

"Owen, do you want to make love with me? Because I want to make love with you. I'm not asking for commitments or anything. At least once, I want to be with someone I like and trust.

"Before you answer, you should know, I've seen a lot at my mom's clubs. But I was only with the one boy. I now know I was a job to him, and I don't think he was really into me. I'm not sure how good I'll be. As hot as you are, I'm pretty sure you've had a lot more experience. But I'm a quick learner and there's no obligation. I realize I'm not voluptuous—"

Owen reached out and placed a finger over her lips. "You're worried you'll end up back under Dracon's thumb. You're scared he plans to rape you and keep you for his own use now that your mother is out of the picture. You want memories of your own choice. I understand. I don't think I should be the guy."

He stopped her from speaking. "Trust me. I won't let you go back to him. If we're separated, I will move all of hell to get to you."

"Isn't that supposed to be heaven and hell?" she asked nervously, praying she wasn't being turned down. She wanted more than memories.

She saw past his good-natured smiles and mild manners. She saw the despair and sadness in his lonely eyes. He was as damaged as she was, and she wanted to know why. She wanted to ease his pain.

"Men like me don't get to have heaven. Now go get to sleep. I've got work I need to do."

She closed her eyes and dropped her gaze. She wasn't enough. Nothing new there. Grandma was the only one who'd ever loved her. Everyone else wanted to use her talents, or in the case of her one boyfriend, for her connections.

Opening her eyes, she realized how close she stood to Owen. His broad chest was inches from her face. Confronted with his perfectly muscled pectorals, so evident, even beneath his T-shirt, she needed to touch what she'd sculpted in her mind. Without thinking, she reached out and placed a palm over his left pec. His heart thundered in rhythm with her own escalated heartbeat. He did want her. As much as she wanted him. "Don't lie. Not now, after you've been honest about everything else. You do want me."

He placed a hand over hers on his chest and the other against her cheek, forcing her to make eye contact. "I don't think I can take one more taste of you and survive. I want you so badly I could explode. To me, you are the most exquisite woman I've ever met. I want to lay you on my bed and make slow, sweet love to you, then catch a breath and make mad passionate love to you. I want to touch you everywhere, kiss you everywhere and make you cum a thousand times.

"And I'm scared, damn it." He placed both palms on her shoulders. "Because if I touch you... if I taste you again... if I have you, I may never be able to let you go. I'm at least ten years older. I'm jaded and tarnished. I don't deserve someone sweet and innocent. And you sure as hell deserve better than me."

The good man, who only saw his damaged parts, couldn't recognize the value of his kindness and character. "Don't I get to be the judge of what I need, and what I want. Why do you get to tell me 'no', making the choice for both of us? We're both consenting adults. I am an adult. I've been deprived of my own decisions for long enough. The life I lived was far from Sunnybrook Farm. I grew up with strippers, call girls and junkies. Not to mention the bullies and thugs, con artists and thieves who populated my upbringing. I was coerced to commit a crime. One that shames me. I'm headed to prison, and I deserve to go."

"Keira, I—"

"Tell me this, Mr. Bad Guy. Have you ever hit a woman? Or a child?"

"No."

"Raped one?"

"Hell, no."

"Drugged one up, then held her down while your buddies got off on her?"

"Fuck no, and I'd kill the bastard who did."

Keira continued. "An occupational hazard of being in the military is that there's a good chance you will have to take a life. Unless you did that with joy in your heart, I'd say you're not evil."

He let his arms fall to his side and stepped back. "But I have, Keira. I killed the monster who murdered my baby sister after he kidnapped and raped her. There was revenge in my heart, and I don't regret it one damn bit."

CHAPTER 10

Keira studied the anguish in his eyes, not anguish for what he'd done, but for his sister. "How many lives had this monster taken?"

"More than I care to count. He tormented Hunter with dead bodies for two years. He almost got Ruby."

"Did you murder him in cold blood?"

He paused. "Officially, the monster died resisting arrest."

"Unofficially?" she prodded.

"I gave him the option of prison or a one-on-one fight with me. Weapon of his choice. I knew what he'd go for. He chose knives. When he attacked me, I fought back. He lost."

"You killed him like he killed your sister and the other girls," Keira stated.

Owen shifted, pinning her with his gaze. "Yes. Exactly like he sliced them open. No feeling. No emotion. No regrets."

She tilted her head. "That's the point, when you're a monster hunter, isn't it? Some people are bad, but foolish. They're easy to catch and lock away, like the men who wanted to attack me the other night. They attempted to accost me in the open, thinking no one would care or stand up to them.

"Then there are the monsters, who are very good at being bad, and good at getting away with it. Those are the truly evil ones, like Dracon and the one who murdered your sister. The ones who cleverly hide their wickedness behind civility and false moral values. The powerful ones.

"The discerning monster hunter searches his heart and makes a decision as to which are insignificant and which deserve to die. Unfortunately, the honorable hunter pays a penance for each job that must be done—a piece of his soul.

"You made your own decision—a job to do."

"You have a vivid imagination, which I'm sure is good for your painting," he said. "But I'm no hero."

"I realize you think I'm naive and not very worldly, and that's partly true. I have been sheltered in many ways." She glanced up to lock eyes. "I've seen more than you think. Experienced more than it appears. I know true evil."

She slipped her arms around his neck. "Mom was always chasing money and position in the community. Grandma pretty much raised me. I grew up on her stories of the dragon guardians, the monster hunters. And I've experienced the monster first hand, Owen. To me, you are a hero, a true dragon guardian watching out for all your family."

A muscle twitched in his jaw. She pressed closer to his body.

He didn't recognize his own worth. Rescuing a soaked stranger, giving them shelter, food, protection, kindness was his nature. He didn't realize that the love he'd given her was more than she'd encountered in years.

Even if he didn't want forever, she'd learn to live with the memories they could make now. If this was all she ever had, like Grandma, remembrances would sustain her.

Owen dipped, sliding an arm under her knees and lifting her against his chest. "Hold on and don't let go."

Flipping the coverlet back, he lay her in the middle of the bed. Turning to the bedside table, he lit a candle, rounded the end of the bed and lit one on the other side. Tugging off his T-shirt and dropping it on the floor, he grabbed a foil pack from the drawer. He turned back to the bed. She'd propped the pillows and removed her own clothing. Lying on her side in the shadowed light, knees bent, she studied him.

"I've wanted to see your body since I met you. I'd love to paint or sculpt you." She smiled. "But you've always been modest, keeping your shirt on around me and around the children who come here."

He shrugged, embarrassment flushing his cheeks above his beard. "If I'm working out or sparring with Gage or Ivy, I don't wear a shirt. With the little kids, it seemed like the right thing to do."

"I wondered." She sat up on her knees. "I watched you the other night when you were beating the crap out of the big bag. You'd stripped down to shorts. I noticed you had a tattoo on your chest. I couldn't see it clearly."

When she placed a palm on his rib cage and slid it upward to the head of the dragon tattooed on his chest, Owen sucked in a breath. With the tip of her finger, she traced the fangs, then the eyes, and followed the scales along the spine.

"Magnificent. Bold. Brave. Like you." Keira glanced up and met his gaze. "I should have guessed. I've nothing to fear from this dragon. In fact, I give myself gladly to him. To you, my dragon guardian."

Lifting her hands, she speared her fingers into his hair before covering his lips with hers.

Owen was as lost as he'd known he would be. There'd be no holding back. God help him, he was going to do all in his power to possess every part of her, to ensure she would someday come to crave and need him as he did her. Clasping the back of her head with one palm to keep their lips entwined, he slid the other to the waist of his sweatpants and pushed them to the floor. Leaning forward, he helped her stretch out on the mattress before following her down, careful not to crush her.

She chuckled. "I won't break."

"You're such a little thing. I'll be careful. Don't let me hurt you."

She clasped his face in her palms. "I'm not afraid of you. You'd never hurt me. Now please, make love to me."

Owen nuzzled her neck, then nibbled her earlobe. Her shiver of reaction spurred him on. Licking and nibbling, he traversed a path down her neck, across the sweet spot between her neck and shoulder, over the gentle rise of her breast to her sweet berry where he paused to suckle. Her delicious scent filled his head, entrancing his senses.

"Yes. Oh yes," she cried.

Lying between her spread legs with his chest against her belly, he rested on his elbows. Stroking and cupping the satin soft flesh of her breast in each hand, he worshiped one, then the other, repeating his attention again and again. Her hips bucked against his belly; her voice cried out for more. "Now. Please, I need you inside me. Now."

Shifting, he knelt up and gazed down at her glistening warmth. So sensual. So expressive. He reached for the foil pack laying on the mattress and ripped it open.

She bolted upright, kneeling before him. "Wait. I want to touch you first."

He met her eyes, then nodded, resting his palms against his thighs. She flicked her tongue against his nipple. He sucked in a ragged breath.

"I always wondered if men's nipples were as sensitive as a woman's."

He groaned when she suckled the other side. "Does that answer your question?"

He felt her smile against his flesh. Her murmured 'yes' hummed against his sensitive spot, dragging another groan from his chest and causing his cock to jerk between them. Her gaze dropped, followed by the gentle warmth of her hand against his heated erection.

"Oh, Little-bit, I won't be able to handle much of that. Not this first time. I've wanted you since the moment our eyes met."

She glanced up. "The first night when you rescued me?"

He nodded.

Smiling, she nodded. "Yes, me too. Insta-lust."

Instant love, he thought, but nodded.

"Promise—next time I get to do the exploring."

Lifting an eyebrow, he smiled. "Next time I'm all yours."

She lay back against the pillows, folding her arms above her head.

Damn, she was a siren surrounded by a billowy sea of grey sheets. Sheathing himself, he shifted to the side of her, then resting a broad palm over her cheek, he brought his lips to hers. He savored her taste as he gently ran his hand down her neck, pausing to cup and knead her breast, plucking the nipple and drawing a moan of desire from her throat. Following his hand with his lips, he drew his tongue over her skin and trailed his fingers over her belly. His thumb skimmed a linear scar on her tender flesh, then another and another. There were several on her belly and thighs. He hesitated and glanced up to question her. "What are these?"

She placed a palm over his hand and whispered. "Don't ask. Not tonight."

Lowering his gaze, he kissed a narrow scar as he lowered his hand to glide over the heart of her desire.

Her fevered gasp and arching body urged him on.

Reaching his goal, he used her wetness to coat his fingers as he teased and tantalized the bud of her arousal. Brushing the ball of his thumb over her sensitive flesh, he slowly breached her core with one, then two fingers, gently searching for the special spot with each thrust.

Her hips jerked. "Oh yes. Oh yes. Now."

Sliding down the mattress, he trailed kisses down her torso until he reached the object of his desire. Drawing circles around her clit with his tongue, he slowly licked her throbbing bud.

"Don't stop. Don't stop. I've never...." She gasped, and her body trembled beneath his ministrations. "Owen. Yes, Owen!"

At the sound of his name on her lips as she exploded, his heart expanded and almost burst with joy.

Beautiful. Perfect. He watched the pleasure of her orgasm slowly dissipate from her face and her body melt into the bedding. Gradually, she opened her eyes and smiled.

"That was almost perfect," she murmured.

He raised an eyebrow. "If it wasn't the best orgasm you've ever had, I'll have to try harder."

She smiled and ran her fingers through his hair. "That was the only orgasm I've had that wasn't battery operated."

He leaned up on one elbow and smiled at her. "Well, let's see if I can do better this time."

She tightened her finger in his hair and lifted his face to hers. Slipping her leg between his thighs she stroked his erection with her calf. "The only thing that could make it better right now, is for you to fill me and we cum together."

He hesitated for a brief second, knowing there'd be no going back for him. Hell, who was he kidding? It was already too late.

He knelt between her legs, sliding her hips onto his thighs

positioning his cock at her entrance and eased forward. "I'll go slow. Tell me when you're ready for more."

Grasping his forearms, she rolled her hips a fraction and caught her lip between her teeth. "More."

A few minutes later, when he was fully seated, he kissed her forehead, then her brow, the tip of her nose. Her lips. His restraint was about to break, but he couldn't hurt her.

She tugged his ear. "What're you doing?"

"Making sure you're okay."

"You're the kindest, gentlest man I've ever met. I'm not that fragile. You may make me die of need though, if you don't move."

He met her smile with a grin of his own. Slowly, he rocked his hips back and forth. "Damn, you feel good. Warm. Perfect."

"More, Owen. More. I want all of you."

Control snapping in the heat of her words, he thrust harder and deeper until her scream of release sent him flying over the cliff—a freefall from heaven—together.

Keira lay with her head on his chest and a leg thrown over his waist. His powerful arm wrapped around her with his palm cupping her hip. A sigh of contentment escaped her lips. Now she understood what the fuss was about. The euphoria of their joining followed by the contentment of being cradled in his warmth was nirvana itself. This was a memory worth cherishing.

MONDAY EVENING, the family waited in the loft for the call from Grandma Quang. Owen studied the normally unflappable Ace as he paced back and forth in front of the breakfast bar.

Owen was worried for the older man. Hope was a double-edged sword

His original plan to run with Keira was no longer an option. With what they were learning about Dracon, Owen needed to stay and help protect Ace and the rest of the family. Keira would be safer with the group intact.

"We've got to think like he does." Owen paced his own path across the loft. "Tell me how his relationship started with your mother?"

Keira glanced up. "He's smart. A sweet talker. He pretends to be less than he is, to let people think they can manipulate him. He plays people by giving them what they think they want, like praise, value, security, power. He becomes their friend, their confidante. He sees everyone as a tool he will find a way to use and manipulate."

"What did he use on your mom?"

"Power, success, social standing. He has powerful friends she loved to hobnob with. He praised her for a well-run business and her schemes. He planted hints and let her think they were her ideas. Like using the back rooms to record and blackmail the local VIPs. There were other improvements she wanted to implement, and he suggested a partnership. He offered to help her with expenses. He quickly took it to the bedroom. She was excited to find someone to support her who was also driven by financial gain. The two of them expanded the business quickly, and she had more money than she'd expected. They got married to seal the deal."

"Do you know what their other businesses were?"

"No. I didn't want to know. I suspected part of what he sold was drugs. Before I quit working at the club, the behavior of several of the regular patrons changed." She hesitated. "Mom and Dracon bought the apartment building across the street from the club. I'm sure some of the dancers were using it for sex work."

Hunter interrupted. "The local cops didn't stop it?"

Keira snorted. "The cops were going in and out pretty often on their own, but they never stopped anything. Dracon has a lot of reach and plenty of influential friends."

"There has to be files somewhere," Owen spoke out loud. "Blackmail takes serious proof to be effective. If Dracon ever appeared in a photo or film with one of his blackmail victims, we might be able to use it to incriminate him. I'd love to get my hands on those files. He's smart enough not to keep them online."

Owen glanced at Keira. "Did he have one place where he kept a computer with no internet, or an offline server?"

"I'm guessing his office. I never went inside any of his private quarters. I know there were no windows, and he always kept it locked. Even my mother was never allowed inside."

Owen nodded. "Sounds like the right room. I've tried to locate blueprints of the house, but can't get them. Could you draw me a floor plan?"

"Yes. There are rooms I've never entered, but from walking the halls I can give you door locations and estimate from there."

The phone resting on the coffee table rang. She looked up at Owen, and he nodded. They'd gone over the plan several times.

Keira answered the call, placing the phone on speaker. "Hello?"

"Keira, is that you?" Grandma asked in her native language.

"Yes. Are you well?"

"Yes. Did you find the shop I told you to visit and the object I told you about?"

"Yes, Grandma. Are you alone?"

"Yes. Now you will be safe. I think he may be suspicious.

He's making me go to the doctor again on Friday." She paused.

Keira heard the shaky indrawn breath.

"Ace—he is well? Did he remember me?"

At the sound of his name, Ace reached down and picked up the phone, bringing it closer to his lips as if it brought the woman closer. In halting Vietnamese, he spoke to the woman he'd lost so long ago.

Keira glanced at Owen.

He shook his head. "Let them have their time. Only translate what isn't personal," he whispered.

She listened carefully. Her heart broke at the pain and loss both expressed. Both shared regret and guilt. Their "I love you's" increased her determination to give them the rest of their lives.

She glanced at Owen, meeting his gaze. Could she have a love so true?

The tone changed, and the words became more strained. Keira turned to Owen and Hunter. "Last week she had to dump the burner in the toilet at the doctor's office. Today she searched the tank and the phone was gone. She's afraid someone told Dracon. He's been acting strange. He must know we are communicating."

"Ask if she's been sleeping more than usual?"

Keira asked, then nodded her response.

Owen shifted. "She needs to be careful. He's probably drugging her to make her responses slower. Does she have access to food? Is there a staff member she can trust or a friend who can come visit and bring her food and water from outside?"

"She can go to the kitchen for snacks, but since Mother died, meals are brought to her. She has a friend he lets come once a week to keep up appearances. They have supervised visits in the garden where they cut flowers and talk," Keira replied.

Owen tapped Ace on the shoulder. "Tell her not to eat or drink anything she can't prepare for herself. If they bring her a meal, flush it down the toilet. Get her friend's phone number, and Keira will call her to sneak in more food. And find out what time she's calling on Friday."

After Ace relayed the instructions, Owen continued. "Tell her to stay in bed after a meal, as if she's too tired to get up. See how they act when they check in on her. Tell her to check the next burner twice a day to see if we've left her a message. She should use phone six to call Friday."

As the older man repeated his words to Quang, Owen realized the longer they were on the phone, the more likely Dracon's staff would be able to trace it back to him at the barn. He and Hunter had talked earlier, and both agreed it would be beneficial to force Dracon to come to them. In Spencer they had their own network of contacts.

Ace hung up a couple moments later. "I need to go to her. I'm her husband. She's frightened. I'm going to get her in the morning."

I'm her husband. Something flickered in his mind. Shaking it off, Owen turned to his friend. "Ace, we're all worried about you, about Quang, and Keira. We have to think this through. We need to think like Dracon does. What can he use against us? What can we prove against him?"

Owen turned. "Hunter, the legal help Jakob recommended, are they in Denver?"

"Yes," Hunter said.

"Is there any way your grandfather could get them here tomorrow?"

"I'll text Jakob now. What're you thinking?" Hunter asked.

"I don't care what he's thinking. I'm going to get my wife. He can't refuse me." Ace cut in angrily.

Owen straightened to his full height, shoulders squared and his arms crossed over his chest. "Okay Ace, let's play this out. What's your plan?"

"I'll catch a flight in the morning, rent a car at the airport and drive to get her."

"You think he's going to let you walk away with the only bargaining chip he has to get his cash cow back? Are you willing to hand over Keira, your only granddaughter? Keira is also looking at serious time in prison if he decides to get vindictive. How do you think Quang will feel about that?"

"I'm her husband. He'll have to let her come with me."

"The husband who seemingly deserted her for almost fifty years? No contact, no money, no support. Now you show up when she and her granddaughter may have inherited a considerable amount of money. Seems pretty opportunistic to me."

"It wasn't like that," Ace exclaimed.

"We all know that. But do you really think he's going to open the door and let you take the woman who has a claim on half his fortune? We already know he's got judges, lawyers and doctors in his pocket. The police officers he pays off will drag you away when he complains you're making false accusations and threatening him. He'll ask for twenty-four hours to prove you're lying. Which is all he needs to come up with documents. You go there, and he's fighting on his home turf."

Owen rested a hand on Ace's shoulder. "Ace, we know the truth. We know you tried. Those were terrible times, and a lot of people were hurt, lost and left behind. But Dracon is scum, and he'll twist the facts to get what he wants. And he wants your granddaughter."

Owen studied his friend. He didn't burden Ace with his suspicion that his daughter was murdered because the monster now lusted after Keira. "We need to get Dracon to come here. We need to start pulling our proof to make sure our records are on file before accusations are made. We need the lawyers, judges, doctors and cops who know *us* to be ready and willing to help."

"Quang is his best bet to get Keira back. He won't do anything to hurt her at this point." He waited for Ace to absorb his words. "Ace, I know you're worried and angry. We all are. But we need to stick together. Are you willing to work with us and help come up with a plan to free them both?"

He waited and watched countless emotions flash in the older man's eyes before Ace finally nodded. Owen clarified, "You will wait?"

"Yes. I'll wait, but not long," Ace conceded.

Owen glanced at Hunter. "Did you get the DNA results?"

Hunter shook his head. "They promised we would see them tomorrow."

Ivy walked through the door leading in from the barn. "Donavan knows someone at the DEA who's been trying to nail Dracon for years. But they can't get anyone to flip. The two who agreed to speak up never made it to the meet. Nor have they been seen since. The FBI is looking into him for art fraud, but they keep missing him. They think he has someone inside the bureau tipping him off. Donavan is getting us contacts we can hopefully trust."

Owen sat at the table. "Let's start with the legal. If he's getting fake medical documents and power of attorney, we need to ensure we have verifiable records. The lawyer can collect the forms and records and validate our information to prove what we have is legit and has been on file for years. Have him—"

"Her," Hunter interrupted. "And she responded to Jakob. She'll be here at ten tomorrow."

Owen nodded. "Ace's military records and proof of marriage papers. She can check that there was never a divorce decree for Ace and Quang in Texas or here. We want all of that before Dracon has even a hint of Ace. We also need Grandma Quang's citizenship papers." He paused and glanced at Keira. "Where were you born? We'll need a copy of your birth certificate."

"I was born in Texas. I brought the original with me and copies of Grandma's and Mom's papers."

Owen reached out and covered her hand. "Perfect. We need to get those documents locked up somewhere." He glanced at Hunter. "The safe at the lodge?"

"Makes sense. Especially for the lawyer. I know her. She's tough and doesn't back down for anyone. She'll want to meet with Keira and Ace to form her own opinion and decisions. Once she's in, she's all-in."

"Good. We've got nothing to hide." Owen glanced at his watch. "Time to get back to the Wild Card. Ace, we'll pick you up in the morning. Bring your marriage certificate and your discharge papers. Once we talk to the attorney, we'll have a better idea of what else she'll want." Standing, he glanced around the table, thankful for everyone's nod of buy-in for the plan.

He tried to lock down his own desperate feeling. They were running out of time.

CHAPTER 11

*W*alking into the barn after closing down the saloon, Owen double-checked the security settings. "I'm going to do a quick visual check down here. Will you wait for me on the stairs? I don't want you going up to the loft alone."

Keira nodded and waited patiently for her dragon. Although he moved with his customary loose saunter, she knew he was wound tight. All night while they waited on customers, he'd watched her. She could almost see the myriad of scenarios racing through his mind.

His decision to keep his hands off of her was obvious. She smiled. She had her own plan. Grandma taught her to be a realist. Her days with her lover were numbered. She intended to create as many memories as she could.

When he returned, they walked the stairs together. He had her wait on the landing while he checked the loft. Once he was assured they were alone, she followed him inside. Knowing his habits, she crossed to the kitchen and reached into her backpack. "I brought a couple sandwiches from the sports bar for you. While you eat, I'm going to throw in a load of clothes. I'll throw yours in with mine for a full load."

He shot her a sheepish grin as he sat at the bar. "Thanks."

She smiled as she plated the food and poured him a glass of milk. Placing both in front of him, she ran a palm over his chest. "You need the calories to keep your body fueled. I happen to like your body the way it is."

Dropping a kiss on his neck, she moved past him.

He cleared his throat.

"I ah, Keira. I—I don't think I should sleep with you tonight. We—ah—have an early morning tomorrow, and you need your rest."

Pausing on her way through the loft, she turned to him. "Okay. You shower first while I work on the laundry."

Emptying her dirty clothes from her backpack, she also removed her sketchpad and pencils for later. For days, she'd itched to draw him. Now that he knew her secret, she could sketch the images racing through her mind. More memories for the years ahead.

Once he entered the bathroom, she crossed to the bed and flipped back the coverlet and sheets. Opening the bedside table, she removed two condoms and slipped one under the pillow, then lit the candles as he'd done the night before. Shucking her clothing, she took a fortifying breath and went to join him. She knew what she wanted and what she needed. He was right. Time was running out.

Keira stopped in the open doorway and absorbed the sight of him. He stood under the rainfall faucet. One hand braced against the wall with his head dropped forward the water beating against his neck and shoulders. His tension was visible.

He was magnificent. Broad shoulders bulging with muscle, tapered down to a narrow waist leading to firm buttocks, massive thighs and strong calves. Her hands ached to examine every inch of him. She needed to memorize the strength and musculature, the feel of every perfect inch. Someday, even if only in her mind, she'd sculpt him.

He thought of himself as an oversized hulking monster. But he was a gentle giant. The owner of her heart. She intended to show him how she felt.

He must have sensed her entering the glass enclosure. "Keira, I'm trying to do the right thing."

Placing the foil pack on the inset soap tray, she rested her palms on his taut shoulders, slid them downward over his back, around his sides to his waist and up to flatten against his chest. Leaning her cheek against his back, she pressed her body along his. "Then touch me. Let me touch you. Make love to me. And hold me like you never want to let me go. Let me memorize the smell of you, the warmth of your touch. That's all I ask."

Releasing a shuddering breath, he slowly turned in her grasp. His fingers holding her face, he studied her.

Too afraid to speak the words, she prayed he could see the love in her eyes.

"Mine," he whispered before capturing her mouth with his.

His kiss blasted over her senses, lighting her on fire. Desire consumed her, yet gave her life. His touch, his need was the breath she craved.

"Do you even realize what you do to me?" he gasped, kissing a trail down her neck to the hollow of her shoulder. "I get a whiff of you and I'm rock hard. I can't breathe or think. Or, God help me, let you go."

Kissing the dragon on his chest, she licked a trail down his torso, circling and dipping into his navel. She slowly lowered to her knees, trailing kisses to her destination.

When he would've stepped back, she shifted her right hand to his buttock and held him in place. His body went taut and he sucked in a breath as she gripped his shaft.

This was her turn, her chance to learn what he liked, what he wanted, what he needed. Tonight, she wanted to explore and experience the joy of pleasing the man who gave of himself. Her man.

She stroked his length until he leaned back against the wall with a groan and worked his fingers into her hair, lightly grasping her head. Free to use both hands she cupped, kissed and sucked until his legs quivered and his chest heaved. Sliding her lips over his girth once more, she glanced up, into his blue eyes.

"No more. I can't take anymore." Leaning forward, he grasped her under her thighs and effortlessly lifted her up, where she wrapped her legs around his waist. "Damn Little-bit, you're killing me. Your sweetness and innocence urge me to be tender. Then you look at me with those dark sensual eyes, and I need to take you, pleasure you so completely you'll never want anyone but me. You're all I'll ever want. I'm nothing without you."

A ripple of fear washed over her. Did he realize what he'd said? Could she accidentally destroy this man? Did she mean as much to him as he did to her? What if her stepfather won? Wrapping her arms around his neck, she rained kisses on his neck and shoulder. "Now. Please now, Owen."

Lowering her so she could stand, he swiped the condom from the shelf, and sitting on the built-in bench, sheathed himself before settling her astride his hips. "Yes. That's it. Ride me, Little-bit. Take us both all the way."

Later, lying spooned on the bed, one arm wrapped over her, Owen stroked the slim ridges on her abdomen with his thumb.

"Who is Oona?" she asked, tracing the name on his inner bicep.

He swallowed the pain before he could speak. "Oona was my little sister."

"Will you tell me?"

"She was twelve years younger than me. Big blue eyes, long pale blond hair like our mother."

"Like the tattoo on your arm."

He nodded. "She was tall, lanky. Smart as a whip. When she smiled, she looked like an angel. Innocent."

Pausing, he thought of the last time he'd seen Oona alive. He'd been shipping out, and she'd pleaded with him not to go. She'd said she knew something terrible was going to happen, and she begged him to stay. Oona was afraid for him. He, in his young, brash, cavalier style had ruffled her hair and told her not to worry because he could take care of himself. There hadn't been anyone to take care of her.

"My parents were older when she was born, and we tended to be pretty protective of her. We lived in Chicago. I joined the military to get the benefits and maybe a college education.

"Turns out I've a knack for war and an innate ability for strategic planning. My commanders were making recommendations. I'd just signed the papers to re-up for another six years. I was going to be a career man. I served in some pretty remote areas overseas. It was five months before I got the notice that Oona had gone missing. She'd been out with friends for a birthday party. She went to the restroom and never came back. So much time had already passed, and I couldn't get leave. I talked to my parents and the cops in charge of the case. I knew the statistics about the first 24 hours. I was already months behind what had happened, but I started piecing together what I could and researching other female disappearances in the area."

He rolled to his back, hooking an arm over his head, and shifted Keira to his side. She draped a leg over his thigh and placed a gentle palm on his chest. Staring at the darkened ceiling, he forced himself to continue. "I tried to talk to my parents as often as possible, and I wrote weekly. My mom got sick. She'd already lost hope we'd ever find Oona, and she ignored the cancer. She gave up and let death take her. My dad made the funeral arrangements, went home and killed himself. He couldn't live without Mom.

"I kept in touch with the detective in charge. He explained someone was coercing girls into sex work with drugs and promises of a better life. The really young ones were flat-out stolen and sold. Drugged into compliance, the girls were used and abused until they became unmarketable.

"The detective admitted several girls from the area had disappeared over a period of a few years. The sick sonofabitch running the girls would kill them and dump them into the lake or a river before they could talk. It was usually months before their bodies were found. There were no leads on who was in charge."

He thought of the list of names he kept on his computer, each one, while Keira gave him quiet, breathing through the memories with him. How long he lay lost in the darkness, he didn't know.

Keira raised onto her elbow and brushed the soft hair of his stubble beard. "Tell me."

"Months later, my commanding officer notified me I was approved for a brief leave to go home and ID a body they thought was my sister. A fisherman found her. The Detective was excited because the body had only been in the water about twenty-four hours when it was found. It was my baby sister. There were track marks on Oona's arms and—" Images of her mutilated body flashed in his mind.

"Finish it," Keira coached.

"The bastard stole her innocence and when he was done, he gutted her like a fish. Like he did all the other girls he dumped."

"How'd you find the monster?"

"When I got out of the service, it took me two years to figure out who he was. I worked jobs with the lowlifes who ran in that world. Whenever I found something, I leaked info to the Chicago PD. Around the same time, Hunter went undercover, trying to bust the guy. His cover was blown, and he was officially off the case. That's when the bastard started taunting Hunter with dead bodies.

"I went deeper underground to get the guy. That's how I met Ruby and Hunter. I caught up with them here in Spencer, and we worked together with Ivy to catch the sonofabitch. I told you, I'm not a good person, Keira. And someday I'll pay the price. I've come to terms with the fact that the world sometimes needs people like me.

"But I swear on my life, I'll protect you and somehow get you safely out of this situation. I'll get you and your grandmother and Ace free, to have a life."

"And who protects you?"

"I don't need protection. I'm the monster hunter."

ENTERING through the gates at Aspen Gold Lodge the following morning, Keira was awestruck by the simple sophisticated grandeur of the estate and the lodge. The grounds were immaculately groomed, and she saw several guests walking or riding horses in the distance. "This is beautiful."

"We came through the family entrance. If you think this is spectacular, wait until you see the front," Owen remarked.

"Why would we come through the family access?" she asked as Hunter walked up to them.

Owen snorted and nodded to his friend. "Because he's family. His grandpa is Jakob Spencer."

It struck her that she'd never questioned or wondered about the people who'd offered to help her. She'd simply accepted Owen's explanation that they were his family. At the saloon they had all seemed like normal working people. It was enough of a shock to learn that Ruby was married to the chief of police, but now to learn Hunter was the grandson of the richest man in the area, if not the state, was a little unsettling. Money and power had proved suspect in her experience.

Keira was ushered into Jakob Spencer's private office. Owen, Ace and Hunter followed. Jakob Spencer himself, dressed in boots, jeans, and a chambray western shirt, greeted them and led them to a sitting alcove set up with coffee, tea and pastries. "Mac is getting organized in the private boardroom. She'll be right with us. Grab something while we wait."

He turned to Keira. "My wife, Willa, remembered she judged one of your pieces in an art contest when you were in your first year of college. She was impressed with your talent and is looking forward to catching up with you." He smiled and winked. "In truth, I think she wants to talk you into showing your work in her studio."

Before he could expound, a slender woman with long thick curly dark hair strode purposely into the room. Her intelligent amber gaze scanned the occupants. "Good morning everyone. I'm Mac Walker, and from what I understand, we've a lot to cover today and a limited timeframe in which to build our case." She nodded toward Hunter and crossed to Ace. "Mr. Joseph, would you please come with me first? From what Hunter tells me, this starts with you."

An hour later, Ace and Mac returned. Mac placed a comforting hand on the older man's shoulder. "Andi, Jakob's assistant, is making copies of your documents now. There'll be a set for you and for me. The originals will be locked in Jakob's safe. The staff at my office in Denver are already validating all of the documents and getting judicial sign-offs. We need to make sure there is no change of documentation before we present. I know you want to see your wife, but you'll need to be patient for a couple more days."

Hunter glanced up from his phone. "Ace, Keira, the tests are back. DNA confirms your Mom was Ace's daughter and you're his granddaughter."

Keira was surprised by the sense of relief that coursed through her. She hadn't realized that she secretly worried maybe she and Grandma had made a mistake. Ace turned to her and opened his arms. She rushed into his embrace. His willing acceptance and soft-spoken words of endearment filled her with joy and hope for a real family.

"You'll send me that report?" Mac asked.

"Already have." Hunter responded. "As you requested, I have swab kits with me. We can do tests for you to send back to Denver, and the remaining hair strands Keira's grandmother provided."

"I want another independent test from a second facility," Mac explained. "We need to avoid speculation that Hunter used sympathetic sources. We're covering our bases." Mac glanced across the room. "You're up, Keira."

Keira followed the woman into the boardroom and took a seat at the table. Covertly studying the lawyer as she prepared her laptop, Keira guessed the woman to be in her late thirties-early forties. She noted the expensive, professional slacks and silk top, and the brand name, yet practical shoes. Three bangle bracelets, one copper, gold and silver graced her left wrist. Beautiful diamond and ruby earrings peeked from beneath her curly hair. The woman was attractive, polished and commanding. Keira plucked at the sleeve of her cotton blouse and swallowed back the shame of her own past, having grown up in a gentlemen's club and painting forgeries. Why would this woman care about her? She couldn't even pay her.

Mac opened her laptop, pressed a key, then met Keira's gaze. "I'm going to record our session. I'll also occasionally type notes while we talk."

"Are you going to help us?" Keira asked. "Can you get my grandmother away from Dracon Escott to be with Ace?"

Mac leaned back in her chair, and the morning light hit her face at a different angle. Keira caught a glimpse of a well-disguised scythe-shaped scar starting at the corner of the woman's lip and extending under her cheekbone. Not wanting to be caught staring, she shifted her gaze back to the women's eyes.

"I understand from Willa that you're an exceptionally talented artist. Tell me about your stepfather and the forgeries. Then we'll make a decision on where to go from here."

From her backpack, Keira retrieved a copy of the list of paintings Owen had asked her to prepare and slid them to the lawyer. "It started when he convinced my mom to have me paint a gift for my grandmother."

Well over an hour later, Mac rose from her chair and crossed to the credenza under the window. Obviously contemplating the situation, it was several silent minutes before she poured two glasses of water and came back to the table. "You realize what you've done is a federal offense?"

"Yes. I know I'll go to prison. I'm prepared to testify. I'll do anything if you can protect my grandmother. I want this over."

"Have you ever had a psych evaluation? Seen a psychiatric doctor?"

"I've seen the doctors on Dracon's payroll. I'm sure he has their false documentation." Keira studied her folded hands for a moment before meeting Mac's gaze. "I'm not mental. I was tired and lonely and sad. Yes, there was a TV, music and books to keep me company, but no friends to see or talk to, no freedom. I was a prisoner. There was nothing I could do to reach out. If I'd tried to escape, he would have hurt my grandma. I got sick with the flu or something. They didn't notice for almost three weeks."

"When was this?"

"Almost nine months ago. He brought in a man who said he was a doctor and a nurse to stay with me. He told them I'd tried to commit suicide. They kept me in bed and hooked me up to IVs. He visited me every day."

"He?" Mac asked.

"Dracon."

"And your mom?"

"Once."

"Go on."

"When I didn't get better right away, he threatened Grandma."

"How?"

"His threats are never obvious, not like 'I'll beat her up.' His tactics are more insidious. 'I think your grandmother quit eating like you did. She's quite weak. I hope she doesn't fall down the stairs and get hurt. Too bad you can't see her until you get well and are painting again.'

"Dracon claimed the doctor was a psychiatrist, but the man never once talked to me or asked me questions. If my stepfather has documents stating otherwise, they were made up."

Mac leaned forward on her elbows. "I need you to have a psych eval. I've talked to a local doctor that I know, Paige Rasmussen. She'll get you in today. Do you agree to go?"

Keira nodded.

"I also want you to get a physical and submit to drug testing. Is that going to be a problem?"

"I hardly ever drink and have never done drugs. But I don't have a doctor in town."

"Dr. Reggie Jurek, an internal medicine doctor will see you this afternoon. She's a friend of Dr. Rasmussen." She handed Keira a business card with names and times of the appointments.

Heart thumping, Keira asked, "You'll help us?"

Mac studied her. "I have two warnings for potential clients. Don't withhold information from me, no matter how bad it makes you appear. Don't lie to me. Have you done either of those two?"

"No ma'am," Keira answered.

"Keep it that way and you have a lawyer."

"How do I pay you? I don't have money and may never get my inheritance."

"Jakob and I have that worked out."

"When will we talk again?"

"I'm staying the night. The doctors will get back with me later today. I'd like to meet with you again in the morning. Same time?"

Keira nodded and walked toward the door with the other woman. Mac paused with her hand on the knob. "One last question. What part does Owen Strong play in all of this?"

"He's the first person I've ever met who didn't want something from me, or plan to use me in some way." She thought about the need for honesty. "He's the one love of my life."

"You haven't known each other long. And you may be emotionally vulnerable right now. I'd advise you to be careful."

Keira turned, straightened her shoulders and met Mac's

stare head on. "I've made bad choices and some big mistakes. Owen is the only thing I've done right. I have nothing to fear from him. I only hope I'm not putting him in danger. I need you to promise that no matter what happens to me, you will protect, defend, fight for my grandma, Ace and Owen."

Mac held her gaze until something flittered across her face. Keira glanced at the woman's facial scar and realized if anyone would understand her request, it might well be this woman. A seed of courage sprouted from the depths of her hell.

Owen paced the outer office. Keira and the lawyer had been sequestered for almost two hours. Concern, doubt and fear found permanent residence in his gut, and he couldn't sit still. The weight of what-ifs was killing him.

What if this lawyer turned them down? Ace said she'd told him his marriage papers gave him a solid case. Mac felt confident that if they could get Grandma away from Dracon, she'd never be sent back, as long as she could verbally confirm she wanted to be with Ace.

But what if they couldn't get to Quang? He, Deke and Hunter spent a good part of the time brainstorming rescue ideas. They needed more info. He'd placed calls to Dog, imploring help.

What if Mac wouldn't defend Keira? Jakob said the lawyer was a straight shooter. What if she didn't believe Keira had been forced into committing a crime?

What if he couldn't protect Keira from Dracon until they saw him locked away in jail? What if Dracon had enough fake papers to have her turned back over to him? All he'd need to do was get his hands on her and he could make her disappear.

She's my wife. I have legal rights. Ace's words echoed once again in Owen's mind. A husband could protect his wife.

The door to the office opened and Keira and Mac filed

out. Owen crossed the space in four easy strides. Keira opened her arms and snuggled into his embrace. She was back. She was his, for now. He kissed the top of her head. "You okay?"

"Yes, now I'm better." She gave him a squeeze and rubbed her nose on his chest taking a deep breath before glancing up. The smile she gave him threatened to burst his heart. "Mac will help. I need to have a psych eval, medical checkup and drug tests. She has the appointments lined up this afternoon."

"Don't worry. We've got this. I'll get you there." He glanced over her head to where the lawyer watched him. "Ms. Walker, do we have time for me to speak to you before I take Keira to her appointments?"

The woman nodded and turned back to the other room.

Owen glanced at his friend.

"Come with me, Keira, I'm going to introduce you to the best chef in the world." Hunter placed a friendly arm over her shoulder and ushered her to the door. "And after you smile at him, I'm hoping we both score one of his latest desserts."

"Since you're no relation to my client, I can't share with you." Mac stated. Arms crossed over her waist, she stood in front of her laptop.

Owen nodded. Stopping a good ten feet from where she waited, he relaxed his shoulders and slid his hands in his pants pockets. "I understand. However, I can share information with you. There're things she doesn't realize she knows."

She lifted a brow. "And why wouldn't she know?"

"Because she's not a man. She's actually pretty innocent, considering her mother had her working in her gentlemen's club before she was eighteen. Not servicing men, but present. Her mom only asked her to do two lap dances when she was a freshman in college. After that, she quit working for her mom."

"She didn't tell me."

"Why would she? That life was normal for her growing up. The club was the family business."

Mac studied him for another minute before sitting and opening her computer. She started typing. "What else?"

"Dracon started spending more time with her this last year. They already tricked her into doing the paintings, and she believed his attention was to keep a closer eye on her. I think something else happened, but she hasn't shared that with me yet.

"She told me he asked her to paint a portrait of him. It took weeks because he kept making her start over. A few weeks ago, he asked her to paint a picture from a photo. The photo was of her, and she was naked. I'm guessing he'd installed hidden cameras in her suite. He'd probably been watching and filming her for a while."

"Bastard." Mac typed faster. "What else?"

"That was a few weeks before her mother died. I don't think her death was a coincidence."

Mac sat back in her chair and regarded him. "What are you saying?"

"I'm saying, he got tired of the mother and didn't need her anymore. Keira is his cash cow, and he's got a raging lust for her. He plans to get her back to his home and into his bed. With the mom out of the way, no one else would or could run interference. Grandma is his leverage."

"And you came to this conclusion because you're another man who wants to take advantage of her. But she's already in your bed, isn't she?" Mac lifted an eyebrow.

He gave her a crooked smile and turned for the door. "I like your style, Mac."

He stopped with his hand on the knob. Her words twisted

like a knife in his chest. The truth always hurt. He never lied to himself. He looked over his shoulder. "Dracon was the one she gave the lap dances to, before he married her mother. His motto is 'business before pleasure', timing is everything. To answer your question, I know how he thinks. Monsters are my specialty."

CHAPTER 12

*O*wen dropped Ace at the Wild Card, then headed to Pearl's Café. When he shut off the truck, Keira glanced at him and laughed.

"We have over an hour before your first appointment. You weren't able to eat this morning, so you need food, and you know my appetite." He grinned.

Unhooking her seatbelt, she placed a palm on his face. "I know you have a voracious appetite. But I'm still learning what you like."

Leaning forward, she covered his lips with hers. Warm, gentle, comforting until she escalated the heat by slipping inside to do battle with his tongue. At his groan, she leaned back.

"Stop. You keep that up and I won't be able to walk into the café."

She laughed and reached for the door handle. "I guess I need to learn how to cook, too."

It took him a moment to get her teasing. He smiled. "Only you could make me forget about food."

He was at her side of the vehicle before she could slide to

the ground. Lifting her out as though she weighed nothing, he raised her even higher and she placed her hands on his shoulders. "My mom taught me to be a gentleman and get the door for a lady. My truck is like jumping off a ledge for you. Wait for me to help."

"I think you're showing off your muscles for the people at the window."

Wide-eyed, he glanced to the side. His forehead furrowed before he lowered her to the ground. "I forgot where we were. You have that effect on me."

She smiled and wrapped an arm around his waist as they walked inside. The waitress with a long blond ponytail showed them to a booth toward the back. She glanced at Owen. "Is this okay?"

"Great. Thank you, Piper." Owen smiled.

The woman studied him fondly. Keira's heart skipped a beat. Had they dated? Was she an old girlfriend? Had Keira messed up his life and a relationship when she'd come here?

Trying to calm her thoughts and doubts, she attempted to read the menu and covertly glance across the table. He sat silently studying her, patiently waiting for her attention. Friendship, commitment, care, and love were clearly visible to her. Owen wasn't about notches on a bedpost. He was fidelity and honor. A forever guy.

"You okay now?" he asked as he veiled his emotions once again.

She smiled and took his hand in hers. "Yeah. I'm good."

After eating half of her soup, she waited for Owen to finish his sandwiches. Thanking the waitress for her iced tea refill, she let her mind wander to the psych meeting.

"Which appointment has you worried?" His low voice interrupted her anxieties as he pushed his plate to the edge of the table.

"I'm not worried."

He glanced pointedly at the stack of miniature jellies she'd used to build a fortress. "You're safe with me."

He was putting his job and possibly his life on hold to help her. She owed him the whole truth. "I'm—ashamed and embarrassed."

"Not with me. Never with me." He pulled several bills from his wallet and dropped them on the table. "Come on. We'll sit in the park."

Taking her hand in his much larger one, he led her to the bench in front of the bandstand. The gentle breeze soothed her jitters. He positioned them so they faced each other.

"Around the first of the year, I got sick and couldn't eat. Since they left me alone in my studio to work, they didn't notice. When they finally realized, I was in serious condition.

"I wasn't actively trying to starve myself. I just kept throwing up, and then all I wanted to do was sleep. The more I slept, the less I cared. What was the point? I didn't have a life."

"Did they take you to the doctor?" Owen asked.

"The cook who brought my meals was the one who eventually realized something was wrong. Dracon came in with his private doctor. My recovery took a while. He—" With her gaze focused on her lap, she plucked at the sleeve of her shirt. Inhaling deeply, she forced herself to continue. "He told the doctor I was emotionally unstable and a threat to myself. That I tried to starve myself to death. They strapped me to the bed."

Glancing up she noticed a twitch in Owen's cheek. She forced herself to continue. "He came to my room every day and spent hours with me. He watched as the nurse and doctor administered the IVs and bathed me."

"Did he rape you?" Owen asked softly.

"When we were alone, he pulled the sheets back and

looked at me. I knew he wanted to, but he didn't. Every day, I expected him to do it, but he never did."

Owen covered her hand with his much larger one. "He was torturing you. Mind games are worse than the actual physical abuse."

Keira raised her gaze to his face. "After I got better, he continued his daily visits. He told me how sick I was and how disappointed he was that I'd tried to commit suicide. How I was mentally unbalanced and needed someone to watch over me. I was still weak in the beginning, easily restrained."

"The scars on your belly and thighs, did he do that?" Owen interrupted.

She nodded, whispering. "You guessed."

"He cut you to make you look unstable. Even then he was making a case to get control of you." His rage vibrated in his tone. "Dracon controlled the doctor, but he needed solid proof."

Silent tears rolled down her cheeks.

"Come close, Little-bit. I need to hold you."

She snuggled onto his lap and leaned into his chest. He held her as the sobs shook her.

Owen was a little surprised, yet honored when Keira put him down as her contact for emergencies and HIPAA, in addition to the release of information to her lawyer. Before she went to the exam room, he asked her to tell the doctor how she got the scars and have her take pictures.

At the psych appointment, he reminded her that this doctor was on her side and being forthcoming was in her best interest. No one, least of all the doctor, was going to judge her. He liked Dr. Rasmussen immediately. Still, the two-hour wait wore on his nerves. Keira walked out of the appointment and straight into his arms. Looking over her head, he assessed the doctor's expression. Her smile and nod released whatever had been squeezing his chest. He could breathe again.

"I'll get my report to Mac this evening," she said. "I understand we're on an escalated timeframe. I've also given Keira the name of a second doctor should you require another responsible evaluation, but there's no need. Her situation is obvious." She placed a comforting hand on Keira's shoulder. "You have my number. Call if you need me. When the situation settles down, I'll be more than happy to meet with you again."

They walked to the truck, hand in hand. Once settled, Keira turned to him. "She said I'm not crazy or self-destructive."

"Well hell, I told you that." He smiled.

"I think I'd like to go back. She's really easy to talk to." She cleared her throat. "She said what he did to me wasn't my fault."

He guided the truck to the side of the road and took her hand. "None of this is your fault. You're the victim here. We'll get you your life back. Then you can decide what you want to do, and who you want to be. Life will be about your choices."

IN THE MORNING, Owen met with Deke, Hunter and Ace in Jakob's office, while Keira met with the lawyer. Owen laid out the drawings Keira had made of Dracon's compound and the interior of the house.

He pointed to a quadrant on the second story. "This is Quang's set of suites. She has a small kitchenette, bathroom, bedroom and sitting room. You can see there's a balcony big enough for a small table, two chairs and a couple of plants. Keira's guessing on the footage, but the roof overhang extends past the patio by a couple feet, maybe three." He glanced at Hunter. "It makes rappelling from the roof a little more awkward, but not impossible. The inside security is the biggest unknown. From what Keira says, there are a lot of oversized bodyguards disguised as butlers, gardeners, and service staff. We have to assume everyone is trained, including the maids and cooks. If Ace can cause enough of a distraction at the front, and we can get to Quang, that will be half the battle. Once in place, we wait for the Feds to take over and provide backup.

"This monolith was Keira's prison. The stolen paintings and forgeries are stored on the first floor. She doesn't know what is on the second. She was held hostage on the third. On her floor, there's a door with a keypad that leads to the roof. She gave me the number, but they've probably changed it. Every door in this building has a guard.

"She was never allowed on the elevator unescorted. The elevator shows the second-floor button, but the guards also used a key. Once, shortly after she was taken to live there, she and her guard were on the elevator when another guard came running and slipped in before the door shut. Her guard forced her to face the corner, blocking her view and movement with his body. He placed his hands over her ears while they stopped on two. She thought she smelled something burning. She was never on the elevator in a situation like that again. A couple of times she was taken off the elevator and made to wait."

Owen glanced at Hunter. "My guess is it's the lab or where they cut the drugs. Are the FBI and DEA willing to work with us?"

"Let's say we've piqued their interest. Mac has the list of

paintings and her discussions with Keira. She's handling the initial interface with both agencies. She's trying to cut a deal."

"We need to get my wife to safety, first," Ace interrupted.

Hunter glanced up. "We will. Can I take these diagrams to Ivy? She may have ideas."

Owen nodded, then glanced at Deke. "Any word from Dog?"

"He's in, but he's on the move. Said he'd check in later. He wants to stay away from a connection to you. I'll be his point of contact. One of the missing informants was his friend. He said he'll start reconnaissance tonight." Deke pulled his phone from his pocket and frowned. Standing, he headed for the door. "I'll be back."

Owen started pacing. Once Deke left the room, his chest tightened—they couldn't afford the op going south. He glanced to the door leading to the board room. He needed to make sure Keira was protected.

Twenty minutes later, Deke came back, followed by Jakob. "The group in Australia started getting soft hits about four hours ago. They've picked up in intensity recently."

"They can't trace anything back to the lodge, right?" Owen asked.

"Correct," Deke assured him. "Australia made it difficult to find the little info they got. We've only leaked the parts of your backstory we agreed to give them."

The boardroom door opened and Owen waved Deke to silence.

Mac and Keira both studied the group in front of them. Mac spoke first. "Which one of you swallowed the canary?"

Keira crossed to Owen. "What have you done?"

"Everything is fine. No worries."

"Don't tell me that. I know you."

"We have a plan, ladies." Jakob waved toward the sitting area. "Join us, and Owen will explain. He's the strategist."

An hour later, Owen glanced at Mac. "Can you get the FBI and DEA to go along with us?"

"This scheme of yours seems risky to me, but you say you have back up from another government agency. On the upside, if you pull it off, they'll put Dracon away for years." She paused and glanced at Keira. "How do you feel about this plan?"

"I trust Owen. I trust his family."

Mac stood. "I'll make calls."

"Ms. Walker, may I speak with you for a moment?" Owen asked.

Following her into the boardroom, he shut the door and leaned against it. "I've been wondering if Dracon Escott has been married before and what might have happened to those women. You have someone who could check?"

"Umm, good question. I'll get my staff on it right away." She arched her brow. "Is there something else?"

"We need to make sure that no matter what happens, Keira and her grandmother are protected. Ace has me thinking. Would Keira be more protected if she and I married?" He held up a hand. "Before you go all *lawyer* on me, hear me out. If she and I marry, I'd have you draw up an ironclad prenup so I couldn't go after her current assets or future assets. I'll also put in writing that she can get an annulment as soon as this is over, or a divorce that I'll agree not to contest."

"Why are you talking to me about this?" Mac asked. "I work for her."

"Because you understand what's going on, and the fewer people involved, the fewer leaks. Believe me, if he learns you're her lawyer, Dracon will be digging up every tidbit he can find on you. Are you good with that?"

Owen detected a slight hesitancy flicker across her face, but her response was solid. "Let him bring it on."

"Would she be safer?" he repeated.

"Yes. If he pushes that she isn't in her right mind, your marriage would make the whole medical power of attorney simpler. We'll have her sign documents giving you clear jurisdiction. With the added legal responsibilities as her husband, it will be your decision to seek medical evaluations, not a step-father's. The doctor reports I received are in our favor. Should Dracon contest the medical evaluations we procured, we will ask the court to assign independent doctors to reevaluate."

"Did the medical doc send you photos?"

"Yes. Keira insisted they be included in the report. I'm guessing that was at your request. Why?"

"Those pictures are proof."

"Our doctor indicated they looked to be non-suicidal self-injury, but that could be explained by the unrelenting stress she was under."

"That's why the cuts were inflicted. He wanted to indicate she was unstable. Dracon did it. He cut her."

"The pictures don't prove that," Mac argued. "They could both say the other lied."

"And you'll contact a specialist who understands knife work and wounds."

"Are you the expert?"

"I could be, but you'd want an outsider. Look at the scars, Mac. Keira's left-handed."

She paled.

"Start the paperwork for a prenup. I'll talk to Keira today. I won't force her, but I'd feel better knowing we've taken every precaution." He laid a card on the table. "This is my accountant. After this goes down, send him your invoices. I've already given him instructions that you're to be paid without question, regardless of what happens, but I don't want any more paper trails until we're done. I'd appreciate it if you could do a lot of this yourself, rather than outsourcing to staff. Again, it prevents potential leaks."

Reaching for the door handle, he paused. "One more thing. I need a will, leaving all my assets to Keira. I won't require a prenup from her."

Hunter walked into the boardroom after Ace, Owen and Keira left. "I've got a couple numbers you can give your DEA and FBI contacts."

Turning from the window, Mac studied Hunter. "Who, or should I ask what is Owen Strong? My people haven't found anything. Is he a spook?"

Hunter dropped the paper he held onto her desk and smiled. "Officially, he's a damn good mechanic over at Rollie's Auto Body. The guy can fix anything. He also mans the tow truck if you ever need one."

Incredulous, she met his gaze. "You're serious? You trust him?"

Hunter sobered. "With my life. He's already saved me and Ruby once. He's a natural strategist. Would've gone far in the military, if he hadn't left. Keira's in good hands, Mac."

KEIRA LED the way up the stairs to the loft after their shift at the Wild Card. She understood Owen's reasoning that everyone needed to proceed as normal. But the three days of early mornings and late nights, topped off by stress, were taking a toll.

He kissed the top of her head. "I'll meet you in bed."

Later, she felt the mattress dip. Rolling over, she snuggled along the side of his body, her leg over his hips and her head on his chest under his chin. This position was her safe zone. Her home.

She woke to an empty bed. After a trip to the restroom,

she started the electric water kettle and glanced at the stove clock. Noon? Obviously, she'd needed the sleep. She wondered when Owen had gotten up.

Crossing to the window overlooking the gym, she watched Owen and Ivy fighting. No, he called it sparring. He glistened with sweat, and there were welts on his sides, back and chest. Ivy carried similar marks.

He swung at Ivy's jaw. She twisted, avoiding the punch and dropped to the mat, sweeping his legs out from under him. Keira's heart stopped as they both lay unmoving. Ivy rose on her elbows first and said something. Owen rolled and pushed to his knees. He glanced up, unerringly meeting Keira's observation through the glass. He smiled, then said something to Ivy. She looked up, nodded and jumped to her feet, heading to the back of the barn.

Keira watched as Owen grabbed a towel from the weight bench and rubbed it across his body as he headed to the loft stairs. He stopped in front of her, dropping a light kiss on her lips.

"Let me get cleaned-up, then we can go to town for lunch before we need to be at the Wild Card."

He walked out of the closet with his shirt still open and his shoes and socks in his hand. Keira met him and brushed the shirt to the side. She brushed her fingers under one of the still-visible welts. "Doesn't that hurt?"

"I'm used to the pain. Sparring helps condition your body. It teaches the mind how to ignore the injuries during a real fight, allowing you to concentrate on defending yourself."

She was terrified by the cost he was prepared to pay. Grasping each side of his shirt, she buttoned from the bottom. "You're extremely stubborn and cocky."

"Don't talk dirty to me or we'll never get lunch before work."

Chuckling, she shoved him aside. "Button your own shirt. I'm getting my shoes and bag."

After lunch at Maria's restaurant, Owen suggested they stroll around the shops until their shift started. Parking by the saloon, he helped her out of the truck and took her hand. "Do you like ice cream? Curly's Cone shop has the best."

"Who doesn't like ice cream?" she laughed. "But I'm stuffed after that lunch. Maybe another time."

How many days did they have? How soon before she was forced back into Dracon's grasp or shipped off to prison?

"Keira, I need to talk to you about something. Can we sit?" He led her to a park bench and turned to meet her gaze.

"I need to guarantee you'll be safe. The lawyer says your tests and evaluations all came back in our favor, but I don't want to leave anything to chance. There's one more option."

His obvious nervousness was frightening her. Was he going to send her away? "Say it, Owen. You're scaring me."

"Keira, you could marry me. It doesn't have to be forever. I'll let you go whenever you're free of the situation, or I'll be committed for as long as you need me to be your husband. I'll sign a prenup. You don't have to worry that I'll try to get the money that is rightfully yours and your grandmother's. I won't demand anything. Mac said it would help if Dracon tried to push any medical concerns. With me as your husband, he'd have no justification for guardianship rights."

Her breath caught in her chest. A roaring sound echoed in her ears. She placed trembling fingers over his lips. "Stop. Just stop. I don't want to hear anymore."

CHAPTER 13

*E*uphoria battled despair. She loved him, but his proposal was a strategic op. He'd created the plan only to keep her safe, not make her a real wife. His plan slashed her dreams to shreds.

He wanted her to marry him so he could shield her, as an obligation.

She wanted him for a lifetime.

Keira stood and walked a few steps away, arms wrapped around her waist. What should she do? She knew he cared about her, wanted her, but did he love her? If she married him, could his caring turn to love? Or once Grandma and Ace were safe, would he want her to release him?

If Grandma stayed in Spencer with Ace, she'd also want to be close to the new family she'd found. Losing Owen, seeing him with someone else, giving him up, would destroy her. Why did he even bring it up if it couldn't be real?

Cherish the memories, my child.

"I'm not trying to put you on the spot. Just consider it, okay? But we'd need to decide soon." Owen spoke from behind her, his warmth filling the space between their bodies. His scent comforted her. Tears filled her throat. She nodded.

He took her hand and led her to the Wild Card. She couldn't meet his eyes.

OWEN WIPED the table in the corner as he watched Keira move from customer to customer. Damn. He'd made a mess of things. She probably thought he was as bad as Dracon and trying to use her.

Dracon didn't need what he was stealing from them. After Keira's mother died, he could have let them walk away. The greedy bastard had enough money in his own right. People like Dracon never saw it that way. No matter how much they had, it was never enough. No one else should take what they thought was their entitlement.

But it wasn't about the money anymore. What Dracon wanted was Keira. He needed to own her, possess her like the paintings he bought or stole.

He'd fucked up. Now Keira saw him as the same type of slime as Dracon. It was too late to explain he didn't need or want her money. During his search for Oona's killer, he worked as a bounty hunter and underground fighter, earning and investing money for years. On top of the insurance payout for the building his parents left, he was damn near set up for life. He didn't give a shit about money. He'd rather have a humble life with the woman he loved.

Someone clunked a beer on the table as he took another swipe with his rag.

"Sit down and talk to me, before you wear the wood on that table down to the legs," Hunter demanded. "If you don't stop, Ace is going to come over here and it will be ugly. He wants to know what you did to upset his granddaughter."

Owen glanced at the clock above the bar. Almost time for last call. Most of the regulars were already gone. He glanced over as Ruby went to help Keira clear tables.

He dropped onto the chair next to Hunter and took a long pull of the beer. "I fucked up, man."

"No shit. That's been pretty obvious all night. Man-up and fix it."

"I don't think I can."

"What did you do?"

"I talked to Mac. If Keira and I marry, it strengthens our case to keep her away from Dracon."

"You dumb fuck. Instead of telling her you were in love with her, you let her think you were marrying her to protect her, as a tactic. Oh damn, I do not want to be there when Ruby gets her hands on you."

Owen stared at his friend in disbelief. "What are you saying? Why would Ruby be mad at me?"

"Are you trying to tell me *you* don't know that you're in love with Keira? Hell, *we all* know. The whole family has discussed it. Well, except Ace."

Rolling the cold bottle against his brow, Owen glanced up. "I know. It's too soon to tell her. She has too many worries. Besides, she deserves better than me."

Hunter nodded and took a pull of his own beer. "I hear ya there, man. The same goes for me and Ruby. But I'll tell you this. Ruby said she wanted me, too. There's no way in hell I'm letting anyone take her from me. So, I get my undeserving ass up each day, thank god she's mine, and work harder than the day before to be the man she deserves."

"How do I fix this?"

"Hell if I know. You made a pretty bad mess of it. I'd start with telling her the truth, the whole truth. Then, I assume a large dose of groveling will be required. Followed by flowers and chocolate. And more groveling." Hunter got to his feet. "You need to try and smooth it over with Ace."

Just before closing, Owen followed Ace to the supply room in the back. "Need some help?"

Ace glared at him. "What I need is to know what you did to upset my granddaughter. You damn well better not have hurt her, or they'll be looking for you for a long time."

"I love Keira. I want to marry her."

"Then why is she so upset? Did you force yourself on her?"

Owen held up his palms. "Ace, give me a second to explain. I've never done this before, and I'm a little nervous. I want your permission to marry her. But I did sort of ask her already."

Ace crossed his arms. "You'd best be at the explaining part, son."

"I love Keira. She's it for me. I know that. I wasn't sure how she felt about me, since we only met a week ago. I thought that us getting married would offer more protection for her. Like you and your wife. So, I put it to her as more of a safeguard plan, instead of a real proposal. I was thinking it'd give me time to show her how I felt and maybe give her time to love me."

"Damn fool." Ace huffed and reached for three bottles of Crown. "I see the look in your eyes. You got my permission. Be prepared to atone. I hope she puts you through the ringer. I don't want to have to kick your ass."

KEIRA COULDN'T CONCENTRATE. Between the pain in her heart and the constant threat of tears, she'd barely functioned through the whole shift. She'd messed up more than one order and had to go back and check with the customer.

"Thank goodness it's almost time to go home." Ruby's voice interrupted her self-disgust.

She glanced up. "How do you do it? You're always pleasant and happy? You're so close to your due date, and yet you move like you aren't even pregnant? How do you deal with everything?"

Ruby took the tray from her grip and placed it on the nearest table, then led her into the pizza garden. "Sit. Now tell me what's wrong."

"My life." She shook her head. "Nothing. I—something unexpected happened today, that's all." Shoving her hand into her server's apron, she pulled out a wadded napkin and swiped at her tears.

"I'd say a lot of unexpected things have happened to you lately. When life reaches this point on the suck-o-meter it's best to find a friend and share. I'd like to be that friend for you." Ruby placed a hand on top of hers.

Keira glanced up. "It's not nice. It's ugly and awful and monstrous and terrible and—and I'm so damn tired of it."

"Aw honey, I know." Ruby slipped off one of her bracelets, extending her arm into the candlelight showing Keira the scars. "I ran into some trouble and felt pretty much like you do. Then I came here. I made friends who also understood ugly, awful and monstrous things happen. I made a home. I found a family in Ace, Owen, Deke, Ivy and Gage. I know you have your grandma and Ace is your grandfather now, but I think maybe there's more for you here. Does he know you love him? Have you told him?"

Keira's gaze shot to Ruby's. Slowly she shook her head. "That's the problem. He asked me to marry him, but only to protect me."

Ruby shook her head in disgust. "Owen is a little complicated. Has he told you about Oona?"

Keira nodded.

"Well, that's a start. He can play the part of whomever he needs to be and make it seem natural. When it comes to the real him—his demons—he's tight-lipped. The fact he shared his sister's story with you means he has deep feelings for you.

"I don't know how much you've dated, but men aren't that different from women. Oh, they pretend to be tough and uncaring, but deep down they're searching for the same things we want. Love, commitment, a partner. They just screw it up when they tie it to the need-to-protect and act all macho. Most men don't learn how to verbally express themselves. Study his eyes. You'll see the truth."

Ruby stood up, pulling Keira to her feet. "I think you've had a very long week. You need to go home and get some sleep. There's not much left to do here. The rest of us will close up."

Owen met them at the doorway leading to the garden. "Keira, I—"

Ruby interrupted, "Go grab your bag, Keira. I'll keep Owen company until you come back."

After Keira turned the corner into the room with the staff lockers, Ruby turned back to Owen and slapped his chest. "Don't be a fool. Take her home and make this right. Use all the words this time."

Grabbing the tray from the table, she headed to the bar.

Owen was waiting for Keira when she walked down the hall. He took her backpack, slung it over one shoulder, and clasped her hand. Once he settled her into the cab of his truck, he drove in silence to the barn, insisting on his customary inspection. She waited on the steps to the loft, and once inside, she headed straight to the bathroom.

She stopped at the entrance and decided a good long soak was what she needed. Turning on the water for the soaker tub, she added a generous sprinkle of bath salts. Stripping off her clothes, she wrapped her hair in a towel and stepped into the fragrant water. She sank into the warmth and closed her eyes, allowing her mind to float aimlessly.

The gentle massage at her temples softly registered. Raising her eyelids enough to peek out, she studied Owen's reflection in the glass across from the tub. Shirtless, with his hair slicked back as he did after a shower, he sat on a wooden stool behind her. He must have gone downstairs to clean up after she went to his master bath.

Closing her eyes once again, she allowed herself to absorb and memorize his gentle touch. After carefully removing the towel from her hair, his tender caresses gave way to the well-worn bristles of her brush as he stroked it through her hair with soothing repetition. The nurturing attention eased her lonesomeness. She drifted in contentment, vaguely aware he warmed the water a couple times.

Too soon, he whispered near her ear. "Come Little-bit, time to get out."

He helped her stand as the water drained away, placing her palms on his shoulders as he affectionately dried her body. Lifting her against his chest, he carried her to the bed and spooned her. "Sleep. I've got you."

The following morning, Owen and Keira were jerked from sleep by heavy-fisted pounding on the outer loft door. Owen rolled from the bed. "Keira, hide in the closet."

Pulling on his sweatpants, Owen grabbed his knife from the bedside table, noticing the message light on his phone. He padded barefoot to where he could see who was at the door. He called out to Keira. "It's Deke and Hunter. Meet us when you're dressed."

Opening the door, he stepped back as Deke charged inside. "What the fuck? You don't answer your phone? I left you four messages."

"Good morning to you, too. I'll put on coffee." Owen

headed to the coffee pot, hitting the button on the kettle for Keira's tea water as he passed.

"Brew it strong. I've been up for a while." Deke complained.

Owen studied Keira as she walked into the room. Hunter gave her a hug, and Deke patted her shoulder before sitting at the breakfast bar. As she moved toward him, Owen stepped in front of her. Holding his breath, he waited for her to look up at him. The doubt and distance in her gaze sent panic rushing through his veins. "We need to talk. Can I explain?"

"Later," she whispered, grasping her teacup.

Deke reached for the coffee pot, halting the brewing process and filled his cup. "Late last night, Dracon broke through the Australian group's cyber walls like we wanted him to. He's been busy since then. He left four messages for his staff lawyer and contacted what appears to be his personal medical doctor."

"How do we know this?" Owen asked.

"Ivy's ex-boss, Donavan, is in contact with the FBI in Texas. After getting an order to monitor his lines, they've been listening."

"Damn. I'm going to owe D, and I still don't trust him."

"Makes two of us," Hunter chimed in.

We expect Dracon to have your address and history by the end of today, tomorrow morning at the latest." Deke finished.

"Where is Dog?"

Deke swallowed his coffee and reached for the pot again. "He's been monitoring the property from the ground and using a drone for overhead glimpses. By the way, he said he bought cheap drones for some kids in the neighborhood. He asked them to wear them out over the next few days as a test.

He bought a really sweet one for himself. He's sending you the bill."

Owen shrugged.

"He thinks the back-gate guards are the weakest. Once Ivy gets Quang, she plans to head out that way. Everyone else will be distracted by the FBI and DEA raid. A van will be waiting to get Quang and Ivy to safety. Both agencies agreed to interview her here."

"With the proximity to the military base, we think we've lucked out, but Ivy says her helicopter friend is doing flyovers of the compound, starting today until we tell her to stop. The guards should be accustomed to the sound of helicopters already, but especially desensitized by the time Ivy's ready to rappel in. We want her inside with Quang before the raid starts. The FBI is arguing about that part of the plan, but we're a 'go', regardless. Ivy thinks you're right about the safety issue."

"What safety issue?" Keira cut in.

Owen hesitated. "Dracon probably has standard orders in place for people who know too much about his business or about him, should he encounter arrest or prosecution. I want someone we know and trust to protect your grandmother. Ivy volunteered."

Owen waited and watched as Keira processed what he'd said. When she lifted wide eyes to him, he knew she understood the danger to her grandmother.

"You're saying a—" Keira paused.

"A kill order," Owen explained.

Glancing away, she nodded.

"Keira, I'm supposed to ask," Hunter said. "Having grown up in Vietnam, does your grandmother speak or understand French? You've mentioned she'd been forbidden to speak anything but English. Ivy wants to take advantage of Quang's language skills if she needs to talk in front of guards. Ivy knows a tiny bit of Vietnamese, but is much better in French. Also, she'd like to spend time with you today to brush up.

"Yes, Grandma was raised around both, she may be a little rusty on the French. I'm scheduled to work at seven tonight. Any time before then is fine."

"Okay. We'll get you together."

Owen lifted the coffee pot and poured a cup for Hunter. "Are you okay staff-wise, even with short notice?"

Hunter smirked. "Oh yeah. Sage and Levi said to tell you that you owe them big. They're conspiring on what they are going to get from you."

"We have a call with Quang today. If Dracon knows as much as we think, he'll probably try to intercept. Hunter, you and Ace should probably try to be here at the loft a little early. Is Mac still in town?"

"Yes. Jakob convinced her to stay through the weekend. He scheduled a couple spa appointments for her. She had him move a printer into the boardroom. She's been holed up in there since yesterday."

"Invite her to the call. Ivy too, if she can."

Putting their cups in the sink, Deke called out over his shoulder as they walked out. "I'll keep you posted on what we hear from our group in Australia."

"Can she do it? Can Ivy get to Grandma and keep her safe?" Keira asked, clutching her tea cup as though it was her only anchor."

Owen crossed to the barstool where she sat and turned her to face him. "Ivy was a soldier, and after that she did covert missions for a government agency. You've seen her smack me down. And seriously, she holds back on me. She's stealthy and lethal in more ways than one. Opponents always underestimate her."

Keira nodded.

"Ivy is family. She and Ruby are my sisters now. I trust

her to protect Quang. Most importantly, I would trust her to protect the love of my life. You."

At her startled gasp and glance, he continued. "I fucked up the other night because I was afraid—afraid if I told you I loved you, heart and soul, you wouldn't believe me. You'd say it was too soon. That I couldn't be sure.

"Keira, I know my heart. I love you. I want you for my wife. A real wife, not a fake marriage. I don't expect you to feel the same. If you'll give me a chance to prove it and marry me for now, I'll spend the rest of my life showing you my heart. If I can't make you believe, I'll understand later if you want to leave.

"I love you, but I won't deny that I also need to do everything I can think of to keep you safe, and this is one more step we can take."

Keira pushed from the barstool and crossed to the overlook window.

"I'm a criminal. How can you love me?" she asked, turning back to face him.

"You're a survivor."

He dropped to his knees, pulling her into his embrace and laid his head against her midriff. "Thank god you were strong enough to survive. I would've had to wait until the afterlife to know this love."

Tears streamed down her cheeks as she threaded her fingers through his hair and held him. She didn't deserve this man, but she wasn't letting him go without a fight. "How do we get married?"

"You're saying yes?" he questioned. At her nod, he pushed to his feet. Cupping her face, he wiped the tears from her cheeks with his thumbs. "I swear, I'll let you go if you change your mind."

"Don't you see? I love you every bit as much as you say you love me. This is forever. Yes?"

"Forever." He covered her lips, filling his kiss with promise. "Later we'll go to the lodge to get your birth certificate from Jakob's safe and talk to Mac. We'll stop at the jewelry store and then go to the courthouse."

Lifting her against his chest, he crossed to the bed and laid her down. "I need you, love."

"I need you, too," she responded, pulling him down to join her.

MAC, Deke and Jakob were waiting in Jakob's office when Keira and Owen arrived.

"The papers you requested are ready," Mac said. "I'd like to talk to both of you in the boardroom first."

Closing the door behind them, Owen spoke. "I've explained my worries to Keira and she has agreed."

"Did you mention to her the prenup and your will?"

"Will?" Keira flashed him a startled glance.

"Everyone needs one. The prenup is what protects you."

Mac snorted. "I did some checking on you. Quite the military record. Your CO was upset he lost you. He'd recommended you for officer training and felt you would've gone far. I understand you had family issues."

When his only reply was to stare back at her, she slid the papers across the table and stood. "I'll be in Jakob's office when you're done reviewing. There are a few other situations to discuss with Deke."

He read the prenup, signed it and handed it to Keira while he reviewed the will. At the sound of paper ripping, he glanced up. She'd torn the prenup in half and was tearing it into quarters.

"Keira, no. What're you doing?"

"You made me a promise before you took me to your bed. Did you lie?"

"Hell, no!"

"Then we don't need this, and I won't have it between us." She studied the outraged stare he shot her and started to laugh, a deep chest laugh. She realized it had been years since she'd felt free. She laughed until tears fell from her eyes.

"Keira, Keira, what's wrong?"

He lifted her into his massive embrace, cupping her butt in one palm and the back of her head in the other.

He swiped the trail of tears with his thumb. "Tell me, Little-bit. I'll fix it."

"You already have." His love surrounded her with warmth and strength. She would never fear Dracon again. She had her very own dragon.

Several minutes later, they joined the others. Keira glanced at Mac. "We don't need the prenup. We left his will on your computer. I need a will for whatever assets I may receive from my mother. If something happens to me, I want the funds to be used to support my grandmother until she passes. Anything remaining will go to Owen. Can you create those for me, please?"

"Prenup?" Jakob lifted an eyebrow. "When's the wedding?"

"We're going to the courthouse to get the license this afternoon. I'm hoping Judge Albright is in," Owen responded.

Jakob frowned. "Mac and I brought him up to date with what's going on in case we needed a judge. I think he's in court this afternoon. How about this? You get the license today, and I invite him to brunch tomorrow, and we have the wedding here. Ruby would be furious if she wasn't there, and so would Ace."

"I can't believe I didn't think of that. Yes, I want Ace there," Keira spoke up.

Owen nodded. "Okay, we'll make the arrangements today. The call with Quang is tonight. Deke and Mac, you'll be at the loft, right?"

An hour before he and Keira were scheduled to leave the Wild Card to prepare for her grandma's call, his cell phone pinged with a text message from Deke.

He's got a bead on you. Stay frosty.

CHAPTER 14

As per Mac's request to record the conversation, Keira was instructed to put the call from Quang on speaker, even though they wouldn't be speaking English. Ivy was going to translate for Mac.

Keira answered quickly. "Grandma, are you well? Where are you?"

"In my bathroom. The cook brought my food and left me. You were right. They've been putting something in my food. When I quit eating their meals, I was not tired. Something is going on. There was a truck here, and the staff has been tense and busy. I heard yelling. Tell me you are still safe."

"Yes, Grandma, I'm safe. A friend is going to come visit you to make sure you are okay. Her name is Ivy. Please talk to her for a moment. I want you to recognize her voice."

Ivy introduced herself and gave Grandma her description, gently warning her it may be during the night when she visited on the balcony and to expect her in a few days. With a thumbs up, she handed the phone back to Keira.

"Grandma, you can trust Ivy. I want you to go with her."

"I will do as you say. Ace. Is Ace okay?"

"I'm here, my love. Be brave. I'll see you soon," Ace responded.

"I love you—" A door banged. Grandma screeched. "What are you doing here? Get out! Get out!"

Keira panicked. "Grandma? Grandma? What's going on? Grandma!"

A male voice reverberated across the line. "Keira dear, is that you? Are you all right? We've been worried. Did you hurt yourself again? Are you safe? Tell me where you are, and I'll come get you."

Heart thundering in her chest, Keira clutched Owen's hand. Glancing up, she met his steady comforting gaze. She knew what she needed to do. She'd rehearsed during the afternoon with both Owen and Ivy. "You're cutting out. Who is this?"

"Sweetheart, it's Dracon." His voice came across more pronounced. "Sweetheart, I know your mother's death was a shock for you. Running off probably seemed like avoiding the shock and sadness. Come home, and we can deal with our grief together. We all miss her terribly. We miss you."

"That's not my home."

"Your doctor doesn't feel that's wise. Grief is hard enough to deal with when you have the support of family around you. You've already had a difficult year, emotionally, and you're stressed. Come home, and we can talk about changing your living arrangements in a couple months."

"I'm not coming back. I've found my own place."

"Grandma has missed you terribly. She hasn't been doing well since you ran off. Her doctor is concerned. I think having you home would be beneficial for her health. She needs you."

"Then she can come live with me. I'll take care of her."

Dracon's exaggerated sigh made her want to scream.

Owen brushed his palm over her knee. She relaxed. She wasn't alone anymore.

"How will you support the two of you, my dear? Her medical expenses are extensive. If she doesn't get better soon, her doctor's afraid she will require round-the-clock care. You remember how difficult that can be."

There it was, the warning. The threat. She'd known it was coming, still the menace was a punch to her midsection. Yes, she knew how difficult being tied down and drugged could be psychologically and physically. Owen stroked her arm and back.

"Breathe," he mouthed silently. "I've got you."

"Keira, dear, are you still there?" Dracon asked.

"I want Grandma to come stay with me for a while," Keira replied.

"I know you don't mean to be selfish, but she's not well enough to travel right now. You aren't here to see how she's deteriorated. Because she loves you, she would never tell you during your weekly calls. She wouldn't want to burden you. The doctor feels travel could be dangerous for her right now." He paused dramatically. "You must be about out of cash. Where are you? I'll send you money to come home."

"I'm in Colorado, staying with the Strong family."

"Friends? I didn't realize you had friends in Colorado."

"People I met. You don't know them. I've gotta go. Put Grandma back on the phone. I want to say goodbye."

"She's resting dear. She can't come to the phone. Why don't I come get you, and you can come home for a little visit? You can bring your friends. Tell me where you are."

At Owen's nod, she continued. "I've got to go. I need to think."

She disconnected the phone and threw her arms around Owen's neck, trembling. "That bastard."

"I've got you. You did great. You were so brave."

"What if he hurts her?" she cried.

Owen rubbed her back, glancing over her shoulder at an equally furious Ace. "He won't hurt her. Not this time. She's his most powerful asset. Every other time she's been threatened, you've given in. He was already pleased with the conversation."

She sat up, meeting his gaze. "What do you mean? How do you know?"

"Power and control. He interrupted your call, showing his knowledge and reach. He talked loud enough for someone else to overhear his concern for your health and stability. He threatened your grandmother, at the same time reminding you of your own suffering—double whammy. Then he dug the knife in a little deeper by reminding you how selfish you are, making you the guilty party. The kill shot was getting you to admit you were in Colorado. You played that well, by the way."

"How long before he does something?" Keira asked

"Not long. He kept you on the phone long enough to confirm you're in Spencer. The conversation validated what he already suspected. Now the question is, will he come himself or send someone? I'm betting he comes himself."

Keira realized her grandmother had sounded strong and well. She knew Grandma was a fighter. Waiting was torture. The confrontation couldn't come soon enough. Now the rescue plan had to fall into place.

SATURDAY MORNING, Owen waited in Jakob's office, his heart full of love as his beautiful bride walked into the room on Ace's arm. Seeing her for the first time since their arrival that morning, she took his breath away. Dressed in a form-fitting, above-the-knee, red dress with touches of ivory, she was stunning. Her hair laced into an intricate crown, studded with red and white flowers encircling her head. She carried a bouquet of the same blooms.

"Who will give away the bride?" Judge Albright asked.

"I will, her grandfather," replied Ace, a crack in his voice.

Owen slipped her hand into his and led her to a position in front of the judge. Repeating their vows, he slid the simple braided band of white, yellow, and rose gold onto her delicate finger. Seeing his ring on her hand sent a pounding pressure into his chest, threatening to drop him to his knees. His wife. She placed her left hand over his heart, and he remembered to breathe.

He vaguely remembered the judge pronouncing them man and wife. Then she was in his arms, kissing him, holding him, loving him.

Too soon, voices interrupted their embrace. Judge Albright had them sign the marriage certificate with Hunter and Ruby as witnesses. Keira was tugged from his grasp, and Ruby and Mac were hugging her. Hell, even Ivy gave her a quick embrace. Gage, Hunter and Deke each gave the blushing bride a kiss on the cheek.

Normally taciturn, Ace glowed with pride. "She reminds me of Quang and our wedding. The dress is almost the same color as the traditional red gown. And today's date is lucky. Quang will be pleased."

Keira had been thrilled when Ruby told her about the stunning red and cream dress she'd found for her to wear. Now he understood.

Jakob and Judge Albright joined Owen and Ace as the rest of the family gathered around Keira. Owen studied the mimosa Jakob handed him, wishing for something a little stronger.

"That's all we get. Drink it, Son. Willa said this is brunch, not poker night at the Wild Card. Besides, we need to keep our wits about us," Jakob admonished.

Owen jerked his gaze up to meet the other man's. "Something's happened?"

"Hunter got some intel." He waved his drink at the gathering. "Not now. Enjoy your wedding. We'll talk later."

Gathered around the seating area in Jakob's office after eating and celebrating, Owen listened to Hunter.

"After the call yesterday and talking to the FBI and DEA, we decided to see what would happen if we poked the dragon. Late last night, at my request, Keira sent a text message in Vietnamese to the phone her grandmother used yesterday. She told her she missed her and loved her, but she was married now and couldn't come to visit without talking it over with her husband. She begged her to please stay well, because it might be weeks before they could come."

Hunter chuckled. "According to Dog, all hell broke loose about an hour later. The FBI confirmed Dracon's pilot filed a flight plan to Denver, and they've reserved a car rental. His staff tried to reserve a room at Aspen Gold Lodge, but unfortunately there were none available, since it's still peak season. We steered them the direction we wanted, and they took the bait.

"Keane Dagleish is letting us use his family cabin on Lake Louise. He's been staying out there since the construction started on that new Honeymoon Escapes project. He wants to make sure the groundwork is to code.

"Dracon's people booked his cabin for Sunday, Monday and Tuesday, although they indicated they wouldn't be arriving until late tomorrow, which concurs with the flight plan.

"Dog and the Feds are watching to make sure Quang doesn't get moved. We want to be certain he's not bringing her here." Hunter paused and glanced at Ivy. "If the arrangements go to plan, we're thinking we'll drop you Monday night. We're sending you out this afternoon, so you can be in place."

She nodded.

"The minute Dracon's compound is hit, he'll know. We need to be on guard for the unexpected. Don't trust anyone. On the off chance he has someone here already, we keep on about our business as usual."

Hunter glanced at everyone. "Be prepared. We know Dracon is a master planner and manipulator. He'll use anyone. Two of my officers, Sage and Levi, volunteered to help out on their own time. Only locals will be aware they are cops. They're going to be working at the bar. There will be two FBI agents posing as customers. We'll meet them later today. Numerous other agents will be moving around or in strategic spots. We all know how quickly a situation can go south. Once they confirm the paintings are still at the compound, the onsite FBI here will be notified to grab Dracon."

Hunter cleared his throat. "Ruby, you aren't going to like this, but you're staying here at the lodge until this is over. I won't let you or the baby be in danger. Lacey is going to cover your shifts. The rest of the staff don't know what is going on. It's safer for them. They think the doc put you on bed rest for a few days."

Reaching over, Ruby placed her hand on his. "You should've talked to me first, but I understand. I need you to be sharp and not worrying about me."

Hunter stood. "Remember, if something goes wrong, speed dial number one on all your phones. It's our panic number, then text 281. Double check right now that your GPS trackers are turned on. I'm not losing anyone to this scumbag."

A<small>FTER CHECKING</small> the security in the lower level of the barn, Owen swept Keira into his arms and carried her up the stairs. It had been a long day. Dropping onto the couch, he settled her astride his lap. "Non-conventional wedding—get married in the morning and then work a full shift at the Wild Card. I promise I'll give you a better wedding when this is over."

"We were surrounded by family. We're husband and wife. What could be more perfect?"

"Your grandma wasn't here."

"No, but Ace was with us. We have a plan to rescue Grandma, which gives us the future."

"I don't know how you stay loving and grateful when life has been shit for you."

"The path I traveled to get to you is nothing compared to the joy and happiness of finding you. For you—for this, I'd do it again in a heartbeat."

Leaning forward, she kissed him.

He studied the intricate crown of her hair. Running a finger over the delicate tresses, he plucked one of the few remaining flowers that had survived the work shift, and brought it to his lips, inhaling deeply. "Hmm, they do smell nice. But not as sweet as you."

"I realize we're just now starting our wedding night at three in the morning. It is a little late for most newlyweds. Sheepishly, he met her gaze. "Will you do something for me? Will you put your dress back on? We didn't—I didn't get to undress you, and it's been my fantasy all day."

Chuckling, she slid from his lap. "I'll get redressed. Why don't you do the same, and we can meet back here? You were rather imposing and quite handsome dressed in your black dress shirt and slacks. I assume Ruby is the one who came up with the red boutonniere."

He blushed slightly. "I don't dress up much. After Ruby picked you up, Ivy and Gage came over. They didn't like my shirts. Gage loaned me one of his. It was a little snug, which is why I didn't wear a tie."

"And couldn't button the top three buttons." She smiled. "I liked your sexy style. Now get going. I want my wedding night."

Waiting for Keira to return, Owen leaned against the breakfast bar and checked his text messages. Based on the flight plan and driving time, Dracon would be in Spencer by five this afternoon. Hunter assured him all backups were in place.

He kicked back the last of his bourbon and set the glass on the counter. Keira was his wife. He made himself a promise that every day he'd earn her love—and no one would take her from him.

"You look pretty serious. Is something wrong?"

Her soft sweet voice whispered as she crossed the room. He glanced at her and smiled. She was stunning. Looking at her standing there in the form-fitting red dress made his heart pick up speed. "No. I was setting goals. Wondering how many times I could make you scream my name tonight."

"Um." Slipping her hands over his chest, she proceeded to undo the remaining buttons on his shirt and pull it from his slacks. "I work tomorrow. If you want more than one, you need to get started."

"Oh babe, you've got me halfway there already." He shifted her hands from the button on his pants and guided them around his neck. Holding her cheeks, he covered her lips with his. As his tongue danced and teased with hers, he slid down the zipper at the back of her dress. Lifting her with one arm around her waist, he stroked her back and shoulders with his other palm as he backstepped her to the wall.

"Let me look at you." Putting space between them, he caressed her body with his eyes, burning the image into his memory. "You're so damn beautiful. So sensual. So perfect."

Stripping his shirt off, he tossed it to the floor and dropped to his knees in front of her. Slowly, he eased the silky fabric off her shoulders and down her torso, exposing her naked breasts. He groaned. Leaning forward, he laved and sucked one perfect berry into his mouth, then gave equal care to the other. Sliding his palms down her sides, he dragged the rest of the dress down. He met her gaze. "No bra, no panties? Were you dressed like this at the wedding? If you were, you're damn lucky I didn't know or Jakob's board room would've gotten a real christening."

"I wore them earlier. I thought we could save time tonight."

Her playful giggle brought a smile to his lips. "What color were they? White?"

She shook her head.

"Black?"

She shook her head again.

"God, don't tell me they were red. I'll cum right now."

Slipping her hand down his torso and under the waist-band of his pants, she gripped his solid erection firmly. Then nodded.

He groaned again. "You're killing me. You're so damn hot. Tomorrow you're going to show me. You're going to put these pretty red heels back on and model what I missed earlier. Promise?"

Darting her tongue over his lips, she leaned back against the wall. "Promise."

He met her gaze with his own wicked smile. "Now you pay for teasing me. Cross your hands over your head."

After she did what he requested, he helped her step out of the dress, which pooled at her feet. Closing his eyes, savoring every inch of her heated flesh, he stroked up the outside of her legs, over her hips and higher to cup and fondle her perfect breasts. The hardened nubs begged for his attention, and he leaned forward, caressing and suckling until her gasping requests for more sent him lower. She trembled as he followed a path below her waist, over her belly and down to the heart of her need. At his first lick, she hissed his name and again when he gently probed her inner core with one, then two fingers. She clutched his head and screamed his name as he sucked her to her first orgasm. After carrying her to their bed, he lost track of the times he was able to coax his name from her quivering lips.

Eventually, he found his own release in her welcoming warmth. Her whispered 'I love you', before she drifted off to sleep, healed something inside his chest, and with her draped over his body, he slipped into peaceful dreams.

CHAPTER 15

*O*utside the barn with his truck hood open, Owen heard the car pull into the drive behind him. He kept his head under the hood. A door opened and slammed, and footsteps crunched on the gravel. "Be right with you."

"I'm looking for Owen Strong," a cultured male voice spoke.

He tinkered with a bolt, then slowly straightened, slipping the wrench in the side pocket of his coveralls. He glanced at the midnight blue high-end luxury vehicle. One hell of a rental. "I'm Owen. What can I do for you?"

"I'm Dracon Escott. My mother-in-law received a text from Keira, implying you married my daughter. I assume that was to get my attention. Well, you have it."

Pulling a rag from his back pocket, Owen wiped his greasy hands. "Dracon Escott. You're my wife's stepfather." He shrugged. "I don't really give a shit about your attention, as long as I've got my wife's."

Owen leaned back against the bumper of the vehicle while Dracon gave the barn and woods a quick once-over.

"Do you own this building?" Dracon asked.

"Rent it, and the upstairs apartment from an LL-some-thing. Got a deal because I watch out for the property. You know, stuff like mowing, cutting trees, doing repairs."

"What are you, a mechanic, a handyman, a gardener?"

"I'm a trained mechanic, thanks to Uncle Sam. It pays the bills. I've done other stuff." He stuffed the oil rag back in his pocket. "Is this about my career choices or my wife? I love your stepdaughter, and she loves me. That's what matters. You want your little girl happy, right?" He paused. "Or do you have a beef with a man who works with his hands?"

"My daughter's happiness is of utmost importance to me, since losing her mother. I sincerely hope the two of you are meant for each other. You did marry in haste. Or was it lust?" He raised an eyebrow. "Or opportunity?"

"What the fuck?" Owen took a step forward. "What are you talking about?"

A burly, flat-footed guy rolled out of the front passenger seat of the expensive car. Now he knew there was at least a driver and one muscle man. He still couldn't see into the back, but from the GQ appearance of Escott, he doubted he'd share his space in the rear. The driver was probably the second guard.

"I assume you realize who I am, what I'm worth. After all, you tried to check on me through the internet."

"I don't give a shit who you are, unless you try to come between me and my wife. I did want to know about the rich asshole she never wanted to see again."

"I want to see my daughter. Is she inside?"

"She's at work, and she doesn't want to see you."

"Work? What could she possibly be doing? All she knows is painting."

Owen screwed up his face. "Painting fancy walls in stores is a hobby. She got tired of doing that work and she's not painting anymore."

Dracon placed his hands on his hips, and dropped his head forward. Taking a deep breath. "We started out all wrong. I've been panic-stricken over where Keira ran off to. I need you to understand I am here for you, when the two of you have issues. I have the resources to help."

"Issues?" Owen asked.

"How did the two of you get married?"

"Like everybody else in the state. We took our IDs and birth certificates to the county clerk, and then the judge married us."

"Those IDs were fake. Didn't it seem odd to you that she carried her birth certificate on vacation?"

Damn this guy was good, Owen thought. No wonder it had taken Dracon a week to get to Spencer once he'd located her. He'd used the time to falsify different contingency plans. Continuing his facade as the opportunistic jerk, Owen scoffed. "The IDs aren't fake. I'm no fool. A buddy ran them for me. I didn't want to get caught with jailbait."

"How much?"

"How much for what?" Owen questioned.

"How much do you want to walk away from this sham of a marriage?" Dracon snapped.

"I ain't walking away from anything. We're in love."

Dracon ran a hand over his face, then rubbed his neck. "You've no idea what you've gotten yourself into. Keira's complicated. You haven't had time to realize she has deep-seated mental issues. She's a little prone to the dramatic and —" he glanced away as though in pain, then back, meeting Owen's gaze. "Self-destructive. Did she tell you she tried to kill herself? If I hadn't found her in time, we'd have lost her. That tendency is one of the reasons we gave her a private residence on our property. Her mother and I were terrified she'd try something again."

Dracon paced in front of him. "She was hysterical when

her mother overdosed on her pain meds. Grandma and I tried to console her, but she wouldn't listen. She went into her fantasy world, making up bogus accusations. She left a note for her grandmother and took off. This fake runaway is her crying out for help. Her grandmother is distraught and emotional, and she's under a doctor's care. Her dementia is growing worse."

"Keira said her mom would never commit suicide. She thought maybe it was drugs."

"Of course, she wouldn't commit suicide. Not knowingly. She was in pain, and I believe she lost track of how much of her prescription meds she took. My wife had an exceptionally difficult childhood in Vietnam. There was hunger and constant fear, which she never got over. Her past, a hip injury, and her own mental issues led her to drink and rely on her meds too much. Her doctor had been concerned for months. Was her death a blatant suicide? We'll never know.

"Because of Keira's own propensity toward instability, she makes up conspiracy stories in her head. Don't get me wrong, she believes them. They just aren't true," Dracon shrugged. "I can prove it. I brought her medical records. You can read them and understand what you'll be dealing with going forward. Her doctor is with me to help her and explain her condition to you. He's concerned she could be a danger to herself and urges you to get her back under his care as soon as possible. He needs to talk to her."

Dracon gave Owen a compassionate look. "I've dealt with Keira and her mother for years. I know how difficult your future will be. After studying the medical records and talking to the doctor, if you wish to have the marriage annulled, I'll have my lawyers help. I'll make sure that there is no financial hardship to you."

"Ain't letting my wife go."

"Then I propose the two of you reside in her private residence on my property in Houston. Rent free. Since this is a rental, I can have my lawyer work out an agreement for you to break your lease. I hear you aren't afraid to use a little muscle. I'm sure I could find you employment in one of my businesses. That way, when you need my help—and you will —I'll be there."

"Wow man, you're all over the place. Let me catch up. First you tell me my girl don't know what she's doing 'cause her mom died. Then you tell me she's mental. You offer me a house and a job if I bring her back to your place. And you've been her step-daddy for what? Five years? She tells me there's no love lost between you two. Seems messed up to me.

"I got a real sweet deal here, you know. With this place to live, a good job with the biggest auto body place in town, and now my baby girl. Why would I want to move? What's the advantage for me?" Owen crossed his arms over his chest and cocked his head. "Sounds to me like she's got something you want real bad. What, you get locked out of her momma's will? She get one of those prenup papers you hear about on TV?"

Dracon stiffened. "Listen, you prick. I know what you are, you opportunistic thug. You're nothing more than a flea on a mange—" Dracon spun and walked a few feet away and paused. After a few deep breaths, he turned back. "Even if that were the case, I don't need anyone else's money. I have plenty of my own." He moved in front of Owen. "I apologize. I've been worried about her safety. I hadn't realized she knew anyone in Colorado. When did you meet?"

"When she started working at the Wild Card. I took one look at her and thought 'she's mine.'"

"She didn't know you before she got here?"

Dracon didn't seem surprised. Owen wondered if he'd

found out about Ace. "Nope." He held up his hand with his matching wedding ring. "She sure as hell does now."

Owen watched as Dracon's face reddened with fury, knowing he recognized the full implication of the ring and his bed time with her. He'd been right. Dracon could barely contain his perverted lust for Keira. The hate in the man's eyes nearly set the barn on fire.

His own anger threatened his control, and he struggled to retain his relaxed pose. He thought of the mental and physical abuse Keira had suffered at the hands of this degenerate piece of shit. The urge to rip the bastard to pieces nearly consumed him.

"You're right. You're married. We're family now. I'd like to see my daughter for myself to confirm that she's well. I also need to talk to her about my concerns for her grandmother. Quang is still legally my responsibility due to my wife's will. You said Keira works at the Wild Card. I'll stop in and see her, and then we can make arrangements for dinner."

Owen glanced at his phone to check the time and covertly hit the signal to notify the others that Dracon and his men were on the move. "We can go over there now. She's about to get off, and they got good steaks and ice-cold brews. Follow me."

Subtly palming the long-range transmitting device he'd left hidden on the engine, he shut the hood of the truck and climbed behind the wheel. As Dracon crossed to the back seat of the Mercedes, Owen thought he saw another figure move to the opposite side. The doctor? They must not have checked into the cabin, and instead came straight to the barn. Pulling out in front, Owen drove toward Burnham Drive and carefully spoke into the miniature transmitter. "Two guards. The one I saw is definitely carrying. I expect the driver is too. There may have been another person in the backseat, but I didn't get a clear view. He said he brought Keira's doctor. Could be him. On our way to the Wild Card now."

Sliding the device into the pocket behind his oil rag, he glanced at his cell. Hunter was the point of contact on the Houston operation with the assigned local FBI agent. The blank screen indicated he'd had no word yet.

DAMN BUREAUCRATS. Ace paced the Houston hotel room he'd been holed up in for the last twenty-four hours. The monster, Dracon, had left the compound hours ago. But the powers that be wouldn't move until their hotshot people were in place. The original plan had been for Ivy to rappel early that morning, while it was still dark, then make her way to Quang and guard her until the Feds raided. A hot shot from the agency was late getting onsite to the hotel. Now the whole operation was on hold until he arrived. Ivy would be dropping in the daylight.

There was a commotion at the door, and the man Ivy had introduced as her old boss pushed in.

"Grab your gear, Ace. We're headed out," Donavan snapped.

He was followed by a bookish looking guy. Practically running behind Donavan, the smaller man shouted. "I'm in charge, Mr. Donavan. You don't get to say what's going on. I say we wait. Stop. You can't do this."

Two men waited in the hall. Donavan nodded to them as he passed. The first man grabbed the smaller bookish man from behind and slapped handcuffs on him.

"What do you think you're doing? I'm an FBI official."

"You're an informant, a crook, and you're under arrest for drug running and impeding the arrest of a drug runner."

Donavan snapped. "And if anything happens to my people, you will also be charged with murder."

Donavan patted the other man down and removed his cell phone from his pocket, then glanced at Ace. "We need to hurry. I've got Dog covering Ivy until she gets inside to Quang, but we need to get there."

DOG CURSED TO HIMSELF. He'd been stretched out on the tree limb peering through his rifle scope at Dracon Escott's compound in Houston for hours. The call from Donavan finally came through his earbud. They'd caught the federal agent who'd been feeding Dracon information. They didn't know yet how much of today's operation had been compromised.

He switched focus as he heard the helicopter approach. He'd volunteered to cover the man rappelling in to guard the old lady. As they suspected, after five days the sound of the helicopter no longer drew much attention.

He watched the soldier's descent through his scope. Once the rope was free, the rappeler pulled his equipment and then connected the next drop line to take him to the balcony. Curious whether or not he knew the guy, Dog swung his view to the face.

He studied the blonde in his rifle site and jerked back. It couldn't be. What the hell. He positioned his powered scope again and studied the blonde. The rappeler was IrishMist Vaughn. She was supposed to be dead. He struggled to comprehend what he was seeing and glanced again. His sister had been dead to him for ten years.

ACE GLANCED to where Donavan lingered in the shadows and pounded on the massive double mahogany doors once again. The sound of the chopper faded into the distance. A moment later the door flew open, and he was met by a man brandishing a SIG Sauer.

"Who the hell are you, old man? How'd you get past the gate guard?"

"I want my wife. Now! Where is she?"

"Get out of here, you old fart. Nothing of yours is here. Dracon Escott owns this place and everyone in it."

Ace waved the wad of papers he gripped in his hand. "He doesn't own my wife, and I want her. Now. I got papers from the local judge saying you have to let me see Quang."

Donavan tapped his ear piece, gripped his weapon, and nodded at Ace, signaling the other agents were in place and ready to roll.

The guard shook his head, lowering his weapon and pushed on the heavy door. "Get lost, you crazy old fool."

Donavan slammed into the door. Ace let the papers fall away, revealing the bowie knife and pressed it to the guard's throat before the other agents stormed the entrance. A thin trickle of blood trailed from the blade tip. "Where. Is. My. Wife?"

"Up the grand staircase to the second floor. Take a right. Last door on the left."

"How many guards are up there?"

"Three."

"Ace," Donavan spoke. "Ivy's with her. Go."

Ace released the man into Donavan's grasp and headed for the stairs.

Donavan signaled one of the agents to follow.

Taking the stairs two at a time, Ace rounded the corner to the right. A man had been laid out cold, feet and hands zip-tied behind his back. At the opposite end of the hall Ace spotted another pair of bound legs.

Counting the doors on his left, he got to the last door and took a deep breath. Would she still want him? Did she hate him for not finding her? For not saving her? For the suffering she'd endured?

With a shaking hand, he pushed open the door. Another guard sprawled directly inside the door. Ivy crouched beside the bed where a woman sat, hands clutched in her lap.

Sensing his presence, the woman turned, then stood. Shoulder-length black hair sprinkled with silver, delicate shoulders, slender form, the alluring girl of his youth had become a stunningly lovely woman. In his eyes and in his dreams, she'd always been the most beautiful woman. He was afraid to look her in the eyes.

"Ace?" her voice shook.

Taking his courage in hand, he raised his gaze to hers. Tugging the chain from his collar, he dangled the pendant he still cherished. "I love you, Quang. I've missed you and longed for you every day of my life."

As she walked toward him, she lifted a similar chain from under her blouse, showing him the jade wedding band he'd given her. "I have loved you with all my heart. I have never forgotten you."

A spatter of gunfire erupted below, followed by what sounded like an explosion. Ivy crossed to the window and spoke into her comm. She turned back. "I'm sorry. We need to go."

Quang rushed to the closet, tossing aside a blanket from a pile on the floor exposing a hiking backpack. "Can we take my bag? Is it too large?"

Ivy glanced at Ace.

Slipping the straps over his shoulder. He palmed his knife

in his right hand and took Quang's hand in his left. He nodded at Ivy. "Let's go."

Taking the lead, Ivy got them through the house and garden to the back gate, where a black SUV waited. Donavan sat in the passenger seat beside the driver. "We're heading straight to the airport. By now Dracon knows we've seized his property. We found several paintings exactly where Keira said they'd be. We'll compare them with her list when we get to home base.

"Owen was right. The drug lab was on the second level. It was set to blow. We got there in time to stop the worst of the destruction, still there was little evidence left behind. Dracon had already moved the operation. Probably as a precaution after Keira escaped."

Donavan met Ivy's gaze in the mirror, reading her suspicion. Dracon had been tipped off?

"Have you heard from the detail back home?" Ivy asked.

"No." Donavan responded.

"Hunter?" Ace followed up.

"No."

CHAPTER 16

*O*wen sauntered into the Wild Card, knowing Dracon would follow. Hunter and Levi worked behind the bar. Lacey and Sage waited tables, and the FBI team, posing as a couple, sat at the corner booth. He was surprised to see Mac at the end of the bar, eating fries, drinking a beer and clicking away on her laptop.

Keira came down the hall from the back room, backpack hooked over one shoulder. A smile lit her face seconds before the door squeaked behind him. He willed her to be strong. He could tell by the slightest hitch to her step that Dracon walked in behind him.

Keira snuggled into Owen's arms and kissed him.

Nuzzling her neck, he whispered, "You got this. We just need to stall until they take him down." He glanced at Hunter before turning. "Look who showed up at the house searching for you."

Keira met Dracon's gaze. "Why are you here?"

Dracon reached out to pull her into an embrace. Side-stepping his grasp, Keira sat at the reserved table, leaving Owen the chair by the wall.

Dracon sat across from her. "You're my daughter, Keira darling. Of course, I wanted to check on you. You ran off after the emotional crisis of your mother dying, and I haven't heard from you. Didn't know where you were. Didn't know if you were safe or who may be taking advantage of you." He glanced pointedly at Owen. "Grandma and I have been beside ourselves with worry. We were pleasantly surprised when you called the other night."

"There was no need. I'm fine." She watched the telltale muscle twitch below Dracon's left eye. The same tic had acted up when her mother disagreed or argued with him. A sense of doubt rushed over her. Had her mother fallen under Dracon's control? She had always seemed in charge, a force of nature. Had she been as much a victim as Keira?

"I promised your grandmother I'd come speak with you and try to convince you to come home for a visit. A short one. She needs to see you for herself."

"Why didn't you bring her with you?"

"She's too sick to travel. As I told you on the phone, her doctor has serious concerns about her health."

Keira met his gaze. The lying bastard. If Grandma was sick, it was because he was giving her something that made her sick. Anger welled in her chest. No more. Remembering his insidious manipulations, his mental abuse, his physical brutality over the years sent fear and resentment coursing through her veins. She wanted to lash out and strike back for what she'd endured. "Your quack doctor?"

Dragon ignored her comment when Levi stopped at the table to take their drink orders.

Owen leaned back in his chair, wrapping his arm over her shoulder, stroking her collar bone, soothing her nerves. She wasn't alone anymore. Owen would never let her go back to the monster.

"I am home, Dracon. Here, with my husband." The truth

of her words sank in, calming her even more. "We'd love to have Grandma come visit us. We could give you a break from the responsibility for a while, and you can go about doing whatever you do."

Levi came back with their drinks. As he placed them on the table, Dracon casually glanced at his phone, then back to Keira. "That's not possible right now. Perhaps when I get back home, we could arrange a video call. Then you can see how badly she's deteriorated."

Owen studied the other man carefully. If Dracon had received info regarding the raid at his compound, his reaction was unnatural. That coupled with no update from Ivy or Ace, had him on edge. They should've heard by now.

Something was off. The raid in Houston had to be over. Why the hell hadn't the local Feds taken Dracon into custody? He looked more closely. Dracon's pupils were dilated. He was excited. He thought he'd won.

Scanning the room, he noticed Sage wiping tables near the undercover agents. They indicated they wanted a refill, and the female lead agent headed to the restroom. His chest tightened. "Hey baby girl, this beer isn't doing it for me. Would you go tell Hunter I need an IrishMist?"

Keira hesitated then smiled and went for his order. Once she was out of earshot, he turned to Dracon. "How bad is the old lady? Is she gonna die? Keira said she'd have to go home for a little while if her grandma passed because of wills and inheritance stuff."

"So, you did marry my stepdaughter for money, as I suspected." Dracon raised a brow and took a sip of his Crown Royal. He shrugged. "You wouldn't be the first to try and cash in on an inheritance. Just curious, how much do you want to walk away?"

"I married her 'cause she's fine, and I love her." Owen

took a pull of his beer and met Dracon's eyes. He nodded and let a smile tease his lips. "So, the old lady is dying."

"She has some time." Dracon smirked and finished his drink. "We all die, Owen."

He knew. Somehow the bastard knew. He'd been tipped off.

Keira came back to the table with a shot glass filled with amber liquid. Sitting down, she slid her hand under the table to squeeze his thigh. "He said to tell you it's the last shot, but he'll send Sage to the storeroom to see if there's another bottle."

Owen nodded, lifted the glass and shot the whiskey down. He shook his head as the drink landed. A fleeting glance assured him that Hunter had got the message. By the hard set of his jaw, he had the same concerns.

"Baby girl, Dracon thinks your grandma is really bad. Maybe we should go for a quick visit. You and me. It could be our honeymoon. I've got a friend with a camper." He continued to play the part, hoping Dracon would underestimate him.

"Can we talk later at home? Maybe tomorrow."

"You staying in town, Dracon?" Owen asked.

"Yes, I've got a cabin for a couple of days." He turned to Keira. "It's been a long day. I'm going to retire for the night. I'd like to spend time with you tomorrow. Let's skip dinner and perhaps meet for breakfast somewhere. It's such a relief knowing you're safe. Do you still have the phone you used to call your grandma?"

She nodded.

"I'll call in the morning. Shall we walk out together?" He rose from the chair.

Owen led Keira to his truck. Lifting her, he kissed her neck as he whispered. "Don't say anything. They could've bugged the truck while we were inside."

Dracon's SUV traveled past in the opposite direction as though going to the cabin on Lake Louise.

As he pulled into his driveway, Owen's phone lit up with a security breach message. He keyed in the team's panic number. Hunter replied with a private code. Owen braked the truck and threw it in reverse. Dracon's SUV pulled in behind him blocking the exit. Two men jumped from the car with semi-automatics.

Fuck. He shook his head when Keira would've spoken. Running a dozen scenarios in his mind for what could happen inside, he visualized every hidden and potential weapon in the gym and loft. Dracon wanted her alive, so Keira was safe. If something happened to him, Hunter was on the way. He needed to buy time.

Dracon leisurely climbed from his vehicle followed by the lead female FBI agent from the bar and the driver. He smiled triumphantly. "I so love a well-laid plan. Why don't we all go inside?"

Keira waited as Owen slid the barn door open and flipped on the lights. She gasped. Four of Dracon's armed men stood side by side, and his crooked doctor sat on the weight bench.

Dracon pointed at Owen. "Search and restrain him."

"You bastard." Keira snapped, moving closer to Owen.

"Tsk tsk, Keira. Such language. Learning new tricks with this bruiser? You always were so easy to manipulate."

Glancing around at the gym equipment dismissively, he glanced to where Owen stood between two guards with his hands zip-tied behind him.

"Put him on his knees and secure his feet. He's a fucking martial artist, you fool. Why do you think I bothered to bring so many of you? And check him for weapons."

Two men shoved Owen to the ground, and the third checked his pockets only finding the wrench and oil rag, then secured his feet.

Keira glared at the man who'd made her life a living hell for years. Hate vibrated through her veins. "I'd guess you brought so many men with you because if you're not terrorizing women, you need backup."

He turned on her, body tense with anger. His face had become an evil mask of hate and lust. "I've been so gentle with you, my dear. Soon you'll know what true terror is. Very soon."

Owen spoke out, "I don't know what you think you can do. The FBI knows about the paintings, and the DEA knows about the drugs. You're done."

"Yes, by now they know about all the forgeries Keira painted and sold. And the drugs her mother was selling. As I tried to explain, the two of them truly have mental issues. Alas, I was simply another pawn in their schemes."

"You liar. It was all you." Keira snapped.

Dracon laughed. "But all the documents they found will point to you and your mother. I will need to relocate for a while, but Dubai is quite promising. There are always new opportunities for those of us with skills."

"If what you say is true, you don't need me. You won't be able to sell my paintings."

The look he turned on her sent shivers down her spine. She took a step closer to where Owen was restrained.

"Yes, you ruined that little endeavor for me. It will be my pleasure to make you pay for that. Who knows? Maybe in a few years, under a different name, we can try again."

Keira swallowed. "What've you done with Grandma?"

"Well, that's up to you. The meddlesome bitch could be on her way to Dubai to meet up with us. Or, she could be in a burning crater somewhere between Houston and Denver.

"You see Keira, dear, life is about changes and going with the flow. You've forced me to make changes. Now you get a choice for the changes in your life."

Dracon removed a weapon from his pocket and pointed the barrel at Owen's chest. "Get over here, Keira. Now."

"No, Keira. Don't," Owen ordered. "He's going to kill us both anyway."

With tear-filled eyes, she glanced at him before crossing to within Dracon's reach. "I did this. It's my fault you're in danger."

Keeping the Glock pointed at Owen, Dracon grabbed Keira by the throat and pulled her in for a ruthless kiss. When he released her, she spit in his face. He backhanded her in response, and she sprawled to the floor, head throbbing.

Owen growled and tried to rise. One of the guards kicked him in the ribs, and he fell to his side.

Dracon leered down, wrapping her braid in his left hand. "Look at me." When she didn't comply, he jerked her hair hard, forcing her to raise her head. "You've grown a little backbone. But you're still weak and malleable. I will enjoy beating disobedience out of you. Once we're in our new home, you'll learn to obey.

"Dubai is quite pleasant, my dear. I've had business there for a while now. You'll be able to paint to your heart's content. Bonus for you, no extradition for your crimes there. Here, you would surely go to prison."

Using her rope of hair, he dragged her to her feet. Wrapping his forearm over her collarbone, he motioned with the weapon in his right hand for the guards to pull Owen to his knees.

"So now, darling, the consequences for your behavior. You can save one. Grandma or your husband. You choose."

"Leave them both alone, and I'll go with you willingly. I won't try to run again. I'll paint whatever you ask. I'll do anything you ask."

He laughed. "Of course, you will. I'll make sure you do."

"Please. They did nothing to you. Let them both go. I'll never speak to either of them again. I promise. Please."

He slid the barrel of the gun over her belly. "Umm, there are some things about this new you I like. You're learning to be much prettier as you beg. But I wouldn't be a good father if I didn't teach you the consequences of your actions."

Clenching her jaw, she stifled the words of rage threatening to erupt. God, she hated this man. This evil, greedy, monster of a man. Hopefully by now, after a lifetime of loneliness, Grandma and Ace had found each other. Ivy had promised to take care of them.

She glanced at the man she loved with her whole heart. Why should he pay for her failure? Meeting Owen's gaze, he smiled and winked. He had strength. Was she strong enough to do what she needed to do?

Dracon snapped at the guard behind Owen. "Get the phone out and have the number queued up to set off the explosion."

Keira dropped her head forward, placing her hand on her stomach under her shirt. She felt sick. She had to be strong. She needed to hope.

Dracon squeezed her collarbone more tightly, almost suffocating her.

"Last chance to pick or they both die. You caused this, so it's your choice."

Keira glanced across the distance and looked into Owen's blue eyes. "I remember the rules. I love you."

With her right hand, she grabbed Dracon's wrist and pushed his aim away from Owen's chest. In a split second, she dropped her left fist down and back, aiming her field knife at Dracon's thigh or belly—anywhere she could reach. The blade breached resistance and sank to its hilt, eliciting a yowl of pain. Quickly, she pulled her arm back and struck again.

"Stand down. Stand down. Now! Drop your weapons or we fire," someone yelled in the distance.

A deafening shot exploded near her ear. Another exploded from a distance, and Dracon lurched right. His weight dragged her with him as he fell sideways. In her peripheral vision, Owen dove left, taking out one guard. Arms free, he twisted, taking out the other guard with the sweep of his legs.

Dracon's weight crushed her against the floor, and her head slammed against the cement.

"Keira, Keira wake up. Come on. Wake up."

Something cool floated over her face. Her eyes fluttered. She saw Owen surrounded by a golden halo. "Did we die?"

"No. You saved us. You were so brave. Can you sit up so I can hold you?"

"No, she can't," another voice cut in. "Get out of my way. I need to check her."

Owen's face was pushed from her view to be replaced by Gage's. "Hey Keira, sweetie. You hit your head. I'm going to make sure you're ok. Owen is going to talk with Hunter for a minute, but he's not leaving you. Okay?"

She blinked, unable to find her voice or move.

Owen hovered behind Gage and waited for Hunter to approach.

He nodded toward Keira. "Is she okay?"

"She must have hit her head when they went down. I couldn't find any wounds. Gage is going to examine her."

Hunter lifted his chin. "Coroner's on the way. I finally got in touch with Ivy. They'll be here in a couple hours. Our pilot saw Dracon's man plant the bomb on the plane. They disarmed the device before takeoff. They have the guy in custody and he's ready to sing. Dracon's plane is on lock-down in Denver. Donavan has his own crew coming in to take charge until we know how many other FBI agents were on his payroll. For us, it looks like it was only the female lead. Mac is on her way over with the FBI lawyer. Ought to be a fun night."

"Hunter," Owen called before the man could walk away. "Thanks for being here. For taking the shot. I owe you."

"You already paid."

OWEN GLANCED over to where Keira rested. Mac and the FBI lawyer had left about twenty minutes ago. Ivy texted that she, Ace and Quang were close.

"I'm not letting you out of my sight tonight. If your grandmother doesn't want to stay with Ace, I'll set her up at Zoe's."

He knew it was selfish, but he needed her in his arms tonight. He expected to have nightmares of her dying for the rest of his life.

"I changed the sheets this morning. Grandma could stay here, and you and I could sleep downstairs on the crash mats."

Of course, she'd want her grandmother close, what was he thinking? Shaking his head, he acknowledged he'd sleep standing up if she asked, as long as he could keep his eyes on her all night. "Whatever makes you comfortable".

Owen peered out the window at the back of the barn. He'd texted Ivy to bring Ace and Quang up from the outside stairs and not through the barn. The coroner had taken Dracon's body, but Owen couldn't get a cleanup team in until tomorrow. He didn't want his family to witness the violent remains.

He glanced at Keira, huddled on the couch. His family. His heart.

Lights flickered over the gravel drive, and a vehicle parked beside the barn. Ace climbed out of the back and assisted a small woman. Ivy climbed from behind the wheel, and Gage emerged from the passenger side. Knowing how emotional the meeting could be, Ruby had called and insisted Gage be present.

"They're here," Owen announced.

Keira threw the blanket off and sprang from the couch, rushing to the door and throwing it open.

"Grandma." Keira launched into her grandmother's arms as she entered the loft. After several moments of conversation he didn't understand, covert glances and a couple of snorts from Ivy, the greetings seemed to settle down. Keira reached for his hand and tugged him forward.

"Grandma, this is my husband, Owen. He is a good honorable man and the love of my life."

"Ma'am." He glanced down at the shorter older version of Keira, older but equally as lovely and vibrant.

Quang studied him in silence, then took his hand in both of hers. "You married my granddaughter. Why?"

He felt awkward standing over her. Leading her to the couch, he sat beside her, making it easier for her to meet his eyes. He covered her hands with his other palm. "Because I finally found her. It feels like I've searched for her forever. I don't know how to explain it, but I knew the minute I looked into her eyes, she was my one and only. I love her for this lifetime and every one after."

Quang nodded once, then placed a palm on his cheek and leaned to kiss the other. Glancing over her shoulder, she reached out for Ace. "As it was for us."

She pushed to her feet. "We all have much to discuss, but the day has been long, and we need sleep" she paused. "Later, we will get together and visit. Now that I see for myself, you're safe, I can rest."

"Grandma, where are you going?" Keira asked.

Still smiling, Grandma squeezed Ace's hand. "Home with my husband."

At the door, Ace looked back. "In true Ruby style, shifts are arranged for today, and none of us are supposed to show up for work. We're expected for family dinner at seven tonight."

Owen stood behind Keira, his arms wrapped around her as she watched Ace help her grandmother into the car. "You okay with her leaving? Ace has extra rooms. Do you want us to go with them?"

Keira shook her head against his chest. "No. I think she deserves this time. A lot has changed for her. The shadows are gone from her eyes, she's happy. After all these years, she's reunited with her lost love."

a ce's hand trembled against Quang's back as he pushed open the door to his house. What would she think of his home? His gaze took in the faded paint and aged wallpaper in the hall. All these years, he'd never paid attention to the place where he slept. Without his love, it had never been a home. He'd preferred to spend his time at work where he wasn't reminded of what he didn't have.

"Give me your bag," Gage said from behind him. He'd insisted on carrying Quang's backpack to the house. "I'm going to run both of these up the stairs and put them in the hallway. Ivy and I will take off, but call if you need anything."

Slipping his pack off his shoulder, Ace handed it to the younger man. Watching him take the stairs two at a time, he realized that Gage too, had become an integral part of his life.

Returning to stand at the door, Gage turned. "See you both later tonight at dinner. Quang it was nice to meet you."

The door closed behind him, leaving them alone for the first time.

Quang glanced around and crossed into the parlor. "This is your home?"

Uncertain, Ace followed her. "This house has been in my family since the 1800s. I grew up here. Other than my time in the Navy, I've never lived anywhere else."

Realizing his accidental reference to his time in Vietnam, he cleared his throat. "I know it's late, and it's been a stressful day, but would you like some tea?"

"Yes, please," she responded.

Now that he'd made the offer, he frantically hoped he had some tea that wasn't too old to offer her. Had he put away his dirty dishes before he'd left? Passing through the doorway to the kitchen at the back of the house, he relaxed.

Inhaling, he took in the sweet scent of orange and pine. The kitchen sparkled, and a vase of flowers sat on the table. A box of green tea and the teapot, along with two cups were arranged on the counter with a covered plate of cookies. He glanced at the shiny wood floor and crystal-clear window over the sink.

Ruby. Of course, she'd worked her magic. He had no doubt the whole house had been dusted, scrubbed and buffed from top to bottom.

"I'll put the kettle on." He pointed to the opposite side from where they'd entered. "Go right at that doorway, and the restroom is on the left. Take your time and walk around while the water heats. On the other side, down here is a living room and office. All the bedrooms are upstairs."

Quang returned as he was filling the cups at the table. "We have cookies, but there's more food in the refrigerator if you want a meal."

She sat with a smile and reached for her cup. "This is perfect. We probably shouldn't stay up much later. The lawyers will be here at noon, and I need to be fresh to answer their questions. I must be sure my—" She gave him a timorous smile. "Our granddaughter is protected."

Ace glanced up from his own tea. She was here, after all these years, sitting across from him as she had in his dreams. He'd longed for her laughter, her gentle teasing as they planned the upcoming day. Already the house felt more like a home than it ever had before. He hesitated.

"Say it, Ace. Just ask." Quang softly encouraged.

"Why Quang? Why didn't you find me? Did you not love me as I loved you?"

Clutching her hands on the table, she met his gaze. "I did then, and I do love you now with all my heart."

"Then why? Keira says you have been here since the late '70s."

"Saigon fell shortly after you left. My family found out we had married against their wishes. They demanded I deny you and marry my betrothed when he returned. I refused, so when they fled the city, they left me behind. I knew I had to hide or I would end up in a camp. I fled to the forest. There I met others who were also fleeing."

"They told me you were dead. Your name was one of many on a camp internment list. I didn't want to believe." Ace tried to keep the doubt from his voice.

"There was much confusion at the time. Later I heard from a cousin that the family also thought I had died. My name is not an uncommon one. I am sorry for the woman who did die."

"How did you survive?"

"Many of those who fled were also women who had been with American men. We stayed together. At first, I didn't know I carried your child. I was always tired and sick. One of the other women realized before I did. Even then, there were stories that American men did not want us and would not claim our children. She tried to convince me to get rid of the baby. She was angry and bitter because her man had refused her."

"I would never have done that. I loved you." Ace whispered.

She reached across the table and covered his hand with hers. "I never believed for one second that you would not welcome us. My faith in you was strong. It was my belief in myself that wavered.

"There were three other women and we bonded, helping each other. There were two children among us. All the women shared in caring for the girls. Preferring to stay away from cities, we took farm work. Fearful we'd be found, we moved often. Almost five years passed before we finally gained passage on a boat. By then there was only one other woman, myself and our daughter.

"I didn't understand. I had it in my head that you would be waiting for us when the boat arrived. I told our daughter you would come for us."

Her words tore at his heart. " I would have been. I swear, I would have been. No one contacted me."

"I know," she squeezed his hand. "My friend and I were both relocated to Texas. A family took us in and gave us work in their grocery business. Everything was so different. We went where we were taken. My English was not very good and our daughter spoke none. She was frightened at first, then became angry. She believed what the other women from camp had said about American men.

"I kept telling myself I would find you when my English was better. Or when I had repaid the kindness of the people who took us in. I told myself you would find us."

"I failed you." Ace couldn't bear the pain. His tears fell unchecked and splashed on their clasped hands. Her fingertips gently swiped at his tears. He struggled with the knowledge that she had been so close.

"No. No my love, it was not your fault. Listen. Five, maybe six years passed. One of my cousins, who had left the country before Saigon fell, found me by accident when he was looking for other missing family members. He told me everyone had been told I died. He possessed records with my name. He promised to help me find you. Eventually he did, but it took more years.

"I was filled with hope. But our daughter was furious. She wanted nothing to do with you. I tried to explain, but she was stubborn and demanded I never speak of you again. If I proceeded to search for you, she would leave me.

"So many years had passed. What if I found you but lost our daughter, our granddaughter? What if, believing your wife had died, you had remarried? A mother should not have to choose. I doubted. I am so sorry. I'm sorry I lost our daughter." She could no longer contain her sobs.

With gentle hands, Ace guided her from her chair to his lap. She wrapped her arms around his shoulders and buried her face against his neck. Clutching each other, they cried, mourning the lost years.

Long moments later when his heartbreak was spent, Ace cradled his love in his arms. Urging her to look at him, he kissed her forehead, then her lips—the same sweet lips.

"Quang, will you stay with me, live in this house and make it a home with me? We can fill it with the joy of friends and the love of our granddaughter."

"Yes. Ace, will you share your love, your passion, and your bed with me, so that we may make a testament for them to follow? We proved true love does exist and can flourish regardless of time and distance."

"Oh yes, my love. Oh yes."

OWEN LAY IN BED. Keira cuddled against his chest, her leg draped over his hip. After Ace and her grandmother left, he'd urged Keira to get some sleep. She'd refused to go without him. He held her in his arms and she'd instantly succumbed to healing slumber.

Sleep had eluded him.

Over and over, the events of the night terrorized his mind. He could have lost her. She could have been seriously injured.

Something flicked against his nipple. He glanced to where Keira skimmed her fingertip over his tattoo. "I was afraid for you. For what my dragon would do or become if you lost another woman you loved. I know what you feel for Oona is different than the love you hold for me, but even a dragon has limits to the pain they can endure. I prayed to be strong enough, brave enough to give you the opportunity you needed. I never doubted you would save us."

"I didn't. It was all you and Hunter."

"It was your plan. You realized someone sold us out. You alerted Hunter. Your security setup gave us a warning. Your forethought saved us. I never doubted you."

"Now we have each other." She slid her hand down to stroke his growing erection, then straddled his hips. "I think we both need to celebrate life."

Leaning forward, she found his lips, then kissed his chest over his heart.

Three more times during the night, he reached for her, reassuring himself in the most elemental way that his love was still beside him before he finally surrendered to sleep.

Owen woke to pounding on the door that led from the lower area. Keira scooted from the bed and headed to the back, he pulled on his sweats and went to the door, fully prepared to ream the person on the other side.

Deke stood before him, balancing a stack of serving

containers. The glorious smell of bacon and spices greeted Owen. He forgot his ire at being woken.

"Rise and shine, kiddies." Deke called out as he pushed past him into the kitchen. "It's two in the afternoon, and breakfast is here. Put the casserole and potatoes in the oven, and I'll be back in fifteen minutes. Mac is leaving for Denver, but she's stopping by for a few words with the two of you. Make coffee while I finish up in the gym." Deke headed back down stairs.

After putting on the coffee and starting tea water, Owen took his turn in the bathroom. Keira and Deke were already eating when he came out a few minutes later.

"Who made this breakfast casserole? It's delicious," Keira exclaimed. "Do you think they'll give me the recipe?"

"Sure. Yolanda Gonzales shares her recipes all the time. It never seems to taste the same when I cook it. She says it's because she uses extra love. Owen is one of her favorites and because he eats like three men, she likes to feed him.

"If you haven't met her kids already, you will. They come to workout with Owen and Ivy a couple times a week."

"Two girls and two boys. I've seen them, but we haven't been introduced."

Owen crossed to the counter, grabbed coffee, and filled his plate. "You'll meet them on Saturday. I think it'll be good for you to work with Ivy and Alejandra." He took a couple healthy bites of his breakfast, then glanced at Deke. "How does Yolanda always know what's going on? And she's always prepared with food." He studied his plate. "Damn, this is good."

Deke shrugged. "Who cares as long as she keeps feeding us?"

"What're you doing here, anyway?" Owen asked.

Swallowing his bite of food, Deke took a sip of coffee, then glanced quickly at Keira. "Cleaner came early. You didn't answer the knock on the barn door. Since I gave you the phone number for the company, they called me to let them into the barn."

"I stabbed him?" Keira looked up with haunted eyes.

Owen covered Keira's trembling hand. "Let's not—"

"Keira, listen to me." Deke put his fork down and leaned his folded forearms on the counter across from them. Once he had her attention, he continued. "Yes, you did some damage, exactly as you should have. You gave us the edge we needed. But Hunter took the kill shot to the head."

Deke's no-nonsense words took on an even harder edge. "Never doubt for a minute that you did what was necessary. There are wounded people in the world who make very bad decisions. Then there is evil. Dracon was evil. Do not waste one second of regret or remorse on him. He made his own choices and deserved what he got."

"Amen to that," Mac commented, walking in from the landing. "Oh yummy, something smells good."

Deke arranged a stool next to his and grabbed her a plate and cup of coffee.

After enjoying the food and making casual conversation, Mac dabbed her lips with her napkin and pushed her plate to the side. "The FBI lawyer and I debriefed Quang this morning. I must say she's a very impressive woman. She managed to smuggle out several files that belonged to your mother in her backpack. There is more to this case than we initially thought, so investigations will be ongoing. However, I can share some things with you now.

"Let's start with Dracon. Hidden on his plane in Denver, we found several original paintings valued in the millions, that support what you told us about the fakes we found at the compound. The private owners will be thrilled. His computer hard drive was also hidden aboard the plane. They were able to crack his code and are downloading his actual records. The documents left at the compound were meant to implicate you, your mother, and several politicians. So far, we can confirm drugs, detailed blackmail records and digital film, money laundering, human trafficking, murder for hire and art theft—and we've only just started. He'd already moved the drug lab to a new location. The DEA was able to make the raid early today."

Mac took another sip of coffee and looked across the counter. "Owen, the added benefit of the recording you had going in your coverall pocket was the icing on the cake. A little muffled in spots but the Feds say they can clean it up.

"In light of all the evidence we've found, as well as your testimony and documentation, no charges will be brought against you, Keira."

"Nothing?" Keira gasped, excitement lighting her eyes. "I won't go to prison? I'm free?"

Mac smiled. "Yes. As I pointed out, you were physically held hostage. Once you escaped, you willingly came forward to testify. After the information you gave them, the bureau would've looked like asses had they gone after you. Besides, because of you they're swimming in enough career-making lawsuits to last years. They also have enough of their own dirty laundry to clean up. Dracon had at least four federal agents on his payroll."

She glanced at Owen. "You were right. Under different names, Dracon had at least two other wives who were murdered under similar circumstances as Keira's mother. There are also a couple of missing mistresses."

Mac reached across the counter and took Keira's hand in hers. "We won't be able to prove it, but we do believe your mother was murdered. I believe that he duped your mother in the beginning. We may never know if she was forced to go along with him once she knew all he was involved in, or if she willingly stayed."

"We did find documentation in the files Quang brought that your mother was planning to leave him because she was afraid for you. Apparently, she found more photos of you like the one he wanted you to paint.

"Keira, what you need to remember is that your mother did care and did love you. She was willing to walk away to protect you. That's what you have to keep in your heart."

Keira swallowed the lump in her throat and nodded. Her mother had tried to protect her in the end.

KEIRA SLAPPED OWEN'S HAND. "Stay out of the cupcakes. They're for us to take to Ruby's. We'll be leaving in a few minutes."

"You bought a whole dozen. There's only nine of us. We could keep three at home. I could eat one now and there'd be two more when we come back."

"No. It's not proper to show up with a gift of cupcakes and only bring nine. Or eleven. Get out!"

"I'm desperate for something sweet." He pulled her into his arms. "I guess it's going to have to be you." He covered her lips with his, pulling her close. When he finally let her up for air, he groaned. "I don't want cupcakes anymore. I want you. I need you. Call and cancel. Let's go to bed."

"We just got out of bed a little while ago." She laughed. "You're insatiable. We're going. I haven't seen or talked to Grandma or Ace since they stopped by last night. I want to know how they're doing."

"Hopefully they're doing more than we are right now," he grumbled.

She looked at him with a wide-eyed gaze.

He shot her a sheepish glance, then shrugged. "He's a guy."

"She's a woman." Keira's giggle turned into a full-blown laugh.

Owen fell in love all over again. "Every day, I'm going to make you laugh, Little-bit. I love the sound."

Keira studied his hundred-watt smile. Slipping into his arms, she cupped his face. "And every day, I'm going to make you smile, exactly like that. No more lonely eyes."

IN ONE HAND, Owen carried the white box with the pink-and-turquoise checkered label and gripped Keira's in the other, for the walk to Ruby and Hunter's. The night was cooling down. He realized how content he felt.

Ruby greeted them at the door, her face flushed and happy. "You brought Cookie's Cupcakes!"

The house smelled wonderful. "Is that roast beef?"

She laughed. "Yes, one of your favorites. And Gage's. And Hunter's. And Ace's. Oh, and I think Deke's as well. There's also mashed potatoes, gravy, green beans with bacon bits, scalloped corn, wilted spinach and fresh rolls. All the food is on the table. Go on in. Deke said he'd be here in less than five minutes. Dessert goes on the sideboard."

Walking into the dining room, Ivy glanced up and started laughing. Gage looked up and joined her. Pretty soon everyone was laughing.

Owen glanced down to make sure his fly was zipped. He felt Keira tremble beside him. What the hell? Glancing around the room, his gaze fell on the sideboard and the three other white boxes with the pink-and-turquoise checkered labels. "Who got the last dozen blue velvet with the peanut butter cream filling and fresh banana buttercream?"

Hunter raised his hand. "They're the Elvis special."

"I got the last twelve chocolate-cherry with cream cheese icing." Gage preened. "Cookie's signature cupcake."

Ace snorted. "Lemon with lemon curd and lemon buttercream. Lemon overload. Tart and sassy." He gazed lovingly at Quang and winked. "Just how I like them."

Owen straightened his shoulders. "Tiramisu, with the dusted cocoa. My lady's favorite."

The front door banged open, and Deke strode into the room. "Sorry I'm late, Cookie's was out of cupcakes, so I ran over to Curly's and picked up ice cream." He handed the paper bag to Hunter. When the others burst out laughing, he regarded them with a raised eyebrow. Spying the boxes lined up on the sideboard, he smiled and rubbed his hands together. "Awesome! We all get at least two, maybe three."

Hunter filled wine glasses with sparkling grape juice as the food passed around the table. "Pregnancy rules" he explained, lifting his glass. "I'll start the toasts. To my lovely wife for bringing us all together."

Gage added, "To new beginnings."

"To lost love—found," Ace said with a smile that creased his cheeks.

Owen glanced at his friends and then at Keira. "To family."

As the men cleared the table, Ruby and Ivy opened the cupcake boxes.

"Hunter Jakob Lawe," Ruby called.

He replied innocently. "What dear?"

She lifted the box of cupcakes she'd opened. "There are only eleven Elvis specials in this box. As the chief of police, are you aware of how this happened?"

He shrugged his shoulders. "There are only nine of us. I didn't think you'd notice one missing."

The whole family laughed.

Owen glanced at the woman beside him. How had he

gotten so lucky? First Ruby had come into his life, and then Ivy. They didn't replace Oona. But they became sisters of his heart. Through them he'd gained the men he now called brothers. And now, a grandma and grandpa. He chuckled to himself. He wondered how Ace would handle being called granddaddy.

He took Keira's hand and brought it to his lips. She glanced up, laughter and love shining in her eyes. He was home.

Thank You

Thank you for joining me for the story of Owen and Keira.

If you loved the book and have a minute to spare, I would really appreciate a short review on the page or site where you bought the book.

Your help in spreading the word is greatly appreciated. Reviews from readers like you make a huge difference to helping new readers find stories like Lonely Eyes.

Bernadette Jones

Acknowledgment

Writing is a solitary occupation. However, it is not achieved on our own. If not for our intrepid backstage cast, authors wouldn't succeed.

My heartfelt thanks and appreciation for all the Aspen Gold Authors. We dove into this together and kept each other thinking on our feet!

My editor, my friend, my mentor, who prefers to stand in the wings. You continue to teach me and make me a stronger writer. Thank you for all you have taught me and even more special, for the friendship you have given.

My friend, my cohort, my 'strut your stuff' pusher, Mindy. I am thankful the readers do not hear our support conversations! Thank you for believing in me, as I believe in you. I want to be you when I grow up.

My beta reader and supporter, Shauna. You give me hope when I doubt myself. You keep me writing.

To Angela Ann, my drill sergeant. The one who nags me out of bed on the days I want to slack. Every 'The End' is dedicated to your discipline.

To all of you who have suffered bullying, abuse, neglect. Don't give up. Find your courage and hang onto it. Get help.

National Domestic Violence Hotline
1–800–799–7233

If you're an adult who experienced sexual abuse as a child, know that you are not alone. Every nine minutes, a child is sexually assaulted in the U.S., and 93 percent know the perpetrator. Many perpetrators of sexual abuse are in a position of trust or responsible for the child's care, such as a family member, teacher, clergy member, or coach.

No matter what, the abuse was not your fault. It's never too late to start healing from this experience. If you or someone you love is being abused, do not hesitate to reach out.

National Child Abuse Hotline at 800.422.4453

National Sexual Assault Hotline at 800.656.4673

ASPEN GOLD THE SERIES

Dear Reader,

Once upon a time a group of writer friends—helping a member with a particularly difficult thread in a continuity series contrived by her editors—got the grandiose idea to create a continuity series of their own.

Yes, this was us, and we threw ourselves wholeheartedly into developing characters, fashioning families, family dynamics, and a setting, which evolved from one member's love of all things Colorado. We created family trees, character profiles, detailed maps, brainstormed titles and themes. We collected photos and researched and even started the stories. We proposed our idea to a few publishers and got no traction. So, after a time the contracted books came first, two members dropped out of the group, a couple new ones came and went. But the core group remained.

In a tragic turn of events, we lost a beloved friend and cowriter. Grief took the remaining wind from our sails. We recovered slowly, welcomed a new friend to our critique. Then came a day when we got together and said, "We're going to get serious and do this!" Energy built, and the series took on new life. A previous co-creator joined us again. Now, here we are, years after the initial idea, sharing the finished stories with you and hoping you will feel the same intensity and appreciation for this project as we do. We have many more stories to share, and the ideas keep coming.

We welcome you to Spencer, Colorado, to have a look inside the families, to laugh in their good times and cry in their sad times, to follow them as they solve mysteries, expose secrets, recover from their pasts, reach for their goals, and most importantly—as they fall in love.

These Aspen Gold books are independently published by the authors. We thank you for your support, and we take pride in giving you quality books and excellent stories. We're thankful you've chosen to follow us and be part of the AG community.

Reviews help readers discover and connect with new authors. Every review is important to us and is greatly appreciated. Please consider leaving an honest review of this book at your favorite bookseller and Goodreads.

Be sure to follow all the Aspen Gold Series updates at:

Aspen Gold: The Series Website: https://www.aspengoldseries.com/

Rocky Mountain Rumors, the newsletter: https://www.-subscribepage.com/n9n7p3

Aspen Gold twitter: Https://twitter.com/@gold_aspen

Aspen Gold on Facebook: https://www.facebook.com/AspenGoldSeries/

Aspen Gold Pinterest: https://www.pinterest.-com/cheryl_stjohn/aspen-gold-the-series/

Aspen Gold Series on Goodreads: https://www.-goodreads.com/series/301364-aspen-gold

We love to hear from our readers. Contact the Aspen Gold authors at mailto:rumors@aspengoldseries.com

ASPEN GOLD BOOKS:

Dancing In The Dark
He had everything a man could want—except her forgiveness...
Call Me Mandy, Debra Hines
The last man Miranda loved took everything from her...
Ryder's Heart, *lizzie starr
She can't allow secrets to steal love from her...
For Keeps, Barbara Gwen & *lizzie starr
Hiding the truth is like denying the sun...
Second Chances, Donna Kaye
She tried the fairy tale and the fairy tale didn't work...
Sleepin' Alone, Bernadette Jones
Every man is guilty of the good he did not do...
Stay A Little Longer, Bernadette Jones
Death wasn't frightening. Living scared the hell out of him...
Speechless, *lizzie starr
How many peonies does it take to get married?
Close to the Heart, Debra Hines
He'd raised her child as his own...
Finding Hope, Donna Kaye
Is the peace he's found too good to be true?
Fortunate Cookie, *lizzie starr
This woman... wearing frosting... and nothing else...
Lonely Eyes, Bernadette Jones
There is an art to pursuit.
Whisper My Name, Cheryl St.John
She was the girl behind the headlines.
Gorgeous Scars, M.A. Jewell
The rodeo never prepared this cowboy for bodyguard duty.
Another Night Alone, Bernadette Jones
How far will a man go to protect everything he never knew he wanted...
Yesterday's Promise, The Aspen Gold Authors
Romantic short stories from the Aspen Gold Authors

Maybe I'm the One, Chery St.John

Adored by millions, her world has become very small.

Just My Imagination, *lizzie starr

Will magic heal her reality?

And many many more stories to come!

ABOUT THE AUTHOR

Romantic Suspense Writer, Never Give Up-er,
First Wives Club-er, Lifelong Dream Achiever & Mom

Bernadette Jones has been making up stories since she learned to read on her daddy's lap. She has imagined casts of characters everywhere she's called home: Texas, Oregon, Washington, South Dakota, Nebraska, Illinois, Mass-achusetts, and now New York.

Books and music filled her life as she, her dad and two brothers traveled the country. She would sit in the back seat of the car—her older brother always got to ride shotgun—listening to the current music on the radio, looking out the window and spinning a story based on a phrase she'd heard in the lyrics. Traveling the country, the music changed from state to state, as did the stories. To this day, she enjoys a wide variety of music and book genres.

After a career in corporate writing, she's decided to settle down and put pen to paper doing what she loves. Living the dream in her NYC apartment with her canine companion, she's bringing her stories and characters to life.

Links

I love to hear from readers.

Bernadette's Newsletter: http://www.bernadettejones.com/newsletters

Website: https://www.bernadettejones.com/

Email: BernadetteJonesAuthor@gmail.com

Linktree https://linktr.ee/BernadetteJonesAuthor

Please follow me on BookBub and Goodreads.

bookbub.com/authors/bernadette-jones

goodreads.com/author/show/19728724.Bernadette_Jones

SLEEPIN' ALONE

Every man is guilty of the good he did not do....

Undercover cop, Hunter Lawe, knows all there is to know about betrayal. A past full of abandonment and deception taught him to distrust everyone. Seductive Ruby Leigh Dupree may hold the key to his redemption, but never his heart. He's on a quest to right the failures of his past. He'll use anyone to get the enemy, no matter the cost.

Ruby Leigh Dupree, running from a past she can't remember, settles in the town of Spencer, Colorado. Night terrors and scars keep her awake at night. When a man from her past walks in the door of the

Wild Card Saloon, she's forced to confront the demons from her nightmares. As difficult as it is to trust someone—especially a stranger—she has no options. Hunter Lawe says he has the answers.

Will they lead to her past or her death...

ASPEN GOLD SERIES
STAY A LITTLE LONGER

Bernadette Jones

STAY A LITTLE LONGER

Death didn't frighten Gage Ewing. Living scared the hell out of him.

The Healer

Doctor Gage Ewing is on the run from a past he can never forget. No matter how many people he saves in hospitals or on the crime-ridden streets, he can never be forgiven for the one who died. Spencer, Colorado was supposed to be another temporary stop on his neverending road. But he made a mistake. He got involved.

The Soldier

IrishMist "Ivy" Vaughn has been fighting to stay alive since the age of twelve, trained with warrior skills to be whatever is demanded of her. No permanent home. Living out of a duffel bag. Changing personas at the ring of a phone.

Spencer, Colorado was supposed to be a place to bury her past and start over. Will they let her walk away?

Sometimes the past won't let you go.

ANOTHER NIGHT ALONE

She'd had the courage to save her child. Can she do the same for herself?

Avie Hall's dreams of a better future for herself and her daughter are shattered when the shadows of their past threaten their new life. With their dreams on the line once again, Avie knows giving in will cost her everything, but is she strong enough to fight back?

She is the light to his dark….

Deke Ward has witnessed true evil in his life. When he finds the goodness in Avie and her young daughter, he'll do anything to protect them. Their hope starts to heal his lonely heart, and when the evil shadows of their past return to haunt them, he'll go to hell and back to save them.

Even if it means letting them go.

YESTERDAY'S PROMISE

A high-stakes poker game, first meets, a dog rescue, loves lost and rekindled, and life-altering choices fill the history of Spencer, Colorado. Discover the challenges faced in these heartwarming stories crafted by the multi-author group who brings you romantic fiction at its finest in The Aspen Gold Series.

The Card Game, M.A. Jewell

With the winning hand, anything is possible—even love.

Some Days Are Diamonds, *lizzie starr

She sacrificed her happiness for his future. Can their love survive her loss?

Ah, Venice, Debra Hines

Tired of playing it straight, he heads to romantic Italy and takes a chance at love.

First Chance, Donna Kaye

He risks his life daily, but his heart? That's another matter.
Racing Hearts, Bernadette Jones
Sometimes it only takes a heartbeat to fall in love...
Rescue Me, Cheryl St.John
Is she willing to take a risk on business...and